VENOMOUS

VENOMOUS

KAYLA MARIE

This story contains dark content that may be disturbing
or triggering to some readers.

The following is included: Graphic murder, violence
and gore, physical assault and abuse, SA and noncon;
including of a minor (one scene shared in detail from
past memory), physical and emotional child abuse by
a family member, death, explicit sex scenes, dubcon,
human trafficking, BDSM, snakes.

PLAYLIST

DAVID KUSHNER – POISON
2WEI – TOXIC
FREYA RIDINGS – POISON
MEG MYERS – DESIRE
WARREN ZEIDERS – PRETTY LITTLE POISON
SLEEP TOKEN – EVEN IN ARCADIA
SLEEP TOKEN – DANGEROUS
FRACTAL SILENCE – POISON IN MY VEINS
URSINE VULPINE, ANNACA – WICKED GAME
MAX MCNOWN – THE WAY I WANNA
EJAE (RUMI & JINU) – FREE
TOPLOADER – DANCING IN THE MOONLIGHT
WARREN ZEIDERS – SIN SO SWEET
HOZIER – WORK SONG
DROWNING POOL – TEAR AWAY
WARREN ZEIDERS – YOU FOR A REASON
MAZZY STAR – FADE INTO YOU

For all the ladies who wanted more of Venom…
here ya go, you thirsty hoes.

This is book 2 in the Visceral Love Duet. Although each book focuses on a different couple, reading Book 1 first, The Bone Reaper, will give full context and a better experience since Venom is first introduced in Reaper & Charlotte's story and plays an important role. This story also begins from the same moment where the epilogue in The Bone Reaper began.

Happy reading!

CHAPTER ONE

FIVE MONTHS AFTER THE EVENTS IN THE BONE REAPER

"You just wait. Someone's on their way here!" the woman shouts.

"Oh? Who? Your husband? I'm not worried about him."

The man comes barreling through the front door. He storms through the house toward me, and I casually look at my watch.

"Five. Four. Three—"

The man drops to the floor and begins convulsing. The woman shrieks.

"Damn, couple seconds off." I shrug and turn my attention back to the missus. "I apologize for the interruption. You were saying?"

"You fucking psycho! Let me go!"

"Now, now, that's not very nice. Mind your tongue."

The woman rears her head back and spits at me. Her saliva landing across my cheek. "Fuck you!"

I pull a handkerchief from my pocket and wipe my face. What a disgusting vile creature. *Most women are.*

I yank her head back by her hair and force her mouth open with my hand and knife, slicing off her tongue.

I hold the severed appendage in front of her as she screams a hollow sound. I wiggle it in the air, taunting her.

"I said, mind your tongue, woman." I then toss it into her lap. She thrashes in the chair I bound her to as blood continuously falls from her mouth between her monstrous breasts. That poor bra is putting in a lot of work. Perhaps I should set it free. I move in front of her once more and send my knife through the fabric. The bra breaks free and her breasts flop out.

"That's better, don't you think? That poor bra can breathe now."

Maybe I shouldn't have cut out her tongue. It's suddenly awfully lonely with no one to converse with.

How boring.

I pull out a metal compact from my pocket, opening it carefully, and move in front of the woman once more. I blow the powdered substance in the compact into her face, some particles falling onto her tits. Her eyes go wide as her face begins to bubble and melt along with the skin over her giant breasts. Taking a seat across from her, I pull out a toothpick and place it into my mouth as I watch.

More attempted screams and gurgling fill the room as the woman slowly, and might I add, quite painfully dies. When the room falls quiet, I let out a sigh and stand.

This was my last hit before I take a much-needed vacation.

I make my way to the front door when I hear what sounds to be someone yelling *help*.

Strange.

Everyone is surely dead.

I listen again. Sure enough, the word *help* is faintly heard again.

I follow the sound into what appears to be a greenhouse. The voice is louder now, clearer.

I move through the wild foliage of various plants and vines, stroking my fingers across the beauties until I reach the back. Under my boot is a wooden door with a lock attached.

Interesting find.

"Help! Help me! Someone, help!" the voice calls out from below.

I'm not typically one to save people. I'm no hero. Although, recent events have forced a heroic act out of me.

I could walk away, begin my vacation, but my interest is piqued. I look around for a possible key. The couple inside seemed stupid enough to leave it visible. Sure enough, in a potted plant to my right lies two keys attached to a piece of twine. I unlock the latch and swing open the door. Sunlight beams into the dark space, illuminating a ladder.

Has anything good come from someone crawling into a dark hole in the ground?

Sighing, I descend the steps. When my boots reach the dirt floor, I turn my phone's flashlight on and have a look around. I nearly miss her the first time, but as my light shines across the space, I spot a girl in the corner, connected to the wall by a chain around her neck.

She squints at me, trying to see past the light at who saunters toward her.

"Hello?"

It smells of dirt and piss, and I internally scold myself for wearing my new boots down here.

I stand almost directly in front of her, and she rises to her shaky legs.

"Well, what do we have here?"

"Oh god, please! Please help me!" Upon closer inspection, she looks to be in her early to mid-twenties, far too thin with pale skin and copper hair. Her clothes are tattered and covered in dirt and what appears to be dried blood. "You have to get me out of here!"

"Do I now?"

"Please!" she cries.

I take a step forward and that's when the girl attacks. She pounces on me like a wild beast, clawing at me, attempting to sink her teeth into my flesh. My phone is knocked from my grip and drops to the floor.

"Christ, woman!" I toss her off me and she slams into the stone wall but doesn't relent. She charges me again, but I manage to step just far enough out of reach as the chain around her neck yanks her back, sending her onto her ass. She screams a wild sound.

"Let me out! Let me out!"

"Will you stop your damn shrieking? I'm not here to harm you. I have the key to your collar, you beastly thing."

She quiets for a moment as I retrieve my phone.

"I'm sorry. I thought you might be one of their friends."

"Have many of their friends paid you a visit down here?" She nods "How long have you been here?"

"Months. A year. I'm not sure. What's the date?"

"September 20th, 2025."

"Bastards! I've been here for nine months."

"Well alright. I'm gonna take that collar off you. You keep your hands to yourself now."

"Okay."

I move closer to her and push back her long hair to see the keyhole. I unlock the shackle and it drops to the floor as she rubs at her neck.

"Are they home?"

"They sure are."

"Oh god, if they see us, if they catch me—"

"They're dead," I say.

"Did *you* kill them?"

"I did." Smirking, I place a toothpick between my lips.

"Who are you?" she asks, bewildered.

"The name's Marcus, but you, darlin', can call me Venom."

CHAPTER TWO

After making my way out of that dank hole, I fill my lungs with fresh air, dust off my pants and then head to my car.

"Wait! Where are you going?" the girl shouts from behind me.

I stop and turn to face her.

"I thought it was obvious. I'm leaving. My job here is done," I say with a dramatic bow.

"But… where do I go now? You can't just leave me here."

"I most certainly can. And I will."

"You're not going to help me?"

"I've helped enough." I continue walking, but the pesky beast follows.

"Hey! Asshole, I'm talking to you!"

Pausing, I turn to her once more with a smirk. She stops as I stride toward her.

"You know, darlin', there's better things you could do with that mouth of yours than spew insults at the man who saved you."

She scowls and raises a finger at me. "Fuck you."

"Sorry, beast, I don't have much time." At that, she crosses her arms, tossing a glare at me.

Amused, I turn, but a hand grabs my arm. I slowly look down at the dirty limb that has attached itself to me, then meet the eyes of the girl it belongs to. "Remove your hand, if you would like to keep it," I say in a low voice, growing tired of this interaction.

She must see the severity in my expression because she immediately lets go.

"Please. I have nowhere to go. I don't even know where I am. There are dead bodies in the house, I'm barely clothed, I haven't eaten or drank anything in almost three days."

"I don't see how that's my concern. Call the police."

She bristles, her cheeks turning a pretty shade of rose. "Clearly, I don't have a damn phone and I'm not going into that house or being held responsible for their deaths."

"Tell them a very attractive and charming poisoner killed them." When she scoffs, I add, "I am not the hero in your story, darlin'. Make no mistake, I am the villain," I add with a smirk.

"Please, Venom." Her eyes soften, looking at me.

I should leave her here and be done with this. Begin

my much-needed vacation. But hearing my name on her pouty lips sends a flame flickering within me. I search her desperate eyes, which are now much clearer in the afternoon sun.

Striking verdant irises with a blast of golden rays in the center of them. Beautiful. Mesmerizing. Light freckles paint her porcelain face along with dirt and dried blood. Her messy long copper hair shimmers in the sunlight like a blazing fire, and I suddenly have the urge to be burned.

My gaze travels over her body, taking note of the bruises and scabbed over wounds before I meet those stunning eyes again. She's staring at me with an intense expression as she silently begs me.

Battered and bruised but not broken.

Raising a finger up to her flushed cheek, I stop before touching her.

"You remind me of someone," I say softly. She blinks and I turn away from her. "Follow me, beastie."

I don't bother looking back to make sure she's obeying. There's a tightness and heat coming from behind me that lets me know she's indeed following me.

Reaching my car up the dirt road, I open the back door and motion for her to get in.

"I can't sit up front?"

"Little beasties belong in the back." I tilt my head at her and smile, motioning again for her to enter. She grunts and takes a seat in the back.

We surprisingly make it two hours into the drive without speaking another word to each other.

I pull into a gas station and start toward the door, then turn back, grabbing a bottle of water from my trunk before sticking my head back into the car and offering it to her. "Would the beast like a treat for behaving so well?"

She growls, snatching the bottle from my hands. "Stop calling me that. And yes—gummy bears."

I blink. "Gummy bears? Out of everything?"

"They're my favorite," she says around the rim of the bottle, eyes daring me to argue. "I've been without them for way too long."

Without another word, I close the car door and stride inside to get the wild woman some ridiculous gummy bears.

"You smell. And now my car smells," I whine after another four hours of driving.

"Well, what the fuck do you expect? I've been stuck in a fucking hole. I can assure you; I don't like it any more than you, pal."

My eyes meet hers in the rearview mirror. "Your manners certainly reflect that fact that you've been living like an animal."

She bristles. "Fuck you."

Amused, I smile, then focus back on the road, driving in silence for the next two hours before we finally reach my home.

I pull up to the gate of my property, and with a press of a button, it opens, leading us down a long stone driveway.

"Where are we?"

"My home."

"Your actual fucking house?"

"Would you prefer I take you to the pound to be put down as a rabid animal?" I see her scowl at me through the rearview mirror. I smile. "Don't go thanking me though, darlin'. You just signed your death sentence." I park my car outside the garage and exit the vehicle before I hear her response.

She scrambles out of the car, quickly following me up the stairs to the front door.

"You live in a castle? And what do you mean, *I signed my death sentence*?"

"It only looks like a castle on the outside." I ignore her second question and continue to my front door.

She huffs behind me. "If you're just planning on killing me anyway, then what's the point of even helping me in the first place?"

I turn toward her with a grin. "I've been known to play with my food before devouring it." The massive wooden door swings open with a push, and I motion for her to enter first. "Beasts before beauty."

"You're an asshole."

"Oh, darlin', you ain't seen nothing yet." She begrudgingly enters, and the door closes behind us with a loud bang, causing her to jump. "First things first, you need a damn shower. I won't have you infecting my home with your filth. Come." I motion for her to follow me, but before we make it to the stairs, someone rounds the corner from the hall.

"Oh my god, you didn't tell me you lived with your mother."

I scowl. "Evelyn is *not* my mother. How absolutely insulting to say such a thing."

Evelyn comes closer, and I can already tell by her expression that I'm in trouble, which is quite common among us. Her brows pinch as she moves her hands and fingers, signing.

"You scared me! You weren't supposed to be back for a month. Is everything okay?"

"I know. Everything is fine." Side-eyeing the dirty woman standing next me, I continue speaking out loud while signing back to Ev. "Change of plans. We have a guest for a bit. This is…" I look at the redhead once more. "What's your name, little beast?"

"Ivy." I can't control the deep chuckle that escapes me as her brows furrow. "What's so funny?"

"Of course that's your name."

Placing her hands on her curvy hips, she asks, "And what exactly is that supposed to mean?"

"Well, don't ya know you're poison, darlin'?" She rolls her eyes, and I suddenly have the urge to watch them melt from their sockets.

"This is Evelyn, my housekeeper. She keeps things in order while I'm away, and well, when I'm here, she also tries her damndest to keep me in order as well."

"You are impossible. It's an endless task."

"Well yes, but you love it."

She gives a light shake of her head with a growing grin and looks at Ivy.

Ivy gives Evelyn a wave with a small smile, looking shy.

"You can speak to her. She can't hear or speak but she can read lips, rather impressively. In fact, you best watch everything you say around her."

Evelyn gently swats my arm as she tries to suppress a small smile.

"*Shall I prepare a room for her?*"

"Please."

Evelyn nods, then glances at Ivy before disappearing.

"She cares about you." Ivy's voice is soft, but steady, cutting through the charged silence between us.

I huff out a laugh, shaking my head. Of all the conclusions... "You've come to that from that one interaction? I pay her well."

Her brows lift. "Are you saying she doesn't care about you?"

A sigh escapes before I can catch it. My shoulders feel heavier with the admission. "The women in my life have always cared more about what I can do or provide for them rather than anything else."

Ivy doesn't flinch. She just tilts her head, gaze unwavering. "That may have been so but you're blind if you can't see it's different with her."

I study her, searching for a crack, a tell. "Hmm. Maybe. Or maybe I can see people much clearer than you."

Her lips curve into a challenge. "And what do you see when you look at me?"

"Besides a filthy beast?" I take my time with the words, letting the insult hang between us. "You're certainly here for what I can provide you, aren't you? You're all the same."

Her jaw tightens. "Maybe you don't give anyone the chance to show you anything different."

I close the space between us in one step, my shadow swallowing her smaller frame. Her green eyes blaze up at me, daring me to keep going. "I don't allow myself to be deceived."

"You think I will deceive you?" Her arms fold across her chest like armor. "You don't know anything about me," she says, crossing her arms.

"I know enough. And I know that you already have."

"What? I have not!"

I smirk. "You are far from what you pretend to be, darlin'."

"I'm not pretending to be anything! I just need a little help."

"Hmm." I flick a piece of her dirty hair. "I'll add that to the list."

She swats at my hand. "Add what?"

"That you're a liar."

"And what list?!"

I slide my hands into my pockets. "My list of why I should kill you."

"Ya know, I'm sick of you being an asshole to me for no fucking reason!"

"You've ruined my vacation. That's plenty of reason. Now let's go, you need a shower, and I need to get you out of my damn sight and nose for a while."

"You know what, fuck this! I'm out!" She heads for the door, pulling it open.

Before she can open it any further though, I slam it

shut. She whirls on me, and I pin her against the door with a hand to her chest. "You will not be going anywhere."

"Fuck you, asshole." Her palm cracks across my cheek before I even see it coming. Heat blooms in the sting, sharp and satisfying. I bare my teeth in a slow smile.

"You truly have no idea who you are fucking with, little beast."

Her chin lifts, green fire burning in her eyes. "Am I supposed to be afraid of you?"

"Yes." The word rumbles out on a sneer, low and deliberate.

"Surprise, I'm not. So... now what?"

Is she really challenging me? This could actually be fun. "That means I have to change that." I grab her bicep and pull her down the hall.

"Let go! Where are you taking me?!" She fights me, but I'm stronger, especially in her weakened state. But then she drops her body weight, nearly causing me to trip. I stop, let out an annoyed huff, then lift her, roughly throwing her over my shoulder.

"If you're going to continue to behave like a wild beast, then I'll have to lock you up like one."

"You're going to keep me prisoner after just freeing me? How the fuck does that make sense?" She tries kicking at the air, but I hold her legs tightly against me. Her small fists bang against my back in frustration, causing me to grin. Such a wild thing.

"It doesn't have to make sense. It just has to work."

"For what to work?!"

"*Tame the beast*," I say, then drop her like a bag of coal into a room and slam the door shut, locking her in.

She jiggles the knob and pounds on the door, screaming like a banshee.

I pop a toothpick into my mouth and stride off.

So much for my vacation.

CHAPTER THREE

I've been through so much shit in my life; a self-centered prick doesn't faze me anymore.

I rub my aching ass from where I landed when he dropped me like I was nothing more than trash, then look around the small room, finding it completely bare of anything. The room doesn't even have any windows.

How long does he plan on keeping me in here? I suppose it's better than a hole in the ground or chained up like an animal.

As far as captives go, he's already better than *them*.

Although, things could always get worse.

They do always tend to get worse, don't they?

Another thing Venom has over my other captives: looks. I'll admit it—he's a good-looking guy. Annoyingly so. Obnoxious, even. Platinum-blond hair, light blue eyes, a sharp, defined face and that villainous, cocky smile that must make women throw themselves at him. Me? It just makes me want to slap him.

I might be annoyingly all too aware how attractive he is, but he certainly knows it as well which just makes me hate him even more. No good can come from a man looking like *that*.

He may be insanely hot, but the guy is still an asshole.

I hit the door once more. I got a taste of freedom and now I'm a prisoner again. My life is truly a fucking joke.

Maybe I can get the sweet woman to help me. Although, with how adoringly she looked at Venom, I doubt she'd take my side with anything.

At least I'm not in a dirty hole in the ground. That's what I have to keep reminding myself of. I'll happily take anything other than that again.

I'll be ready though when he opens the door. I've spent most of my life as a prisoner, with shitty foster parents, then with one of the worst men I've come across, then that twisted couple. My accommodations are better here, but I won't be a captive any longer, even if I have to die. At least in death, I will finally be free.

I lie down near the door, curled up with my back to the wall and close my eyes, trying to ignore how my stomach aches from only having water and gummy bears.

I JERK WHEN I hear the door unlocking.

Jumping to my feet, I brace myself against the wall.

The door opens and Venom takes one step in before I launch myself at him from behind the door.

He's quick. Ugh, why is he so damn quick!

I land hard on the floor, knocking the air from my lungs. Before I can even catch my breath, Venom's strong thighs are on either side of my body, holding me in place while his hands hold my arms above my head.

Fuck!

"Tsk, tsk. Now here I thought you were going to behave after I gave you some time to think about what a bratty little creature you've been."

"Get off me!" I growl.

"Not yet, darlin'. I think we need to establish some rules first."

"Fuck your rules. Just let me go and you'll never have to deal with me again."

"That's no longer an option."

I hook my legs and shove, every muscle screaming, but it's useless. He looks down and smiles, like he already knows how small and pathetic I feel.

"Keep throwing your hips into me and I might get the wrong idea, darlin'."

"Ugh! I hate you!"

"Yes. I think we've established that. Let's move on, shall we? Rule one: keep your hands to yourself. If you attack me, I will hurt you. Rule two: snoop all you want but try to leave and I will kill you—slowly. Rule three: you can lash out at me with that vicious tongue, but you will not, under any circumstance, disrespect Evelyn. Do that and I will kill you."

"Why would I disrespect her? It's *you* I hate."

He rolls his eyes and continues, "Rule four… fuck, what's rule four?" he muses, looking thoughtful. "Well, damn, I'm out of rules… for now."

Before I even agree to his *rules*, he releases my arms and slips his hand into his pocket. When he moves to dismount me, something pricks my side.

"Ow, what the fuck was that?" I move to stand and lift my shirt, not caring that my underwear is on full display. I spot a thin cut just below my ribs, slightly red with blood. "What the fuck was that?"

He casually flips a small blade in his hand twice before placing both his hands into his pockets and leaning against the wall. "Rule one."

Heat rushes through me, then fades just as quickly, leaving me lightheaded. I stumble back, reaching blindly for the wall, but my knees buckle, and I hit the floor. Panic creeps in as my body grows weaker with every second. "What did you do to me?" My words slur, my tongue thick in my mouth as I try to will my body to stand, but it won't obey.

"Instead of telling you, I thought I'd show you. Sometimes lessons are better taught that way, don't you think? And I do like playing with my food."

I look at him through fuzzy vision. Fear blooms inside me. "V-Venom—"

He squats in front of me, and I can still make out his satisfied smile and bright baby blues boring into me.

"Mmm, not much to say now, darlin'? Agree to my rules and I'll give you the antidote."

What choice do I have anyway?

"O-okay."

"Okay what?"

"I-I a-agree!" The words tear out of me, desperate, broken, as tears threaten to spill from my eyes.

His smile widens as something cool presses to my lips. "Swallow."

I obey, the liquid sliding down my throat.

"That's a good little beast."

Relief trickles in as the sharp, slightly minty liquid burns down my throat. He walks out of the room without another word, leaving the door wide open.

It takes me nearly an hour before feeling close to my normal self and before trusting that I can stand on my feet again.

The bastard poisoned me. It happened so quickly, I never saw it coming. He could do it again. He *would* do it again. Fuck. I'm going to have to rethink my strategy here.

Three rules.

I think I can manage that.

Unless he pisses me off again, which is highly likely. And then my damn mouth and anger will get me completely at his mercy *again*.

Asshole.

On shaky legs, I walk out of the room. I didn't get a welcome tour, so I have no idea where I'm going. As I pass by a room, I spot two couches facing each other and a large fireplace against the wall. On a mantle above are pictures.

I step closer to inspect the photo, lifting it carefully. Two boys stand in a sunlit field, blond hair shining, blue eyes unmistakable. One is a foot taller, grinning wide, while the smaller one stares at the camera with hollow, joyless eyes. Brothers—Venom and his kin, though I can't tell which is which.

Someone taps my shoulder, and I nearly shriek. I spin around to find Evelyn wearing an apologetic smile. "Sorry, you startled me."

She lifts her hand, motioning for me to follow. I follow the older woman up a flight of stairs and down a hall before she leads me into what I assume is a guest room. *Too nice.*

"This is where I'm staying?"

With a smile, she nods and then opens another door connected to the room. Peeking inside, I find a bathroom with a large enough tub for four people and a glass shower stall that could fit even more. I look back to Evelyn as she hands me a towel and lightly pushes me toward the shower.

Ok, I get it. I desperately need a shower. I look disgusting and I certainly smell worse.

"Thank you," I tell her before she leaves.

I strip off my filthy T-shirt and underwear and step into the shower. The water hisses hotter as I crank the handle, wishing I could burn off a layer of skin—take the grime and every unwanted touch from that hole with it.

Small bottles line the corner, like this place is some damn hotel: body wash, shampoo, conditioner. I snatch the shampoo first, working it through my thick hair until the suds sting my eyes. The conditioner's next, and I already know I'll drain the whole bottle. Finally, the body wash. The citrus scent blooms around me, orange and pineapple, sharp and sweet, like I'm somewhere tropical, not here. I close my eyes, let the steam wrap me, and stand under the rush of heat as if it could wash away nine months of hell.

After staying in the shower longer than what's probably considered normal, I make my way back into the bedroom to find clothes laid out for me on the bed.

It's nothing special—black yoga pants, a tank top, a sweater, socks, even new underwear. As I slip them on, everything but the sweater clings tighter around my hips and breasts, though not uncomfortably. I've lost so much weight, yet my wide hips and heavy breasts remain, only now with sharper bones beneath the curves.

Now, it's time to find some food.

VENOM

CHAPTER FOUR

R unning a hand down my face, I sit on the edge of my bed.

That woman... no, that *beast* is already exhausting me.

She shouldn't be bothering me as much as she is but something about her is slithering its way beneath my skin. I know I shouldn't have brought her here, but there's no going back. I might as well have some fun.

The image of her pouty, terror-stricken face flashes before me, and an unpleasant feeling pulses inside my chest.

Strange.

I hear the shower in the next room turn on. Finally, the wild thing is washing herself. I lie on my bed and listen to the stream of the water.

Almost thirty minutes pass, and the shower is still going. While I had her locked away downstairs, I installed a couple cameras in her room to keep an eye on the wild thing.

Curiosity taking over, I grab my phone, open the camera app and click on the view inside the shower. The beast is sitting on the shower floor, knees up to her chest with her head resting on them and her arms wrapped around her legs. Steam billows in the air as the water spills over her, slicking her copper hair to her now pinkish flesh. A shiver coils through me. She looks so small and fragile. Breakable. But this creature is far from how she appears.

Fifteen more minutes pass before she finally stands. Closing her eyes and tilting her head up, she lets the water run over her face once more. She looks serene. She then takes a step back, away from the water stream and her lips part, taking in a deep breath as she runs her hands over her wet hair. Droplets of water fall from her thick dark lashes and travel down her face, neck, and over her luscious breasts. I swallow.

As beastly as she is, she's still a beautiful creature. Too beautiful.

I blink a few times, breaking the spell. My thumb hovers before I exit the app, pulse unsteady.

Closing my eyes, I try to rest. It's been a long day.

A couple minutes later, I hear the guest room door open then close.

Where's the beast off to now?

After waiting a moment, I make my way downstairs to see what my fiery redhead is up to.

I enter the kitchen to find her standing at the open fridge, shoving berries into her mouth.

"Would you like a bowl?"

"Shit!" She startles, placing a hand over her chest, drawing my attention to those luscious curves of hers. My gaze slowly travels back up as I grind my molars. Blackberry juice paints the corner of her mouth and chin. "I was looking for something to eat."

"It appears you found where I keep the food."

She scowls at me as she pops another berry into her mouth and licks her lips. My gaze lingers a bit too long at her juice-coated mouth.

"Evelyn will be cooking dinner soon. You can have a proper meal."

"Are you trying to be nice to me after poisoning me?"

"Nice? No, I wouldn't dare." I saunter closer to her, and she takes a step back, colliding with the fridge door, causing it to shut and her to jump once more. Her wet hair hangs free, droplets of water still falling from the strands.

"You a bit skittish?" I ask with a raise of my brow.

"Being nearly killed by poison can do that to a person," she snaps.

"You wouldn't have died."

"No?"

"Just would have wished you had."

"Right. So, you do this often?"

"You gotta be more specific, darlin'." I tip my head to the side, eyeing her up and down.

"Kidnap and poison people?"

"I'd say so. Though, I wouldn't say I kidnapped you.

If I remember correctly, you begged me to take you with me. You were about to be on your hands and knees before me. I think I would have enjoyed seeing that." I step even closer and take pleasure in seeing her visibly tense.

She scoffs. "That was before I realized what a psychopath you are."

I bring my thumb to her face, and she flinches. Smirking, I wipe the blackberry juice from the corner of her lips as she stares at me with bewilderment, then bring it to my mouth, sucking. "Delicious."

"*Don't* do that again," she says with a murderous expression which I find absolutely delightful.

"Or what?" I challenge.

"Or I'll bite your fucking finger off."

I laugh. "Of course I'd find such a wild beast in the south. Nothing good in my life has ever come from there."

She lifts her chin higher in defiance. "You can insult me all you want. I see right through you."

"You certainly wish you would see through these clothes."

"Ugh. Seriously, get over yourself."

"Just do yourself a favor, don't go falling in love with me."

She laughs, the sound oddly pleasant to my ears. "As if that was ever going to be a possibility."

"Do you not find me charming, darlin'?"

"Not in the least," she says, straightening her back and crossing her arms over her tightly covered breasts.

"You'll need to work on that." Smirking, I turn from her.

"On what?"

"Your lying. Oh, and for the record, I bite back," I say as I leave the kitchen.

WE SIT IN the dining room at opposite ends of a long dark table while Evelyn serves us dinner.

"What is it?" Ivy asks.

"You've never had salmon before?"

"No. As far as seafood goes, I've only ever tried shrimp."

"Ev makes the best lemon garlic salmon. But even if you don't agree, just pretend to love it."

Evelyn takes the dish towel that was over her shoulder and throws it at me, smacking me right in the face.

Ivy laughs as Ev signs, *"Don't tell the girl to lie to me."*

"Just looking out for your feelings, Ev. With them being so old, you might not survive someone telling you your best dishes are shit."

"You know what? I think I liked it better when you were gone."

"Don't go lying to yourself now. You know you missed me." Evelyn finally breaks her scowl and smiles at me.

I look back to Ivy who's just been watching our interaction with fascination. "Go on, try it." She actually obeys, parting those pink lips to slide a piece of salmon onto her tongue. I watch her chew, and when a smile curves her mouth, I lean forward. "Good, right?"

"Wow, yeah. That's really good." She looks at a grinning Evelyn and says, "Thank you, it's delicious."

With a nod, she leaves us.

Ivy begins shoveling the salmon into her mouth, barely taking breaths in between.

"You even eat like a beast."

She glares at me. "I've been practically starved for the past nine months."

"Then you should probably eat slower. Let your body adjust instead of overwhelming it." My jaw ticks as images of her wet body take over my thoughts. She considers my words and slows down. I bring a glass of whiskey to my mouth and take a large sip, pushing away the images. "So, how did you end up with that couple anyway?"

She shoots me a hard look, like she's weighing whether I deserve the truth.

"Are we getting personal now?"

"Oh, we've already gotten pretty personal, don't ya think?"

She rolls her eyes but finally exhales. "I was on the run from someone when that couple found me. I thought they were nice—offered me help." Her voice goes flat, her gazed fixed somewhere past me. "Instead, they lured me back to their place and tossed me in that hole. Turns out they were trying to sell me to the highest bidder. And until then, they made money letting men use me." Her expression doesn't shift, her tone as stone-cold as the words spilling from it. No emotion. Nothing left to give.

"Use you?"

"That's what I said."

"You were raped by these men?" My jaw clenches and fingers squeeze tightly around my fork.

She shakes her head. "No. There were rules. No intercourse. Just... other stuff. I was to remain..." She breaks eye contact. "A virgin."

I drop my utensil, the clang against the plate making her glance up and meet my eyes. "You're a virgin?" The words slip out before I can catch them. I hadn't expected that.

"Yup. Still worth a lot of money. You thinking of changing your plans and selling me too?"

"I have enough money."

She doesn't respond, but something flickers across her face, subtle enough most people would miss it. For a couple of breaths, we just stare at each other, the silence heavy, until she clears her throat and takes a slow sip of water.

"So, what are your plans for me then?"

Ignoring her question, I ask one of my own. "Who were you on the run from?"

"That doesn't matter," she says a bit too quickly, causing my curiosity to pique.

"I told you; you need to work on your lying. Don't be shy now, darlin'."

"How about you answer one of my questions first?"

"Fine."

"So, you're some kind of serial killer? Why poison?"

I smirk, then lean back in my chair. "I prefer assassin. And ever since a young age I've been fascinated by pretty, remarkable things that can easily kill you. I also happen to be immune to poison."

"All poison?"

"So far all the ones I've come across." Which happens to be quite a lot.

"You've tested them on yourself willingly? What if you died?" she asks with furrowed brows.

"When you have nothing to live for, it becomes rather easy to risk your life." She looks surprised at my answer. "Now, back to you. Who were you running from?"

"It's a long story."

"Give me the cliff notes."

With a long sigh, she brings her hands to her thighs as if to steady herself. "That couple... they weren't the first to lock me up." Her voice falters, and she swallows before forcing herself on. "When I aged out of foster care, I had nothing. No family. No home. Just me, scared and stupid. I trusted the wrong people." Her hands come up in front of her again as she fidgets with her fingers before curling into fists. "And ended up in the hands of someone more psychotic than you. If you can believe that." I raise a brow, but she doesn't meet my eyes. "Anyway..." Her laugh is bitter, shaky. "I got away. Only to end up prisoner once again with those redneck fucks. And now—again, with you."

"Did any of them serve you delicious salmon and look as good as me?" When she rolls her eyes, I add, "Come now, darlin', I ain't so bad."

"Something tells me you're something entirely different. Which isn't exactly a good thing."

I offer a smile before I take a sip of my whiskey.

"I'd like to go to bed now if that's alright with you."

"Go right ahead, *prisoner*." Before she leaves the

dining room, I call out, "I wish you the sweetest dreams, beastie."

She throws up her middle finger at me before disappearing.

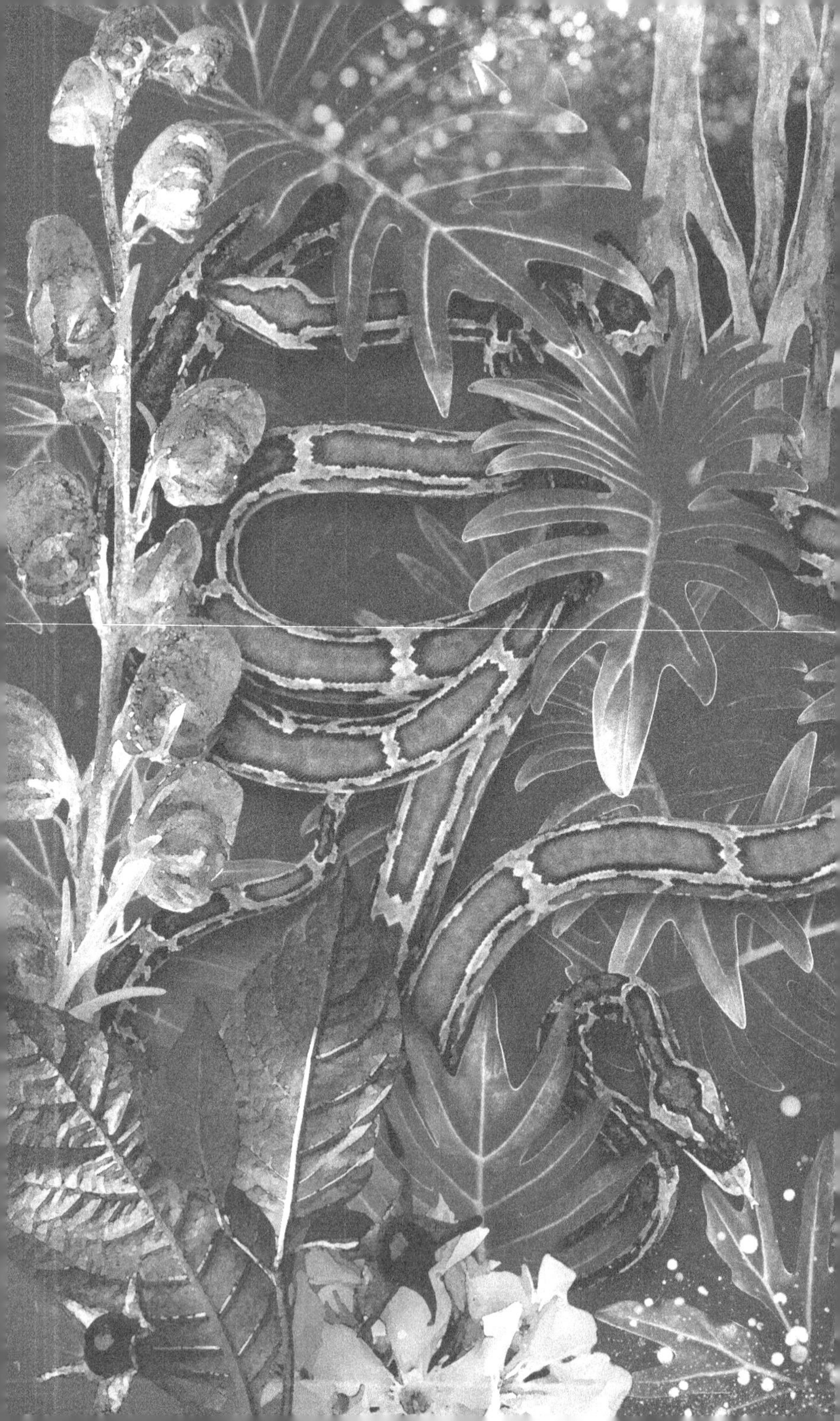

CHAPTER FIVE

14 YEARS OLD

The belt comes down across my bare back, and I grunt. Another blow, and I scramble for anything to bite, but only the TV remote is in reach. I jam it between my teeth and brace for the lashes. When the punishment ends, I'm thrown back into my dark hole.

"Get in your room!" my mother screams as she shoves me inside and turns the lock. She calls it my room, but it's just a closet—big enough for a toddler-size mattress and too small for my long legs.

I flick on my flashlight and press a loose board until it opens. I pull out the three books I stole over the years: *The BFG*, *The Lion, the Witch and the Wardrobe*, and *Harry*

Potter and the Sorcerer's Stone.

When I was little, I pretended I was Harry, waiting for my Hogwarts letter.

No owl ever came. No bearded giant.

The books still comfort me, but I've accepted my life now. The only thing I hope for is that one day my mother goes too far and kills me—only then would I be free.

CHAPTER SIX

Last night, I slept like the dead and woke up feeling like I was a young child with all the energy in the world.

I've decided to explore more of this castle-like house today since I'll be staying here for who knows how long.

Arriving on the first level, I pass the seating area once more, only to find another living room, this one cozier with one long gray couch, a black coffee table, and a TV mounted on the wall. Moving on, I pass the kitchen, another bathroom, and then make my way down a long hall until I reach the frosted glass door at the end. I nearly gasp at the scene.

Before me is a massive greenhouse of sorts. I take in the array of lush green plants all around with big banana leaves and other foliage. Various flowering plants also stand out in vibrant colors of deep pinks, bright yellows and orange, reds and purples, adding pops of eye-catching colors. There are orchids, plumerias, hibiscus and other exotic flowers I don't recognize but are still so beautiful.

Two small butterflies flutter over me with their delicate white wings, bringing my attention to baskets that hang from the ceiling with ferns and fuchsias and pansies, swaying slightly from a breeze. I follow a plant's vines snaking their way up the side of the glass wall, reaching the impressive clear glass dome roof that lets in the natural morning sunlight. There are even trees planted into the dirt grown near the stone pathways, and somewhere in the near distance, I hear the trickle of running water like there might be a pond in here too.

I walk down an aisle flanked by potted plants, their leaves deep purple, burgundy, and bright green. It feels like stepping into a tropical jungle, the air earthy and laced with soft floral notes. Warmth and humidity cling to my skin—nothing like the crisp fall outside. Obviously, the place is temperature regulated, cared for with meticulous attention. Every leaf gleams, every stem thriving. This is the work of someone who loves nature deeply.

I never would've suspected that someone to be Venom.

I lightly touch some glossy green leaves as I walk down the stone path, inspecting more of the beauty of this place. At the end of the aisle, I look to my right and spot a seating area with a little tree near it with delicate pink flowers. I look around finding more tables and equipment, making it look like a science lab. Microscopes, test tubes, beakers, syringes, small blades and many other things I'm not familiar with that scream *dangerous*.

Someone clears their throat from behind me, and I whirl to find Venom casually leaning against a table with a toothpick in his mouth.

"What is all this? Are you some kind of mad scientist?" I ask.

"Perhaps I'm more of a wizard, a potions master, if you will."

"Oh yeah? Where's your wizard hat then?"

"In the closet," he deadpans.

"Uh-huh. And your wand?"

"In my pants. Care to see?"

"No thanks." I grimace.

"Are you sure, darlin'? I can cast quite the spell with it." He tips his head to the side, eyeing me like prey.

"I'll take your word for it, *Professor*."

He smiles, showing his perfectly straight white teeth.

"So really, what's going on with all this?"

"It's what I do. They don't call me The Southern Poisoner for nothing. Be careful touching things though, could very well be the last thing you do."

I internally cringe and wipe my hands on my pants nervously. He smirks.

"Come, let me show you my pets."

He leads me deeper into the greenhouse until we reach the back wall lined with glass cases. Snakes. And other creatures that make my skin crawl.

"This here is Black Betty." He gestures to a thick coil of scales shifting behind the glass. "She's a mean one. Doesn't like new people—gets defensive fast. Best leave her be. We had a few arguments at the start, but I'd say we're on decent terms now."

"*Black* Betty? But she's gray."

"The inside of her mouth is nearly black. But if she goes showing you that, you're in trouble, darlin'. She's extremely fast and her venom is a neurotoxin, which will cause paralysis and respiratory failure."

"Got it. I'll stay away from her."

"Now, this beauty is Sally. She's an Inland Taipan, a sweet gal but the most venomous snake in the world. My personal favorite of course."

"Of course." I roll my eyes. "So, you've named them all?"

"The ones I've had the longest."

He continues introducing me to several other snakes, mentioning other sorts of toxins they possess as well as a few spiders and an interesting looking-lizard named Shirley.

"Shirley's a Gila monster," he says, nodding toward the thick-bodied lizard behind the glass. "Her venom's a neurotoxin, but it's rarely fatal to humans. They get a bad reputation, when really they just want to be left alone. Don't bother them, and they won't bother you. Funny thing—her venom carries a peptide almost identical to a human hormone that regulates blood sugar. Scientists used it to develop a diabetes medication."

He smirks, the pride in his tone unmistakable. "Creatures like Shirley... venomous or not, they can be remarkable."

I don't miss the way his face lights up as he shares a

few more interesting facts on his *pets*. He then takes a seat in a leather recliner and props his feet up on a matching stool.

"You sure know a lot about… well… a lot."

"I'm a fan of knowledge, understanding things, people… creatures." He raises a brow at me at that last word.

"You're trying to understand me?"

"I'm dissecting you. Don't worry, darlin'. It will be mostly painless."

"When will you let me leave? After your *dissection* is complete?"

"When I trust you or when your corpse is thrown into my trunk. The latter is probably more likely."

"I could just sneak out when you're sleeping or preoccupied with your *pets*."

"You could. But I would find you, and oh what fun I would have with you then." His gaze travels down my body then back up, meeting my eyes.

"I could kill you first. I'd have plenty of opportunities."

He tilts his head with a devilish grin like he enjoys the thought. "Please do try, little beast."

"You know, there's an advantage to being underestimated," I say as I step around one of the tables and move closer to him.

"Oh, you got it wrong, darlin'. I don't underestimate you. You simply overestimate yourself."

I don't respond, just continue staring at him with intense hatred. He then pulls the toothpick from his mouth and stands, towering over me. "Now, you best get out of here before you touch something you shouldn't or upset my pets."

With that, he strides past me and heads for the door. "Oh, and don't forget to put that blade back on the table. Wouldn't want you hurting yourself now."

Fuck, I didn't think he noticed that.

But he's out of the room now, so maybe I will just keep this one in case things get really bad.

Wouldn't be the first time I had to kill a man.

CHAPTER SEVEN

Another evening, another dinner Evelyn makes and serves while I sit at the far end of the long mahogany table from Venom. Tonight, the meal goes by mostly in silence. I'm surprised he can resist taunting me. We make eye contact a few times, but I look away first every time. When his eyes are on me, I can feel him studying, *dissecting*, like I'm some science project.

I'm not.

I just want to get out of here and start a new life for myself. Make the right decisions this time. I'm twenty-three and still have my whole life ahead of me. I could still have a great life.

"You've barely touched your food."

"What's it matter to you? Are you trying to thicken me up?"

"No need to hide my intentions. The answer is yes, so now eat."

"Thicken the pig before the slaughter?"

"Perhaps." He smirks.

Venom's phone rings and he leaves the room to take the call. A moment later he returns, looking irritated.

"Now you're costing me money. Just had to turn down an offer because I need to make sure you stay put and behave."

"I thought you had enough money?" I taunt. "Besides, that's on you. This is your decision."

"I made one poor decision—agreeing to help you. I should have left you in that hole. Let your body rot, your bones become one with the earth."

I slam to my feet; the chair scrapes back and clatters. Venom's eyes snap to mine.

"I've done nothing to you! You've been an asshole for no reason. I just needed a damn ride!" I shout.

He strides forward, long legs closing the space. "Well, you certainly got the ride you wanted. Maybe think twice before hopping into a car with a stranger—especially one who admitted to murdering people. Going off with strangers seems a habit of yours, darlin'. Maybe look in the mirror next time you need someone to blame."

His words sting. Fury burns hotter than fear; I slam my fist into his chest. "Fuck you!"

He smiles that godawful grin. My hand flashes up to slap him, but he catches my wrist.

"Now, now, beastie. Rule one." He rolls his sleeves, forearms taut and veiny.

I shove past him, aiming for the doorway, but his grip yanks me back. He slams me against the wall, one hand at my throat until I can't breathe. Evelyn appears in the doorway, gives an unreadable look, then disappears.

"Forgot the rules? Testing me?" he purrs.

"Or maybe I don't fucking care what you do to me anymore!" I spit.

"No, that's not it. Lies. You need an anger-management crash course." He smirks. "Seen anyone for that before?"

"Fuck you."

"You keep requesting that, I might give in."

I don't think—I reach into my pocket, grab the small knife I swiped from the greenhouse, and drive it into his thigh. He grunts, releases me, and steps back. Blood darkens his jeans. For a beat, I'm frozen, staring.

"My, my. You actually stabbed me," he says, amused.

"You deserved it."

"Well, that's debatable." He groans as he pulls the knife free from his leg and hurls it at me. I sharply inhale as the blade grazes my ear with a sharp, burning sting and sinks into the wall beside my head with a thunk.

I reach for my ear, feeling wetness then look at my blood smeared fingers. "You know you're an asshole," I snap.

"You know you secretly love it."

"Do I need to stab you again? And not miss this time."

His brows lift. "You missed? And where were you aiming?" My gaze flicks down. "No."

"Yup."

"You were going to stab me in the dick? Brutal, even for you, beastie."

"Well, stop pissing me off."

"Are you sure it's me you're pissed at, or yourself because you can't have me?"

I scoff. "I absolutely do not want you. I think I made that *very* clear," I say, staring at the blood seeping into his jeans.

"No?" He steps in, thigh still bleeding, trapping me between him and the wall. He drags a finger across the cut and smears the dark streak over my cheek. "Still a liar. Tsk."

"Venom! What the fuck!"

"You look good covered in my blood." He wrenches the knife from the wall and drops it into my hand. "Want more, little beast? Take it." A strand of platinum hair falls into his eyes as I search his severe blue stare.

"You're insane."

"Come now, darlin'. Don't be shy."

"I'm not playing your games."

"Shame." In a blur, he twists the knife from my grasp and presses the tip to my throat. "What if I still want to play? Maybe I want more of your pretty blood. You've got me all riled up."

"You're sick."

"So I've been told." He presses harder, and adrenaline rockets through me.

"Venom." I force the word out.

"Scared?"

"No," I snap.

"Liar. You think that makes you brave?" He chuckles

before his expression turns deadly serious. "Perhaps you're just a very stupid girl with a death wish."

"Death doesn't scare me."

"No? Then what does the wicked little beast fear?"

"As if I'd tell you," I growl.

"Whether you tell me or not, I'll uncover your fears. I'll discover everything there is to know about you, darlin'. Slowly but surely." His grin is menacing and I wish I could slap him.

"Just let me go!"

"Tell me something true."

"Fuck off."

I feel a sharp sting against my neck as he breaks skin.

"Venom!"

"Don't make me ask again."

"Fine! You psycho." I quickly rack my brain and blurt the first thing that isn't a lie. "Dahlias… my favorite flowers are dahlias. His grin widens like a predator satisfied. "Happy now? Let me go."

He pushes off me, looking calm and collected as if we hadn't just drawn each other's blood. He walks away without another word.

Asshole.

WHILE TAKING A shower, I try to avoid water running over my neck where Venom cut me, but it's proving difficult. How can a small cut sting so bad?

I give up and turn off the water. After drying off, I climb into bed, not bothering with clothes. Then I stare at the ceiling replaying every moment I've had with Venom so far.

I need to find his weakness.

That is, if the psychopath has any.

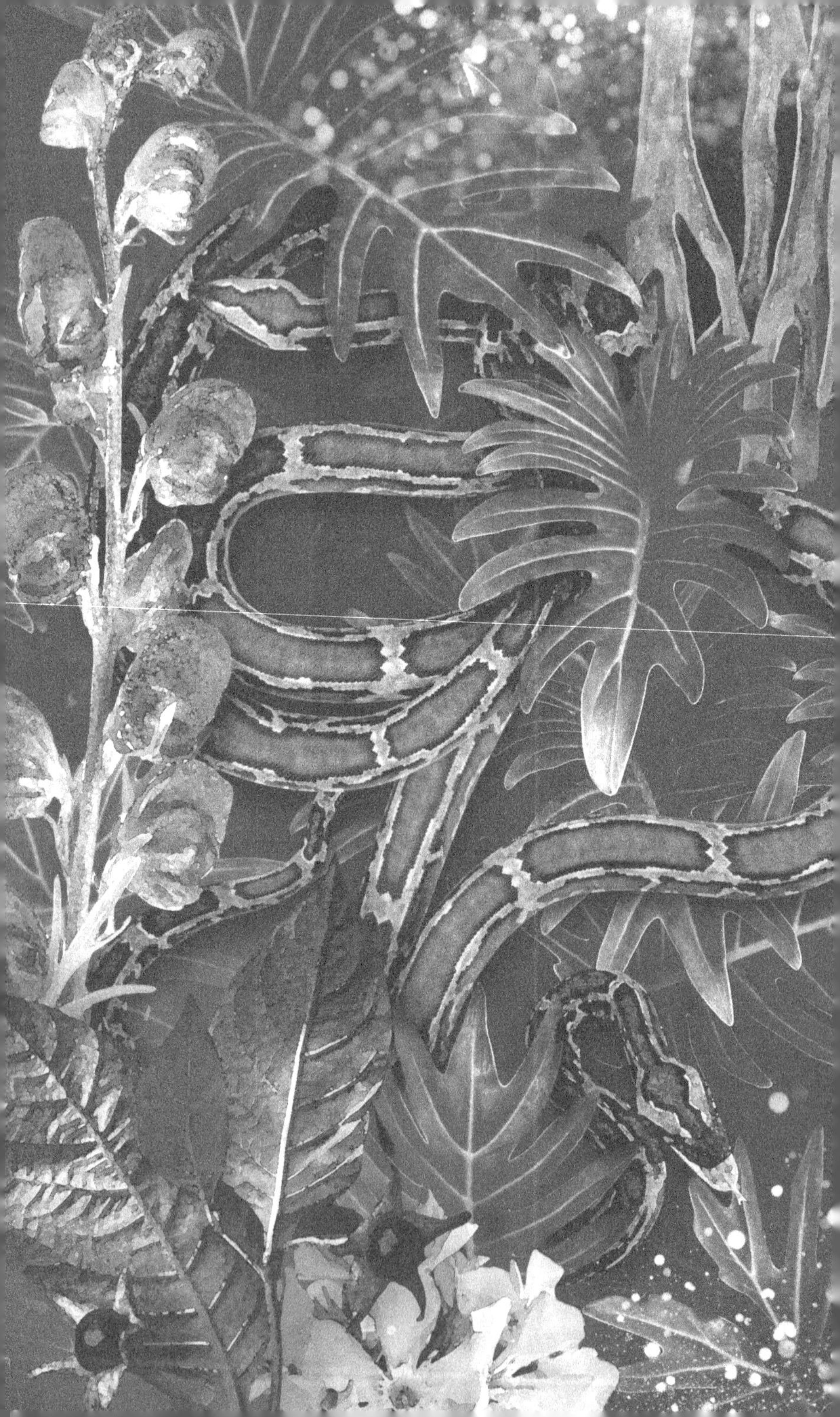

CHAPTER EIGHT

After tending to my wound and bandaging myself up, I leave my workstation in the greenhouse and run into Evelyn waiting for me.

"What?" I ask her.

She's looking at me like she's about to reprimand a child.

"*What are you doing, boy*?" she signs.

"This isn't something you should get involved in. I'm handling it."

Her brows furrow. "*I've seen how you're handling it.*"

"She's infuriating!"

"*And you think you're any better*?"

"Of course. If she stopped acting like some wild thing, maybe things would be different."

She shakes her head. "*You forget that I know you.*"

"And?"

"*You like the girl.*"

I laugh. Really laugh. "Like her? Ev, the beast has attacked me, like what, four times now? She is most definitely set on killing me."

She just smiles at me and pats me on the shoulder as she walks away.

Shaking my head, I make my way upstairs in mild discomfort due to my thigh, but also every movement of that muscle tickles something else inside me. Something that craves to stride into her room right now and hurt her. Make her bleed more just as I have.

But I don't. I walk past her room and into mine. Once I'm in bed, I open my camera app and take a look into her room and find her lying in bed on her back, her hair sprawled around her like a burning halo, and staring at the ceiling, at *me.*

She seems lost in thought.

What could such a wild beast be thinking about?

I stare at her longer than I should. If she knew she was actually looking at me right now, would she still be biting her lip like that?

I need this situation to be over with soon. One way or another before things get out of hand. If tonight proved anything, we're getting closer to a point where she won't come back from.

Morning arrives quicker than I hoped. I feel exhausted and my thigh is sorer and tender. It's a rather annoying reminder of the wild woman living in my home.

I step into the kitchen to find Evelyn and Ivy at the

small corner table. Evelyn's dry erase board rests in front of her, while Ivy's notebook is filled with scribbles and little sketches. Both of them glance up as I pass, but their eyes don't linger.

I head straight for the coffee machine, fix myself a tall mug of black coffee with a swirl of honey, and turn back to them as I take the first sip. Their focus has already shifted from me back to each other.

Evelyn raises both hands and signs *How are you?* Then she writes the words on her board and holds it up for Ivy. She repeats the motion, slower this time, and Ivy mimics her movements. They keep at it, Evelyn correcting with a patient flick of her fingers, Ivy responding with growing confidence as they move on to simple replies.

Ivy hasn't looked at me again, completely focused on Evelyn, seeming eager to learn. I study her for a bit longer. Her copper hair is in a messy bun with wild strands hanging around her face and her dark green tank top fits a bit too tightly against her creamy skin, so much so that I can tell she's not wearing a bra. Perhaps that's because she doesn't have one. I need to send Evelyn out for more clothes. And maybe more shoes, although she seems to always prefer to be barefoot instead of wearing the slip-ons I got her.

I continue watching Ivy's delicate hands copying Evelyn's movements, smiling and laughing when she gets it right and blowing out an exacerbated breath when it takes her more than a few tries to get it. Before I realize it, I find myself smiling at them. At her.

Strange feeling.

I'm not sure what to call it, but it's enough to make me uncomfortable. So I clear my throat and quickly leave the room without another glance at Evelyn and the beastly thing.

CHAPTER NINE

After spending most of the morning and early afternoon with Evelyn, I feel a bit lighter. It was refreshing to be around such a kind person. Where Venom is as cool as ice, the eye of an Arctic storm, Evelyn is the warmth in this home, the kind that wraps you in sunlight and settles into your bones.

There's still so much to learn but I hope I expressed how much I appreciate her taking the time to teach me her language. She said she can teach me more whenever I want, and honestly, it will be a welcomed distraction from the haunting memories and fears in my head. It will also give me something to do here besides wandering Venom's great estate while hoping I don't run into him.

Speaking of, I want to visit the greenhouse again, see the beautiful plants, smell the flowers, and press my toes into the dirt, but I have no idea if he's in there right now.

As much as I want to keep my good mood flowing, I decide to head to the end of the hall, into the tropical heaven, hoping I don't run into the man who so easily gets under my skin.

All my senses light up the moment I step inside the greenhouse. It's nothing like the last one I was imprisoned in—that place reeked of dirt gone sour, rotted plants and piss. This one smells clean, almost sweet, the air so pure I can almost taste it.

Everywhere I look, something beautiful greets me: broad leaves, bursts of color, careful order in the wild. A faint trickle of water drifts from somewhere unseen, and the high, bright notes of a bird echo through the space as if it's made this its sanctuary, just as I wish to.

I could spend hours here, breathing it in, letting the warmth and humid air cling to me, soothe my worries. After nine months of hell, this place feels like another world.

"Like what you see?" Venom says from behind me.

I whirl straight into his chest—half bare. The top buttons of his black shirt hang undone, revealing smooth, toned muscle and the curling head of a snake tattoo, the rest disappearing beneath the fabric.

A bead of sweat trails down the center of his chest, vanishing into the shadow where I can't see. My throat tightens. I clear it and step back, forcing myself to meet his bright blue eyes.

I blink, break the stare, and finally answer his question. "Yes. It really is amazingly beautiful in here. I've never seen anything like it."

"Even though most of the things in here are poisonous?" he asks with a raise of a dark brow.

"Even so."

"It truly is a beautiful thing. Life and Death. These hands plant, nurture and give life. These hands also create death from my very own garden of life." I swallow the sudden lump in my throat. "You know," he continues, taking a step toward me, causing me to bump into a table. He then takes a strand of my hair, twirling it around his finger. "You really are as pretty as a peach, but something tells me if I were to take a bite of you, darlin', I'd end up choking on a type of poison I'm not immune to."

His eyes move from my hair to my wide-eyed gaze. He then tips his head slightly, waiting for a response.

I don't know why words suddenly fail me. Normally, I've got a dozen sharp remarks lined up for him. But now, with his fingers tangled in my hair, his eyes drilling into mine, his body so close the heat rolls off him, I can't get a single one out.

His scent, clean and fresh like spring rain, fills my lungs until my head feels foggy and the air between us grows too thick to breathe.

"Viper got your tongue, darlin'?"

His smooth voice slices easily through my hazy mind and I snap out of it enough to respond with the only thing I can think of.

"How's your leg?" I ask smugly. Venom slowly smirks, then yanks my strand of hair before releasing it. "Ow! That hurt, asshole."

He walks toward the back of the greenhouse, and I follow. "Are you going to cry about it?"

"I don't cry."

"Never?" he asks as he sits in his recliner.

"Not since I was a child."

"Mmm, something we have in common."

"I'm disappointed to hear stabbing you didn't upset you more."

"Pain is an old friend of mine. If you want to upset me, little beast, you're gonna have to figure something else out."

"Is everything a game to you?"

"It sure keeps life from being boring. Now tell me, did you come here searching for me?"

I scoff and cross my arms. "No. In fact I almost didn't come *because* I didn't want to see you."

"Yet here you are, *seeing* me." He winks.

"You should be careful up there on your high horse. It's a long way down if you fall."

"You mean you wouldn't catch me?" He places a hand over his heart, feigning offense.

"I would much rather watch you break your neck in the fall."

He laughs. "Vicious beast." After a few awkward seconds of silence, he walks over to his snakes in their glass homes with his hands in his pockets. "So, Evelyn is teaching you sign language?"

"She is."

"Learn a lot today?"

"A lot to me but probably not according to you. She taught me the important stuff, like how to tell you off."

He turns to me. "My sweet Ev wouldn't teach you such things."

I shrug.

"So how is it you're immune to poison anyway?"

"Besides gradually building up tolerance with non-lethal doses, I also have a particular unique innate immune system, according to doctors. According to me, I'm just very special."

I roll my eyes at that. *What an arrogant prick.*

He turns back toward his pets, but his leg buckles mid-step. He steadies himself, then limps to his chair. Watching him struggle, an unexpected pang twists in my chest—guilt, maybe. For the first time, I almost feel bad.

Why should I feel bad? He deserved it. He deserves worse... I think. Maybe.

"I'm sorry. About stabbing you."

His brows furrow as he stares at me.

"Strange."

"What is?"

"I think you might be actually telling the truth."

"Well, I am. I just... you were right. I kind of have an anger problem."

"You think?"

I exhale. "For as long as I can remember, I've been angry. At my life, at myself for choices I've made, and why I've had to be put through so much."

"Fate only gives the strongest the burden of a rough life."

"I don't see it that way."

"And perhaps that's your problem. At least one of them."

I narrow my eyes, feeling annoyed. "Well, maybe I don't want to be strong then."

"I don't think you can be anything but strong, little beast."

He quickly pulls his dark jeans down, revealing his tight gray boxers and a blood-soaked bandage on his thigh. Shrieking, I turn away.

"Geez, give a girl a warning before you take your pants off."

"You're welcome to look, darlin'. Maybe see something else you like in here."

I shake my head. He never lets up. "Just do whatever you're doing and be done with it."

"I reckon I might need some assistance."

Turning back around, I look at him like he truly has lost his mind. "You expect me to help you now? Can't you ask Evelyn?"

"You were the one to stab me. And you're sorry, aren't ya? Come on, it's at an awkward angle and I clearly did a shit job at stitching myself up."

"You want me to redo it? I don't know how to do that!"

"I'll walk you through it. It'll be easy. Besides, you'll get to inflict pain upon me—your favorite."

"Yeah, but you like it apparently. That's not really a punishment."

"Come now, beastie" he says, holding out his hand.

I begrudgingly accept it. He gently pulls me to him, then sits. Motioning to a cart on wheels next to him, he says, "This has everything you'll need. You'll clean the area and sew me up. It will be fine."

I let out a long sigh and get to work.

With each step, Venom walks me through everything, a few times placing his hand over mine to show me how to do something or to stop me from fucking up. Toward the end, once I get a hang of it, neither of us speaks, but I don't miss the way his gaze never leaves me or the way he stiffens when my fingers graze his bare skin.

Twenty minutes later, his wound does look a lot better than before. I apply a bandage over it, and he stands before I do, putting his groin at my eye level.

Oh fuck. I almost fall back, but he catches my arm and helps me stand.

"Thank you," he says. "That should hold. Unless you attack me again."

"No promises."

"Wouldn't expect anything less. Now run off and go do whatever beastly things you do around here."

Before I turn, I sign, *"Eat a dick, asshole."*

And his shocked expression is the most satisfying thing I might have ever seen.

Thanks, Evelyn.

It's 3AM when I wake up to noises. No, not just noises… yelling? Is that Venom?

I crawl out of bed and leave my room.

"No! No! Please!" Venom screams from the room next to mine.

I walk over to the door and press my ear to it.

"Please, no more!"

I've never heard him so… distraught.

I try the doorknob—it turns easily. Against my better judgment, I ease Venom's door open.

The hallway light spills just far enough inside for me to make him out on the bed. Alone. His body twists, muscles tight, low groans slipping from him as though he's trapped in some unseen struggle.

I step closer, slow and quiet, until I'm standing at his side. Sweat beads on his forehead, platinum strands of hair plastered to his skin, his face contorted in raw agony.

Is he having a nightmare?

"Don't! No more!" he cries out again.

"Venom," I hedge.

Nothing.

His body jerks again.

"Venom. Hey." I reach out. "It's just a nightmare." My hand lands on his chest.

His eyes fly open, and I'm instantly roughly grabbed and twisted onto the bed, a blade placed to my throat.

He heaves above me with fury, his eyes boring into me, wild and murderous.

"Venom." I manage a breathless whisper and raise my hands in surrender.

His eyes soften just a bit but still anger coats them.

"What the fuck are you doing in here?" he snarls.

"I… I heard you. It sounded like something was wrong and you needed help."

"Does it look like I need your fucking help?"

"Um… maybe not so much now but it sure did a moment ago."

His glare intensifies and the blade digs deeper.

"I could have killed you."

"But you didn't."

"Not yet," he says through clenched teeth. "Get out." He pushes off me and stands. He's nude, but I quickly avert my gaze from the shadowed parts of him.

Slowly sitting up, I touch my neck to make sure I'm not bleeding.

"I was just trying to help. You were having a nightmare," I say as I stand, smoothing my shirt down to cover my panties.

He whirls on me again. "I was not having a fucking nightmare! Now, get out!" he shouts.

I say nothing further and leave him.

I know I've only known Venom a short time, but I've never seen him so out of character. He's always so put together—all cocky confidence. Just now though, he was a broken, disheveled man.

CHAPTER TEN

7 YEARS OLD

"Please, no more!" I beg.

I always beg, but it never helps. Mama never shows any mercy. She strikes my back again with the leather belt.

"Say you're sorry!" she demands.

"It was an accident, Mama!"

The belt comes down again on my bare back.

"Say it!"

I accidentally spilled her coffee this morning when I brought it over to her. Tripped on the edge of the rug and sent it spilling on the floor and the side of the sofa. It made her so mad.

Mama is always so mad.

"I'm sorry."

"Louder!" Another lash blazes across my flesh.

"I'm sorry!" I shout through tears. My gaze lands on my brother who sits like a statue on the sofa, afraid to move. He looks away from me, and I hang my head. "I'm sorry, Mama. Please, no more."

My pleas die when the buckle of the belt begins to crash against my back and spine, splitting and bruising my skin in white-hot pain. All there's left to do is hold my body tight and wait for it to end.

When Mama finally leaves me curled up on the floor, my brother finally comes over to me. The first touch of his hand on me sends me flinching and cowering.

"Marcus, it's just me. It's Ben." I lift my head and look at him through blurry eyes. "Come on, let me help you."

I let him slip an arm under me, helping me sit up and then stand. I used to wonder why Ben never stepped in when Mama would hurt me—until the one time he did. She got him real bad. Bad enough that he had to go to the doctor. He came home with his arm wrapped in bright blue, race cars printed across the cast. After that, Ben never tried to stop her again.

CHAPTER ELEVEN

Venom and I have not spoken about that night I entered his room. The next morning, he was back to his usual annoying self as if nothing had ever happened. If he wasn't going to bring it up, I sure wasn't either.

I've spent most of my time with Evelyn. Being drawn to her tender nature and warmth, growing closer to her over these weeks. Continuing to learn sign language and how to make some of her favorite dishes. I think she's the only reason I've kept my sanity in this place. Although, the greenhouse is different.

Besides being around Evelyn, the greenhouse has become a place I feel most calm, where my wild thoughts are a little less loud, where I can breathe easier.

I expect to find Venom there, but he's not around.

I'm not sure if I'm relieved or disappointed. He's kept his distance lately, only having brief interactions when he sees me, still enough to annoy me and leave me flipping him off as he walks away.

The table he works at, which is usually tidier, currently looks as if he left mid-*science project*. Vials of liquid, powdery substances, syringes, and dart-like objects are scattered about. There's also a bowl of juicy-looking dark berries close to the edge of the table. Seems he left his snack too. Must have been in a hurry.

Wanting to irritate him when he returns and finds his snack gone, I pop a berry into my mouth. It's decent, not overly sweet. I continue eating and looking around. I stand in front of one of the large glass cases and put a finger to it, stirring Black Betty's attention. She's cute but not like *I want to pet her* kind of cute.

I finish most of the berries and set the bowl down and get back to looking over all the different containers, saying hello to all Venom's pets.

"Hi there, I'm Ivy," I say, bending to meet a beautiful dark blue snake with light blue stripes and a red head. "You're a redhead too, huh? Are you also a prisoner?" I smile as it sticks out its tongue, probably trying to get a smell of me… or taste.

When I stand, I suddenly become disoriented, my vision blurring and my heart beginning to race.

Woah, did I stand up too fast?

My mouth feels dry and the light is suddenly too bright.

How did—

Where's—
I place a hand on the glass cases to steady myself.
Nothing feels right.
And then I'm falling.
Something crashes along with me as I hit the floor.
The room disappears.

"Ivy? Christ, Ivy!"
In the distance, I can hear my name being called.
Shit, everything hurts.
I try to take a breath in, but it's not deep enough. I need more. Why can't I breathe?
"Ivy! What happened?!" It's a man's voice.
Deep and smooth with a southern accent.
Familiar. So familiar.
Venom.
No, but that can't be right. He's never used my name before. I'm always *beast* or *beastie* or whatever else he uses to insult me.
"Hey, hey, look at me, Ivy. What happened? What did you touch? You need to tell me what you touched."
"B-ber-ry."

I look over at my workstation where I left a bowl of belladonna berries. Empty.
Fuck.
"Oh beast, what have you done?"

"Am… am I g—gonna die?"

"Most definitely, darlin'," I say with a smile.

"A-ass—"

Inspecting more of the area, I notice the shattered glass home belongs to Black Betty, who's now missing.

Ivy groans loudly in pain as I lift her into my arms, glass shards falling away from her. Passing Evelyn and letting her know to grab my black leather bag, I carry Ivy to my room.

She's unconscious by the time we make it.

I gently place her on my bed and get to work removing her clothes and inspecting her body. When I check her back, I'm stunned for a moment. Various linear raised scars scatter her back. Some thin and smooth and others crisscrossing in rougher patches.

This is not something I would have wished to have in common with her.

Who the fuck did this to her?

Before I let my anger consume me at the thought of Ivy being whipped and in pain, I flip my focus back to the urgent matter at hand.

More cuts from the glass reveal down her body, but then I find two puncture wounds on the side of her hip, swollen and red.

Oh, Black Betty.

Double fuck.

CHAPTER TWELVE

My eyes slowly open to a dimly lit room. As I become more aware of my surroundings, I notice a man sitting in a chair near the bed.

Blond hair, smooth, chiseled face, broad shoulders and long legs spread wide in his seat as he reads a book.

Venom.

"Am I dead?" My voice comes out hoarse.

Venom quickly closes his book and sits up. "Is this your idea of heaven? You, naked in my bed?" I look beneath the covers—I am most definitely nude. I quickly grip the sheets against myself and fix my gaze back to him.

"Too late for shyness now, darlin'."

"What happened?"

"Not only did you eat something you shouldn't have, you also seemed to have upset Black Betty when you broke her home."

The berries... the snake. Fuck, I was bitten.

"I told you to be careful in there."

"Shit," I groan, lying my head back down on the pillow.

"Anyway, you nearly died. Surely would have if I didn't get to you when I did. You'll be alright now though."

"You saved me?"

"Surprised? Honestly, it's becoming a rather annoying habit now."

"Thank you."

"You should rest. You've been in and out of consciousness for a couple days, but I don't think you're ready to be up and moving around just yet."

I nod, then stop him before he walks out.

"Why am I naked?"

"You were covered in glass and blood. But don't worry, darlin', your body was respected. Could also be worshipped when you're ready."

"Not a chance."

With another devilish smile my way, he leaves.

AFTER A FEW more days, I'm finally feeling like myself again. The swift care I received saved my life—antivenom to counter Black Betty's bite, activated charcoal, and even some antidote with a name I can't pronounce.

Venom saved my life.

Again.

In the sitting room, I find Venom lounging on the couch, staring into the lit fireplace, lost in thought.

The nights are starting to get cooler, and I must admit, being able to sit by a warm fire is pretty nice.

Venom is usually the one sneaking up on me, but here I am moving closer to him, as he seems unaware. I decide to clear my throat as he would.

"I know you're there, beast."

I sigh and plop down on the other couch. After a moment, he finally diverts his attention to me.

"How are you feeling?"

"Pretty good."

He studies me with furrowed brows. "You look like you want something."

"I do."

"Well, go on with it then."

"It's been weeks, Venom. And I almost died. I need to get out of the house."

"No."

"Please, I've been good lately, haven't I?"

"Suspiciously so," he says as he looks back to the fire. "Unless you count breaking Black Betty's home and causing Evelyn to be a nervous wreck at your severe state."

"Speaking of. Evelyn's birthday is coming up. I wanted to make her a cake."

That snaps his eyes back to me. Exactly what I'd hoped—enough to get his attention, maybe even my way out of the house. He's got a soft spot for her, whether he'll admit it or not.

"I can pick up what you need," he says with a dismissive tone.

"No offense, but when was the last time you went to a grocery store?" He lets out an exasperated breath. "You would be so lost and fuck up what I needed."

"Fine."

I quickly sit up. "Really?"

"But I will chaperone you. And I hope you know; you'll have to finally put on some shoes. No wild barefoot beasts allowed in stores."

I ignore his extra comment, too giddy at him actually agreeing. "You're going to go shopping with me?"

"Did you honestly think I would let you go alone?"

"Well, no. I didn't even think you would agree to this at all."

"For Evelyn. Not for you."

I smile. "Tomorrow morning then?"

"I'll check my schedule and get back to you."

I roll my eyes and leave.

BEING ABLE TO finally leave the house and have new surroundings is refreshing.

The drive to the nearest grocery store is longer than I thought, but I don't mind. I'll soak up every moment out here.

Neither of us speaks. Venom drives and I stare out the window, watching trees pass. Their leaves are beginning to turn, a sure sign that fall is here. It's quite beautiful.

Once Venom parks his car, he turns to me.

"Rule four, you behave yourself out in public or you'll

never see the light of day again. Don't make me regret this."

"Pinky promise," I say, holding up my pinky.

He looks at it with disgust, then exits the car.

The store is surprisingly busy for a Monday morning, and Venom looks instantly out of place. He keeps twisting his broad shoulders to avoid brushing into strangers much smaller than him. Eyes follow us as we move—some admiring, some hungry. Even the men can't help but stare. Venom either doesn't notice or doesn't care. I just shake my head.

As I pull out my list, someone next to me bumps into a table filled with fruit and a container drops to the floor, cherries spilling out and bouncing over my shoes. My heart constricts as the memories slam into me.

"My sweet cherry, you look beautiful as always. Come to me," he says in his Russian accent, patting his lap. I cringe but don't refuse. I'm already walking on eggshells, worried if he will let go of the fact that I refused to join him for dinner last night. I sit on his lap, and his fingers dig into my thigh as his other hand strokes my hair before grabbing a fistful and forcing me to look at him. My face twists in pain. "I haven't forgotten about last night. You denied me, Red. We cannot have that."

"I'm sorry, I told you I wasn't feeling well."

"You did. But you also lie."

"If I ask you to do something, you do it. I thought we established this. Should we start training all over?"

I shake my head. "No. No, I'm sorry. It won't happen again, Nik."

"It won't." He shoves me off his lap, and I crash to the marble floor. My knees hit first, pain jolting up my legs before

my palms catch me just shy of smashing my face. Agony sparks through me, but I don't cry. He'll never get my tears.

"Remove your shirt."

"Nikolai, please. I said I was sorry. It won't happen again."

"I'd like to make sure of that. Now remove. Your. Shirt."

I obey.

He crouches and touches my face lovingly. "When will you cry for me, sweet cherry?" I simply stare forward, bracing for what's to come. He laughs. "You still have that defiance in you. Such fire." He strokes my hair. "Such beauty." Then he reaches for his whip and uncurls it. The sound of it slapping against the marble floor has me flinching and I—

"Hey, you alright?" I'm snapped back into the present, staring down at someone gathering the scattered cherries. When I look up, Venom's eyes are on me, brows furrowed. I shake my head and wave a hand, brushing it off.

"Sorry, yea. Just got a little dizzy. I'm fine." He looks like he doesn't believe me, but he doesn't say anything. I step around the cherries and pull out my list and begin to look for the baking aisle. After going down a couple wrong aisles, I come to the end of one and nearly collide with another man carrying a full basket. *Gosh, what is with me.*

"Sorry," I tell the bulky man.

He takes one good look at me and his annoyed expression changes in a flash.

"No apologies needed, miss. That was my fault."

I offer a small smile and move to step around him, but he stops me with, "Hey, have I seen you here before?"

Shaking my head, I respond, "Nope. First time here." I look past the man to see Venom leaning against a table, fiddling with the toothpick in his mouth while intensely watching our interaction.

"Hmm, maybe I'll run into you again sometime. We could call it serendipity." He chuckles.

"Uh, yea, sure." I take a wide step around him and return to Venom's side. His gaze stays locked on the man, but when I glance back, I catch him still watching me. Most likely, he spent the whole walk staring at my ass.

Fucking creepy-ass men.

Venom finally follows me.

I make it to the baking aisle, grab what I need, and head toward the dairy section. Halfway down an aisle, I spot the same man at the other end. I can't tell if he's following me or just shopping for the same things, but either way, unease prickles under my skin.

I keep browsing, pretending not to notice him until Venom saunters past, stealing my attention in an instant.

Where is he going?

I watch as he times it just right and places himself in a position where he gets nearly pinned between the bulky man and an older couple shopping. They all apologize to each other and keep moving. But something feels off about it.

A moment later, that feeling is confirmed when the man collapses on the ground and begins seizing, foam and blood spilling from his mouth.

Multiple people rush to assist him.

"Call an ambulance," someone shouts.

"Oh my god. Sir, are you alright?" another asks.

He's most definitely not alright.

I briskly walk over to Venom who watches on from the end of the aisle with a smirk. He rounds the corner before I reach him.

"What the fuck did you just do?! Have you completely lost your mind?!" I whisper-shout.

"A long time ago, darlin'."

"You can't just go around killing people in a grocery store, for fuck's sake."

"I can if someone looks at you like he did."

"And how was that?"

"Like he wanted to bend you over the meat display and shove his sausage in you."

I nearly choke on my saliva at his words.

"And since when do you care how I'm looked at?"

"Drop your basket. We need to go."

He turns to leave, but not before snatching a bag of gummy bears off the shelf. Then he strides out of the building without the slightest effort to hide them.

Great. I'm an accomplice to murder and gummy bear theft.

CHAPTER THIRTEEN

"That was really unnecessary," Ivy says from the passenger seat.

"I assure you, darlin', it was necessary and even if it wasn't, I sure did enjoy it."

I don't need to have the gift of mind reading to know what that disgusting ball of grease was thinking while staring at my little beast. "I might prefer killing women, but I will end a man just as quickly for letting his eyes roam all over what is mine."

"What the fuck? I'm not yours."

"Make no mistake, beast. You are most certainly mine."

"I'm not some damn property, ya know."

"You are under my care; therefore, you are mine."

"More like under your captivity. I'm still a prisoner if I'm not free to leave."

"Would you have preferred to run off with that man?"

"Ew. No."

"Alright then." I finally toss the bag of gummy bears into her lap.

"Why'd you grab these?"

"They are your favorite."

She stares at me suspiciously as if I poisoned them.

"They are."

"You're welcome."

Scowling at me, she opens the bag and pops a few in her mouth. "So now what? We didn't get anything for Evelyn's cake."

I pull out my phone, quickly typing in something, then hand it to her. "Order what you need. I'll have it delivered."

"You mean, we could have done this in the first place?"

"You said you needed to get out of the house." I glance at her; she looks surprised. I can feel her gaze on me as I grip the wheel tighter. "I do hope you enjoyed your outing," I add, sarcasm dripping from every word.

A gummy bear pokes near my eyes, bouncing off my cheekbone. I slowly look over at her with a raise of my brow, and she simply smiles and looks away.

She really is so fucking beautiful… and infuriating.

Barely suppressing my smirk, I continue clenching the wheel in an effort not to touch her right now. Strange that most of my thoughts throughout this whole excursion have been about touching her. I almost wish she would attack me so I could wrap my hands around her throat and feel her frantic pulse beneath my fingers.

We're almost home when Ivy finally speaks again.

"So, you kill for fun?"

"That's part of it."

"Money too?"

"It's a nice bonus."

"Does the target matter? Or is it just as long as you're getting paid and can have a good time?"

"Like I said, I prefer women. I don't usually accept hits on men."

"You gonna tell me you kill children and puppies too?"

"I'm certainly not that evil."

"It doesn't matter if they didn't do anything wrong?"

"According to who?"

She huffs out a breath and looks back out the window. "That's fucked up," she says, crossing her arms.

"I never claimed to be a good man. I told you from the beginning, I am the villain."

"But why? You hate us that much?"

"Not exactly." I sigh. "Women are beautiful creatures, but I learned from a very young age that they can also hide viciousness behind a pretty face." I glance at her before continuing.

"Sometimes, beasts need to be tamed. Sometimes, they need to be put down. I love women too much to let the fakes stand among them. Those who mask their monstrous side with a soft smile don't deserve to breathe the same air as the true beauties."

I look over to her once again and she seems to be considering what I just said. Then she turns to me. "Who hurt you?"

"What makes you think I've been hurt?"

"Do you want the whole list?"

"You've been making lists? For me?" I ask with a grin.

"I'm being serious. No one becomes how you are without a troubled past."

"You know a lot about troubled pasts, don't you?"

"Quit deflecting!"

"Are you worried you might be next?" I know I'm riling her up, but I can't help it. She looks more beautiful when she's angry with me. It's certainly more comfortable than when she's looking at me like she might actually… care.

"Should I be worried? You could have let me die twice now. But really, how much longer are we gonna do this? I don't think you're ever going to trust me. So am I just going to be a prisoner forever or are you finally going to grow some balls and kill me?"

"And now you're thinking about my balls."

"Dammit, Venom, can you not be serious for more than five minutes?"

"Do you want me to kill you, little beast?" I ask as I pull into my driveway.

"I just want to be free one way or another."

An admirable answer. One I didn't expect to hear. We truly have a lot more in common than she realizes.

Before she exits the car, she says, "Don't you know villains don't get happy endings?"

"Maybe I've accepted that long ago."

"You could change. Be the hero instead."

"I don't think I have that in me, darlin'."

"Well, that's disappointing." She climbs out and walks into the house.

I drop my keys in a dish by the door before making my way to the small bar located near the kitchen to pour myself a much-needed drink. A moment later, I hear the all too familiar rumble of my car starting back up.

No.

I run to the front, noticing my keys missing in the dish as I throw open the door. Ivy just backed out of the spot in front of the garage and turned the car around the half circle driveway, throwing her middle finger out the window at me.

Oh beast, big mistake.

She begins to drive off down the path when I flip open my jacket and launch multiple small knives at my tires. They land true. As always.

She continues driving, but she won't get far.

I open the garage doors, grab a set of keys off a hook and start up my Corvette, sliding into the dark green custom seats with black stitching and a viper sewed into the back. The engine rumbles as I give chase to her.

She makes it down my long driveway, past the gate and a half mile down the road before she's driving on rims.

I fly past her, maneuvering directly in front of her path and then slam on my brakes. Ivy hits hers at the same time and swerves, nearly colliding with a tree. I quickly exit my car, straighten my jacket and stride over to her, casually leaning against the car and giving a hard knock on the window.

She looks at me through the glass, nostrils flaring.

I try the handle, but of course it's locked.

"Open the door," I demand as I tap on the glass.

"Fuck you!" she yells, then tries to step on the gas, only to realize she's stuck in the dirt.

She bangs on the steering wheel and screams.

"I'll ask one more time. Open the door."

"No!"

Fine.

I walk back to my Corvette, finger the small tool in the glove box, then return to Ivy. I press the device to the window; the glass shatters and she screams.

I shove my hand through the jagged hole, unlocking the door despite a cut ripping along my arm. The door swings open and I grab Ivy by the hair, hauling her out of the car.

"I'm disappointed in you, darlin'. I thought you'd try this sooner."

"Oh, fuck you! Let me go! Just let me fucking go!"

I tsk. "You broke the second rule. I can't let you go now."

I pop open my trunk and lift her up, then stuff her into the small trunk.

"No! Don't you dare!" she yells before I slam the trunk closed.

I make a quick call about my damaged Mercedes while she hollers and bangs inside the trunk. Then I slide back into my Corvette and drive home, taking my time.

The beast doesn't stop screaming, burning through her energy fighting metal, probably hurting herself more than the trunk.

Did I expect her to try to run? Sure. But I thought it would be sooner, and lately I'd started to believe we'd moved past these antics.

Once home, I take a deep breath, smooth back my hair and open the trunk. I'm all too prepared when she nearly pounces on me, clawing and hitting wherever her hands land. It takes some effort, but I finally drag her back inside and toss her on the floor in the entryway.

CHAPTER FOURTEEN

"I thought we were past this."

"Not a chance," I say as I lunge for him again.

Twisting and dodging my attack, he counters with his own and I end up pinned against the wall. Venom's front pushes against my back while my cheek presses into the wall.

He holds my arms behind me in a vise grip as I try to squirm. "My, my, you are an angry one today. Is this any way to thank me for taking you out?"

"Don't act like you did me some kind of favor when I'm still not free."

"Was my company not enjoyable?"

"No!" I growl, heart hammering in my chest.

"Shame. And how about now? Is this the attention you were craving, little beast?" He presses closer, and his body heat unravels me. I hate the way I feel when he's this near—something I can't explain, can't control. My body wants to betray me, and it's confusing as hell. I can't handle those feelings. Not now. Not when anger is safer. Anger is where I'm comfortable.

"Just kill me already!" I shout, not wanting to play these games anymore.

"Is this what it's about? You want me to give you the easy way out? Should I have let Betty's venom and the belladonna kill you?"

"Easy way?" I laugh. "Does this look easy to you?"

"You don't want to know what this looks like to me, darlin'."

"I broke your rule, so do what you have to do."

"I think I have a better idea. I think it's time we try something else."

"What do you mean?" My cheek is beginning to ache from being pressed up against this wall so hard.

"We need to take care of your anger problem. It's not healthy to harbor all that in such a beautiful body. I think it's time for another lesson."

"Fuck you, Venom."

He drops his lips to my ear and whispers, "Mmm, I do love the way you say my name when you're angry." His mouth grazes my skin and goosebumps spike along my arms; something low and wanton wakes in me and I clamp my thighs shut.

I shove my head back into his face. He grunts, surprised, and lets go of my hands as he staggers back. I bolt for the kitchen, snatch a knife, and spin to face him as he comes running in behind me.

"Put that down before you hurt yourself."

"Let me go."

"What do you think you're going to do with that?"

"I'll do what I have to."

He smirks, but then I put the knife to my throat, and his smug smile drops for once.

"What are you doing?"

"I told you, I'm ready to do what I have to."

"Come now, darlin', don't be foolish. You thanked me for saving your life and now you're so quick to try to end it? Put the knife down."

"Let me leave, Venom."

For a moment, he actually looks sympathetic. "I can't do that."

"Fine. So be it."

I press the knife into my skin. Venom moves in a flash, launching something at me. A sharp pain explodes from my wrist as a small blade lands into my flesh, causing me to drop the knife.

And then he's on me once more.

He pins me to the floor, my arms above my head. His grip around my bleeding wrist is painful but it only takes my attention away from my anger for a small moment.

"You will never do that again! You hear me?"

His eyes dart across mine, jaw clenched so tight I can see the muscle twitch. He looks furious—but is that... fear? No. Can't be.

I buck against him, desperate to break free from his grip.

"Stop fighting me, you wild beast!"

"Then let me go!"

"Never, darlin'."

I search his eyes, looking for something malicious, something evil behind them, but I don't find it. Instead, I see something that scares me more. Longing.

My heart thunders with a mix of terror and temptation as the air around us shifts. An invisible string pulls, but I resist, refusing to be swept away in the storm of his eyes, and push away the feelings he keeps coaxing from me.

His expression hardens, and in one swift motion he hauls me off the ground and slings me over his shoulder. He heads for a door I've never seen open before. The hinges creak as it swings wide, revealing a stairwell leading down into darkness.

Oh, fuck. He's really going to kill me now. Please let it be quick.

He pushes me onto my back on a cold table, tying my hands above my head onto a hook.

"What do you think you're doing! Stop! Get off me!" As I continue to squirm and fight, he wrangles my legs and secures my ankles to each corner of the table. No. No. No. "Untie me right now! What the fuck are you doing! Fucking untie me!"

I can't be tied up again. I can't.

Panic seeps in, bringing the memories, the trauma at the forefront.

Venom just stares at me as he leans against the wall with his arms crossed and a sick smile on his face. I hate him!

"I hate you!!!!" I shout with everything I have. "I

fucking hate you!! Let me fucking go! I'll fucking kill you! I swear I'll kill you!"

His smile widens, and he saunters closer. I buck, trying to break free and clobber him.

He pulls a small flat knife and flips it between his fingers, lifting it toward the dim light before waving the blade in front of my face. I freeze for a heartbeat, but then anger surges back, burning away any trace of fear.

"Do it! Fucking kill me then. Put me out of my fucking misery! DO IT!!!"

"Good. Feel your rage." His blade flashes, slicing away my pants, then my underwear, leaving me bare to the cool air and his hungry stare. "Let it fill your veins; let it threaten to consume you."

He sets the weapon aside, pushes my shirt up but leaves my breasts covered, then drags a finger in slow circles around my belly button. His gaze fixes on my stomach, as if lost in thought. "You live in a constant state of survival. And though I know too well the scars trauma leaves, I don't want to watch you keep yourself captive—don't want to see you destroy yourself."

My chest rises and falls too fast, eyes darting over his face, trying to read him.

"You didn't get to choose what happened to you," he murmurs, fingers brushing my skin again, raising goosebumps. Then his eyes lock onto mine. "But you do get to choose what happens now. So tell me"—his touch lingers, searing—"is it time to heal, little beast?"

I look at him with a mix of curiosity and confusion.

"Release your rage. Give it to me, darlin'. All of it.

Relieve yourself of the burden of harboring such toxic anger. Replace it with *this*."

He moves lower, skimming the top of my pussy with a gentle touch and my body stills. "Let me show you."

He doesn't move, as if he's waiting for my permission. I'm still so angry but now something else is beginning to creep its way in. Like a fever taking hold, burning and blurring my thoughts.

I nod, and without hesitation his hand slides between my thighs. Two fingers drive inside me and I gasp at the sudden, hard intrusion. Rage spikes, then shifts, twisting into something else.

Slowly, like a snake, it coils through me, slithering along my flesh before sinking its fangs deep. A different kind of venom floods my veins—soothing, heating, consuming.

My eyes snap to his. I clench around his fingers, breath ragged. His gaze pins me, sharp and unrelenting. There's no cocky smirk, only a tight jaw and a rigid body, like he's fighting himself as much as me.

He curls his fingers, begins to pump into me. My back bows off the table, a gasp tearing from me, and still I can't look away. I don't want to. His stare sears me open, melting away the armor I've carried, leaving me raw, trembling, twisted with desire.

What is happening? This can't be right, but ohh... it feels so good.

"Venom..." I whimper.

"Shhh." He places a finger to my mouth as he continues his movements between my thighs. "Just feel."

And I do. I feel everything. Too much. Things I don't want to be feeling. Things I haven't felt in so, so long. I should still be angry. I hate him... right?

They say there's a fine line between hate and...

A tear escapes my eye for the first time since I was a child and Venom swipes his thumb at it, bringing it to his mouth and licking it.

"You cry so sweetly, darlin'."

He pushes his thumb into my mouth. I wrap my lips around him and suck, swirling my tongue around his warm thumb. He rolls his eyes and lets out a small groan, enough to let me know he's pleased.

My pulse beats frantically. He's in my mouth and in my pussy and I've lost all train of thought. I don't even know what I was so angry about anymore. All I know is I want to just let go and surrender to this moment. Surrender to him as he consumes me.

He picks up his speed and adjusts so the heel of his palm keeps rubbing against my clit. I pull at my restraints.

Oh god.

The coiling inside me is terrifying, a delicious force threatening to sweep me away. But as much as I fear giving in, I also feel desperate for it.

The ache inside me intensifies.

Fuck, it aches so good.

"Do it. Come for me, beast. And don't look away."

I stare at him through the strands of hair falling over his forehead, swaying with each sharp jerk of his hand between my thighs. And god—his words, the way he's staring at me, those damn fingers.

I let go and explode.

My vision tunnels as I cry out around his thumb and bite down on him. He hisses and my body bucks and writhes through the first orgasm I've ever received by a man.

I've been toyed with before, but no man has ever given me an orgasm. None have ever even cared to. It was always about simply using me, and *their* pleasure, *their* twisted desires.

As I come down from the euphoric high, I release him, and he slips out of me. He drags his soaking wet fingers up my legs, around my belly and then across my mouth. Then he swiftly unties me and walks away without a word. Leaving me reeling, confused, and satisfied, yet still craving.... more.

I sit on the table and stare at the stairs he just disappeared from.

Why do I feel like this just changed everything between us? Now I'm more scared than I have ever been.

But it isn't that moment that haunts me later, when I'm lying awake and trying to sleep. It's something else— the memory I wish I could outrun: the first time I met the man who fed me false promises... and revealed himself to be a monster.

"Well, aren't you a pretty little cherry." He strokes his finger over my cheek, then toys with my hair as he circles me.

"Please, don't hurt me. I'm just looking for a job."

"Oh Cherry, I'm not going to hurt you. I'm going to take such good care of you. So much so that you'll never want to leave." He smirks, and I recoil further away from him. "The name is Nikolai. Welcome."

CHAPTER FIFTEEN

T he next day, I sleep in until noon.

I groan and roll over in bed, not wanting to wake up.

I'm not sure I want to see Venom. How can I face him again after what happened yesterday between us. There's too much to process. The things I'm feeling are still too confusing, even more so as I wake up and realize that was not some fucked up dream. It really happened.

I keep expecting to feel anger at the memories, but I don't. I can't. Maybe I'm more fucked up than I thought.

My stomach growls.

I open my door and find a couple of plastic bags filled with items on the floor in front of me. I peek in and find a note.

These arrived this morning. The butter and eggs are in the fridge.

—V

I'd forgotten all about the things I ordered for Evelyn's cake. I'd been so worked up that it completely slipped my mind I was supposed to be doing something nice for her birthday. The realization makes me feel like shit.

She cared for me when I almost died. She worried about me. She's treated me with nothing but kindness.

The least I could've done was wait until after her birthday before trying to run away.

I drop the bags in my room and head downstairs. In the fridge, a plate waits with a sandwich and a sticky note in Evelyn's handwriting. I smile and grab it.

I'm just finishing the last bite when Venom walks into the kitchen—gray sweatpants, black tank top. My eyes widen at what else is draped over him: a blue snake, coiled around his muscular bicep, its head resting where his shoulder meets his neck. He doesn't say a word. Just grabs a water bottle and leaves. No glance, no acknowledgment. As if I'm invisible.

But the moment he stepped in, my heart started racing. My thighs clenched. Nerves fluttered where anger used to sit.

Jesus, Ivy. One orgasm and you forget he's your captor.

Except… maybe he's been more than that. Or less. Maybe I've been seeing this wrong. Maybe he's been keeping me safe—safe from what's out there, safe from myself and the mistakes I'd make.

He's never hurt me unless I struck first. He pulled me out of that hole. Saved my life twice when he could've let me die. He clothed me, gave me a room, fed me meals better than I've had in years. More freedom than I'd known.

My anger blinded me. Whatever hypnosis or voodoo he worked yesterday, it's left me seeing clearer. I've been a bratty beast.

I clean my plate and slip back to my room. I know I need to talk to Venom, but I'm not ready to meet his eyes yet.

When I'm sure Evelyn's asleep—and hopefully Venom too—I take my bags of groceries to the kitchen, ready to bake her birthday cake.

Thankfully, I bought everything I need to make it from scratch. I combine the wet and dry ingredients, stirring quietly, when a door closes somewhere down the hall.

Shit.

Venom strolls into the kitchen and stops when he sees me, looking just as surprised as I am.

I quickly avert my gaze.

"What are you doing?" he asks softly.

"Making Evelyn's cake."

"At this hour?"

"Well, I didn't want her to see. It's supposed to be a surprise."

He steps around me, his arm lightly brushing against

me as he passes, and it sends a burst of warmth through me.

"You're making it from scratch?"

"I am."

"How'd you get a recipe?"

I tap my head. "It's all in here. A recipe my mother taught me." He nods and then his expression shifts to a faraway look.

"Were you close?" The words come out too soft, almost a whisper.

"For a short time, I guess. We used to bake together often. They're the only good memories I have of her before she died of an overdose."

I glance over and find him leaning against the counter, arms crossed, his expression distant, thoughtful.

"How old were you?"

"Twelve. I had a few different foster families until I turned eighteen."

"They didn't treat you well," he says it more like a statement of fact rather than a question.

"Nope. My anger only progressively got worse."

"A hard life can do that to a person."

"Sounds like you would know, except, you don't seem angry."

"Once upon a time I was, but I channeled it into something. Something a bit more wicked." He grins.

I dump the mixture into the cake pan and slide it into the oven. I begin cleaning up when I notice he's still watching me.

"Enjoying the show?"

"Quite."

I roll my eyes.

"Don't you have something else to do?" I'm starting to get more uncomfortable with his lingering presence. Memories from yesterday keep flashing in my mind.

"You look a little flushed, darlin'. Are you alright?" he asks with an amused grin.

"I'm really not in the mood for your games right now." He doesn't respond, just continues staring at me with a tilt. "Look, I know we need to talk about what happened, but—"

"But?"

"I just… I can't right now, okay?" I'm feeling more overwhelmed. My hands beginning to tremble.

How can he so easily stir the chaos within me all while looking unaffected. He's the definition of cool, calm, and collected.

"Now seems like as good a time as any."

"No." God, I swear the room is getting hotter, must be the oven. I'm feeling desperate for fresh air.

He takes a step closer, and I move to the other side of the room. He follows.

Dammit, why can't he just let me be!

I hold up a trembling hand. "Stop. Don't come any closer." He continues stalking toward me like a predator to their prey. "I mean it, Venom!" I should just run back to my room right now and lock the door, but before making that decision, he reaches me as my back hits the wall.

Smirking, he presses his body into mine.

In a panic, my hand snaps out and cracks against his cheek, jerking his head to the side. Slowly, he turns back to me, his expression unreadable. Then his hand clamps around my jaw with a firm grip and he leans close. "Slap me again and I'll consider it foreplay."

"Fuck you." My tone doesn't carry the same harshness it once did, and I pray he doesn't notice.

"Say *please*."

"You disgust me," I lie.

"Your body sings a different tune, darlin'. I think we established that yesterday, right?"

I hate that he's right. Every time he's close, every time those eyes caress over me, my anger wants to dissolve. I want to just let go and surrender to him. Especially now, after yesterday, I'm just left wanting.

I'm a match, wanting nothing more than to be set ablaze by him. But I'll be damned if I admit that right now.

"Let me go, Venom."

He leans into my ear and whispers, "If there's something you desire, use your manners, little beast."

As he pulls away, his lips graze my cheek and my knees weaken. His gaze drops to my mouth, parted as I drag in quick, shallow breaths, before rising to meet his eyes again. I summon what strength I have left to shove off the wall and try to escape him... escape this.

Whatever *this* is between us.

He quickly moves his hand from my jaw down to my neck and slams me back. I grunt and look at him through watery eyes. Why am I about to cry? I'm tougher than this. I've been through worse; I remind myself.

But it's him. Not my foster parents, not Nikolai, not the redneck couple.

Him.

I can't handle these feelings he drags out of me. I can't take any of this anymore. I feel like I'm losing my sanity... what little there is left.

Every pounding heartbeat pushes me closer to the edge.

I don't want to fight him anymore.

I'm exhausted.

His wicked blue eyes bore into me, sending chills through my body. His lips hover above mine and I close my eyes for a moment before I open them back up and try pleading with him.

"*Please*, Venom," I whisper.

Then his lips crash against mine, rough and unyielding.

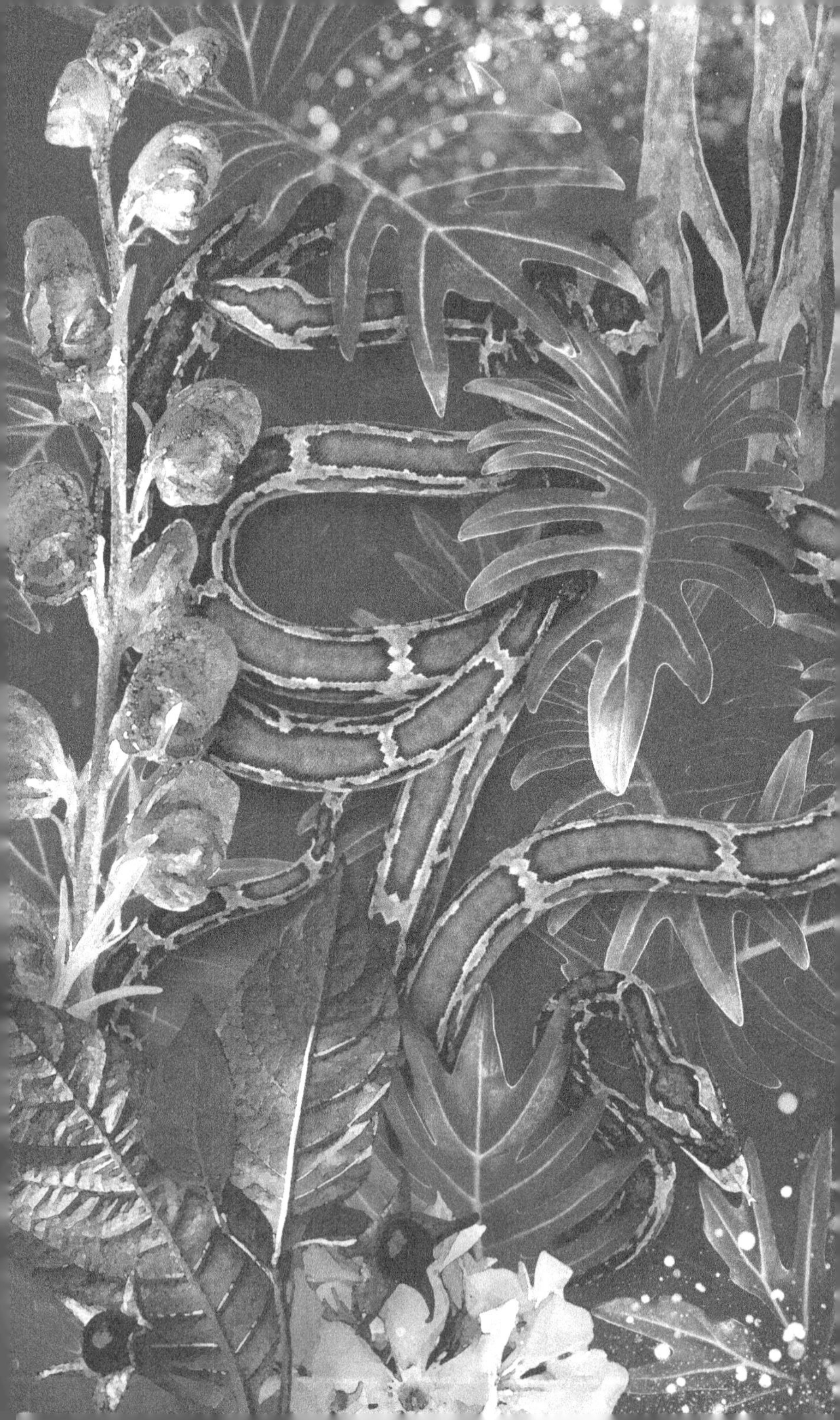

CHAPTER SIXTEEN

Kissing Ivy feels like the sweetest poison entering my bloodstream. I am on fire—too wild to contain.

Fuck, her lips are so soft. When everything about her has been so tough, her lips give me a dose of tenderness.

I've stopped trying to figure out what it is about her that drives me to a state of mind that's so foreign to me. A place where I can't stop thinking about her and wanting my hands all over her body, marking her as mine with my bruises and kisses.

The beast fights me every chance she gets. If it were anyone else, she'd be dead.

But it's *Ivy*.

It's the green-eyed wild thing, with hair like hellfire and a tongue full of venom, who somehow speaks to a part of me I didn't know existed. It's the girl who smells like summer, something I've never cared for outside of my tropical oasis, but her scent has me painfully missing the season whenever she's not near.

We've drawn each other's blood and caused pain, but now, I want her pleasure.

Yesterday's lesson in the basement wasn't enough. If anything, it turned me into an addict. Wanting nothing more than to watch her come for me over and over again. It might have started off as a way to replace her anger with something more satisfying, but all it truly did is fuck me over in the end.

Because now, Ivy is my favorite dose of poison.

For a breath, her shock freezes her in place. I use the moment to drag my tongue along the seam of her pretty mouth, savoring her, and then I bite down on her bottom lip, dragging it into my mouth. She gasps, and to my pleasant surprise, she begins to return the kiss, her arms collaring my neck. I lift her, wrapping her legs around me and smashing her against the wall. Another delicious noise leaves her mouth.

The kiss deepens, becoming frantic and desperate for more. I fist a chunk of her hair and pull, drawing out a breathy groan from her as I walk over to the dining table and then lay her atop it. I pull away from her lips, seeing her eyes wide, feral; just how I like her.

I yank off her sleep shorts and underwear in the same motion and kneel before her, pulling her plump ass to the edge of the table. I give her one last smile before I set my mouth onto her delicate pink pussy.

My tongue sweeps through her as I finally taste the sweet beast. Her back arches off the table and she moans while attempting to grab onto the table. "My, my, you are the sweetest tasting poison," I say, breathing against her.

I dive in, licking and sucking, savoring her light, honeyed taste as my cock throbs painfully hard.

I want more. I need more. I crave her.

Her moans grow louder when I push two fingers into her and suckle on her clit as I pump into her.

"Oh fuck, Venom."

I hum against her sensitive nub, and she whimpers for me.

"Please, Venom… fuck, make me come again."

"I do love when you beg, sweet beast."

I move my free hand from her thigh and reach out to grab her breast under her shirt, tweaking her nipple.

"Yes, harder."

I oblige and pinch her nipple again as I suck her clit and fuck her with my fingers.

Her loud cries fill the dining room as she bursts apart, grabbing my arm and squeezing my head between her thick thighs. I watch her intensely and listen to her sweet cries of pleasure as I lap her juices up.

I slide my fingers from her and grip the edge of the table as my cock threatens to burst from my jeans and take her right here and now. My vision sways, and I feel myself going feral. A viper ready to strike.

I need to get out of here. Away from her.

I wipe my mouth and take one more look at her sprawled out on my dining table, looking like the best meal I've ever eaten in here and, well… ever.

Christ, she's beautiful.

Turning to leave, her voice stops me. "Wait. Where are you going?" she pants when I turn around.

"I need to go."

"Why?"

I dare a look at her and her disappointed expression nearly breaks me.

I take a step towards her, feeling my body tense, hands clenched at my side.

"If I don't leave you right now, then I'm going to shove my cock in you and tear you apart right now. And darlin', as much as I fucking want to, you're a virgin. The way I would fuck you right now is not what you deserve for your first time." With that and all the strength I have, I turn and leave my sweet beast.

FISTING MY THROBBING cock in the shower, I jerk myself hard and fast to the thoughts of what I truly wanted to do to Ivy down there. It's not the most enjoyable orgasm but a necessary one. I don't think Ivy's sweet virgin pussy is ready for me just yet.

I need to better control myself, but hell, the wild woman might just break me in a way no woman has before.

The ways I've been broken before were tragic, painful, but what Ivy could do to me now, I'm not sure I'd survive.

CHAPTER SEVENTEEN

The oven beeps, signaling the cake is done.

I sit up, legs feeling like jelly as they dangle from the table. My eyes trail over to my shorts and underwear lying on the floor where Venom disposed of them.

Letting out a long breath, I run my hands over my face then place one over my heart. God, it's still beating so fast.

I slide off the table, put my bottoms back on and go back into the kitchen to take the cake out before I burn the damn thing. After letting it cool off for a bit, I frost it and set it aside, ready for tomorrow.

I make it back to my room and crawl into bed. Thoughts of Venom between my legs, and the way he looked at me before he left keeps me from falling asleep.

A part of me wished he stayed, did exactly what he desperately wanted to do to me. But another part of me feels strange emotions knowing he wants my first time to be special.

Venom has turned out to be someone I gravely misjudged.

I look to the wall to my right, knowing he's on the other side. Is he lying awake too, unable to sleep because of how everything has changed between us?

Turning on my side, I clutch the covers close to my chest and stare at the wall until at some point, sleep takes me.

"Happy Birthday!" I say and proudly sign to Evelyn. Her surprised expression is everything I hoped for. Tears brim her eyes as she smiles.

"Happy Birthday, Ev. You're officially older than the mountains and got twice as much dust," Venom says.

"Hey! You can't pick on her on her birthday."

"Oh, is that so?"

I shrug. "I didn't make the rules, but we will follow them. Now grab some plates."

I expect him to quip something, but he doesn't. He walks over to the cabinet and grabs the plates. Evelyn gives him a loving smack on his arm as he passes.

We all sit and eat the chocolate cake, and both Venom and Evelyn compliment how delicious it is.

Sitting here at the small circular kitchen table with

them, sharing casual conversation with sign language that I can actually be a part of thanks to Evelyn teaching me, feels good.

I still have more to learn, but for the most part, I keep up. This feels natural with them. It almost feels like I'm part of their small, odd family. A warmth blooms in my chest, a lightness taking over me where I normally feel heavy. I think I feel real happiness right now.

I laugh at an insult Evelyn signs to Venom, and he chuckles too, his eyes finding mine. We stay locked there for several beats, laughter fading to smiles, then to nothing. The air shifts, tension sliding into the space between us as Evelyn glances back and forth, reading it too.

I quickly excuse myself, leaving them staring after me.

I don't wander far though, I step into the living room and make my way over to the mantle above the fireplace, taking a picture frame and looking at the photo of Venom and his brother again.

The air grows thick with tension, a heat cocooning my back and a particular earthy, sweet scent messing with my senses.

"That's my older brother, Ben, in the white shirt," Venom says over my shoulder.

I had a feeling the taller boy was his brother.

"Shouldn't you be smiling?"

"Should I be? Probably."

"But you're sad," I say, stating the obvious.

"I am. Well, I was. It was not a good time in my life."

"Yet you keep this picture as a reminder?"

He moves to my side. "It's the only one I have of my brother. He's dead," he says flatly as he takes the picture frame from my hands and stares at it.

"I'm sorry. I didn't mean—"

"It's fine. He… he deserved what came for him."

What or who? I don't voice my question, though.

"Oh."

"He was still my brother. Our relationship was just…" He takes a breath. "Complicated. Sooner or later, his poor decisions were going to catch up to him."

"You didn't try to talk some sense into him?"

"I only remember one conversation with him about his life choices, and he didn't care to hear advice from his younger brother." He lets out a sardonic laugh. "Ben always did whatever he wanted, no matter the cost to anyone else. Selfish prick."

He sets the picture back on the mantle, his thumb brushing over his brother's face before he slips his hands into his pockets.

"What happened to him?"

"A vigilante took care of him. Knowing who that was, Ben had a very painful death."

"You never thought of getting revenge for his death?"

"I certainly got my own form of revenge in a way. It actually happened earlier this year." A satisfied smile grows across his face as he recalls his *revenge.*

"But the vigilante… he's still alive?"

"Yes, he lives. Dare I say we might be on good terms nowadays." He finally turns toward me and then tucks a strand of hair behind my ear.

The gesture sends my nerves buzzing. Unsure how to react, I quickly break eye contact.

My eyes land on a book lying on the coffee table in front of the couches. "So, you like to read?" I blurt out.

He smiles and retreats, releasing me from the hold his intoxicating energy had on me. "I would think a personal library would surely give that away."

"You have a library?"

"You didn't know? Third floor."

My mouth drops further open. "There's a third floor?"

"What in the world have you been doing around here this whole time?"

"Not exploring enough apparently."

"Spending all your time fighting me instead," he says with a playful raise of a brow.

"Can I see it?"

"You can do more than just see it. Follow me, beastie."

In my defense, the stairs to the third floor were in a room I've never been into.

I follow him up a spiral staircase to a double set of tall doors. He looks back at me before pushing them open in a grand gesture.

Soft lights automatically switch on, casting a dim glow, already making the space feel cozy.

My eyes brighten as I step further in, taking in the grand room. Every wall is lined with floor-to-ceiling shelves crammed with books. In the center lies a large rug patterned with florals and two intertwined snakes, perhaps lovers. A wide black recliner, a burgundy chaise lounge, and a matching loveseat rest atop it. A small table holds a plant with delicate white blossoms I can't name, but it's beautiful all the same.

The air smells like an old bookstore laced with the crisp scent of new pages, softened by a faint trace of vanilla.

"This is impressive."

"This is what it finally took to impress you?"

I roll my eyes and smile. "It's just... not what I expected." *You're* not what I expected, I almost add.

"I've always loved to read since I was a child. At times it was the only thing I could do to escape my reality and keep myself alive."

I eye him curiously. Venom is still an enigma. I keep getting little pieces of him, but I want to know more about him. I want to know how he became who he is. It's not even a want... more like a need. A need to know him on a deep level. I want to peel back his layers and truly see the man behind *Venom*.

"You can talk about it, if you want," I say.

"I don't talk about it."

"You don't or you won't?"

"I've never talked about it with anyone actually."

"Maybe that's the problem. You've kept it all in. Bottled it up, gave it a good shake, and it's been threatening to pop ever since. You might feel better if you share your story, let it out. Let it go."

I don't bring up his nightmares and how it might help those too.

"You know from experience?"

"Ha. If only. I should probably take my own advice."

"Go on then, darlin'. Let it out, let it go."

I look at him thoughtfully for a moment and then I sit and begin speaking.

"Where do I even begin?" My laugh scrapes out hollow. "My life has always been shit. At least... the parts I can remember." I rake a hand through my hair, staring down at the rug. "I wish I could say the worst of it was with my drug-addict mother, but truthfully, that was probably the best. Because at least then... I had a family. I wasn't alone."

My fingers twist in my lap before I push them through my hair again. "After she died, it was foster homes. One after another. Families who treated me more like an animal than a kid. I suppose I did behave quite—"

"Beastly?" Venom smirks, leaning back with his arms sprawled across the loveseat.

"I was angry. Hurt. Scared." My gaze lifts to the high ceiling, lungs tightening with the sigh that leaves me. "Like my entire existence was punishment for something I didn't even do. Just... for being alive." When I glance back, Venom's brows are furrowed, his eyes unexpectedly soft. I push the moment away and keep talking. "The day I turned eighteen, I left. Never looked back. I tried to find work, but it's not easy when you're homeless. Then I met this girl my age. She offered me a place to stay, said she could hook me up with a job, dancing. Good money. Promised I'd be taken care of."

I swallow, my fist curling tight. "That's when she

brought me to the club. And introduced me to Nikolai." Venom's gaze dips to my clenched hands. "He looked at me like he'd just been handed easy prey. Promises poured out of his mouth and I was so desperate, so alone, I believed him. Or maybe I just wanted to."

"I take it that didn't go well?"

I shake my head. "Nope. I was so stupid. He became obsessive. Possessive. I barely danced a few times before he couldn't stand other men looking at me. Touching me. Then he found out I was a virgin." My laugh is sharp and bitter. "The girl who brought me in told him. She was just his rat." The memory forces me to my feet. I start pacing, anger bubbling hot. "That night he dragged me off stage mid-song. I never went back. He locked me in his home, kept me tied up when I disobeyed—which apparently meant refusing to eat with him, talking back, trying to leave, or not falling in love with him fast enough."

Venom says nothing, only watches.

"That's what he wanted," I spit. "Stockholm syndrome or some shit. He wanted me to beg him to take my virginity, to make it seem like I loved him. Like it wasn't my choice." I bark out a laugh.

"He wanted to feel special," Venom adds.

"Well, I sure made him feel special right before I shot him in the head."

Venom sits up straighter, eyes wide. "You did what now?"

I drop back into the chair. "One night, I played along. Seduced him. Convinced him I'd fallen, that I wanted him to be my first. I almost felt bad at how happy he looked." I lift a finger. "Almost. Not enough to stop me. His guard dropped, he set his pistol down on the bedside table. I grabbed it, aimed, and pulled the trigger."

"Vicious beast." Venom's smile is sharp, almost proud.

Despite myself, I smile back. Then shake my head. "I won't pretend I wasn't scared. I was terrified. But I left him and didn't look back. Took cash from his wallet, though I should've had a better plan. I didn't think I'd actually get out. I made it a few states away before I met that couple in Virginia. Sweet on the surface. Offered me work on their farm, a place to stay. Sounded promising."

Venom jaw tightens, his brows furrowed.

I wave a hand. "Anyway, you know how that ended."

"I do. They did not have a pleasant death, just so you know."

I smile at that. "That is oddly comforting. I just wish I was there to witness it too."

"And I wish I had gotten to them sooner, found *you* sooner."

I give him a small smile before I break eye contact.

"Who hired you anyway?"

"I don't look into my clients, but I was curious after I found you. The *who* is not exactly specific, but that vile woman... *that couple*, had been up to these extracurricular activities for quite some time. Trafficking young girls. My client was a disgruntled customer of theirs who was fucked over and felt as though he was scammed."

"Scammed?"

"Apparently, he paid a lot of money for a girl who

was supposed to be a virgin. She was found to be not that. She also died soon after. He received a *used and defective product*." Venom puts his hands up. "Not my own words."

"Fucking men. Do you know how old she was?"

"I do, but I will not say. We don't need to dwell on the past."

"Seems like you're still holding on to your past. That's what we're doing right now, right? Sharing our past and letting it go? I think it's your turn now."

I think he's about to refuse but to my surprise he grins, sits back once more and begins.

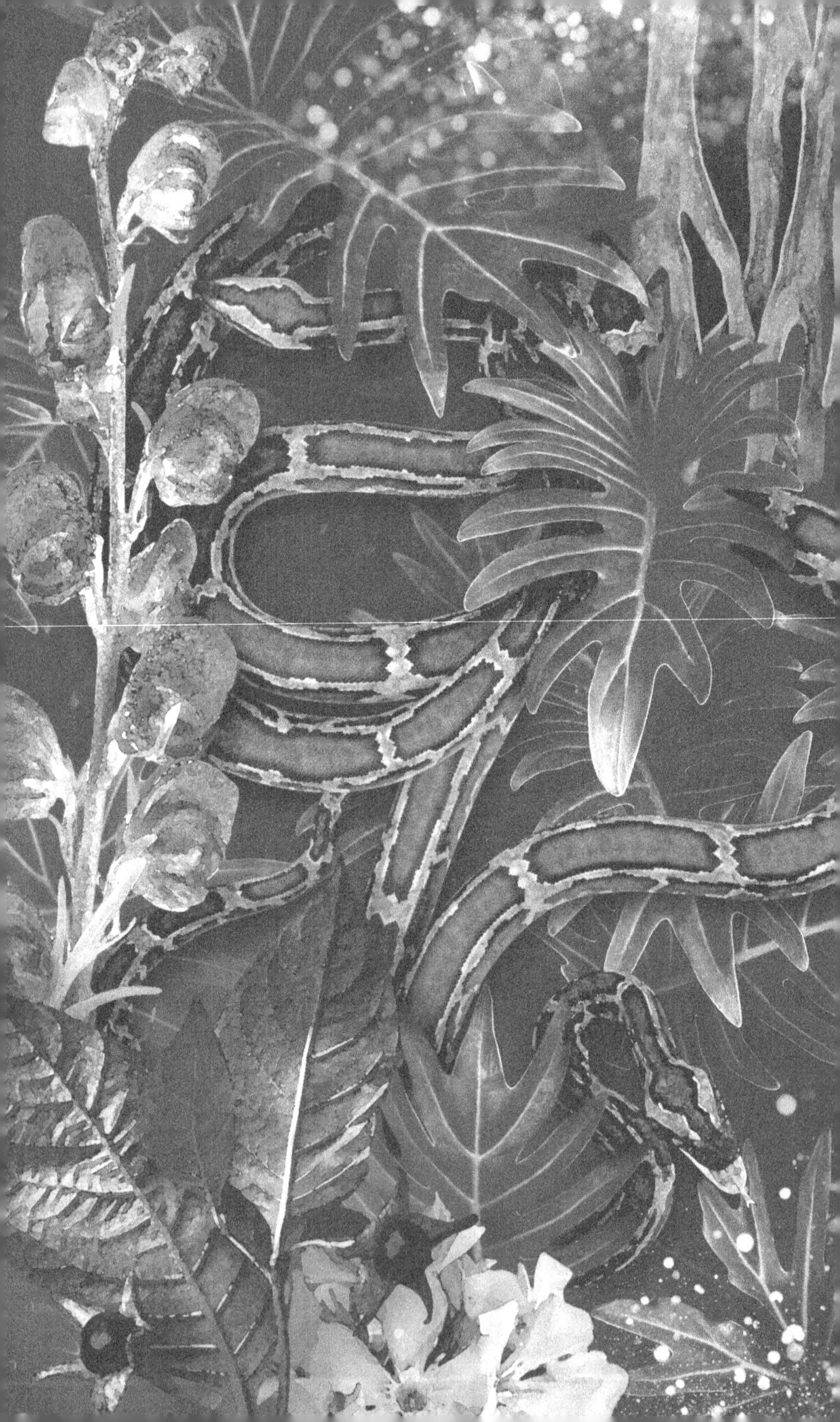

VENOM

CHAPTER EIGHTEEN

"Well, alright then." I lean forward, forearms braced on my thighs, hands clenched so tight my knuckles begin to ache. "My mother was a hateful, wretched woman. She beat me for anything. For nothing. Just to bleed her rage out on me."

I risk a glance at Ivy. She drops her gaze, pushes her copper hair behind her ear like she can tuck away her guilt.

"Ben got less." My lip curls. "Always less. I used to wonder why. What was so wrong with me? Later I learned. Different fathers. Mine was a disgusting nobody, renting out a hole for the night. Ben's? Maybe she cared for him. Maybe not. Doesn't matter now." I let out a low laugh, more breath than humor. "Pain became a friend of mine early on. As did the creatures in the yard and the books I stole for my closet. I would spend my days reading, escaping to faraway places. Anywhere but there. Wizards. Giants. Wardrobes."

The corner of my mouth curves up at the memories, at the comfort those stories brought me.

"That was my escape from the hell I was living." My smile falters and jaw flexes. "As I got older, the stories darkened. Same as my life. My mother started regularly selling herself for cash. Men came and went like smoke. Some patted my head. Some just smiled that sick smile on their way out. I used to think my mother was beautiful. Turns out she was vile and greedy. Greedy for money. For power. For more than she ever deserved."

I stand and walk over to the small bar cart and pour myself a drink before taking a seat again in front of Ivy.

The whiskey burns as it goes down.

Doesn't quiet the memories.

"When I was seventeen, she told me I was a man now. I didn't know what the fuck that meant until Caroline walked in. Sophisticated. Older. Not ugly but certainly not my type." I raise a brow at Ivy, and she presses her lips together. I grin and continue, "She took me to Ben's room. Talked for a bit. Then she started touching me, touching me in ways I had never been touched before."

The glass sweats in my hand. I don't look at Ivy. "She kept telling me to relax, that I would enjoy it and how she was so thrilled to be my first. She told me how young and beautiful my body was as she removed my shirt and stroked her long-painted nails over me. When she pushed me completely down on the bed and undid my pants, I tried to stop her."

I set my glass down and dig my fingers into my palms and swallow the lump in my throat. I stare off at the bookshelves as I recall that night. "I grabbed her wrist, firmly. She only seemed to enjoy that further. With her free hand she began stroking me again over my boxers. I couldn't control how my body felt. It was confusing. I just wanted to get out of there, get away from her and get back to my closet and escape into my books. I felt nauseous... yet parts of me were reacting as if I enjoyed her touch."

I glance back to Ivy to see her reaction. Her lips are pressed tightly together, and her eyes are brimmed with tears. I close my eyes and take a calming breath.

"Eventually I let go of her wrist and she removed the rest of my clothes as well as hers. She used her mouth on me first." I shrug. "Sure, I had seen magazines and videos online that Ben had shown me over the years, but the farthest I had ever gotten with a girl was a kiss. My mother never allowed me enough freedom for anything more. I'm lucky she even allowed me to attend school."

Another bitter laugh escapes me. "So that woman, Caroline, she was my first. I had covered my face nearly the whole time her mouth was on me, trying not to feel, trying to think of anything else. It didn't work."

I tightly close my eyes, as the memories try to overwhelm me. I open them again to meet Ivy's comforting green eyes. They settle something within me. She shifts, eyes glossy.

Ivy then stands, placing a hand to her mouth then to her forehead. "God, Venom. Was it over after that?"

"No. I thought we were done, but she wanted more.

She wanted… everything." I pause. "And she got it. She climbed on top of me and took what my body gave her. When it was done, Caroline paid my mother as she told her what an amazing young man I was and promised she'd be back. My mother looked so damn pleased." I curl my lip in disgust.

"Once Caroline left, my mother told me to shower and get back to my room. It was *my* birthday, but Caroline got what she wanted, my mother got her money. And me? I got what little there was left of myself stripped away. And that was just the start. More women came. My mother's pockets fattened. My anger did too."

"Where was Ben? He was your older brother; he should have protected you!" Ivy says with clenched fists as she paces back and forth.

I stare at the shelves, but I see Ben's back instead. "He left when he turned eighteen. I begged him not to. Begged him to take me with him. He told me he couldn't. Called it kidnapping. Said he didn't even know where he was going. At least I had a roof over my head, he said. I should be grateful." The word tastes like rot. "He promised he'd come back for me when I turned eighteen. He never did."

"He left you there? He should have taken you with him! He knew what your mother was going to do with you next, what she was already doing to you! What an asshole! How could he leave his younger brother like that?!"

"Calm down and sit, beast. We're letting the past go, right?"

She rolls her eyes, huffs out a breath and plops

back down on the couch. "Why didn't you just leave at eighteen too?"

Sighing, I say, "Truthfully, I'm not sure, darlin'. I had barely seen the world outside of school. I think I was more afraid of being alone in the outside world than alone in my closet with my books or in the basement with the critters I collected. I was comfortable with what I was familiar with. If that makes sense."

"It does." She gives me a sad look. "So, what happened? You obviously got out at some point."

I nod and stand, placing my hands in my pockets. "I was used for three years. During that time, something in me changed. Not only did my anger grow but so did my knowledge of the world, people and the effects of... *poison*."

I shoot Ivy a wink. "The women were always so chatty. I used it as an opportunity to learn things. I asked questions. I had meaningful conversations. It didn't take long before I was the one seducing and manipulating. They took from me, but I took so much more from them." My grin is cold. "One of them bought me a laptop. My first secret. I did so much research, devouring everything I could. I was addicted to knowledge. I planned, waited. And when I was twenty, I killed my mother.

Ivy's jaw drops.

"You can't be that surprised, darlin'." I grin. "Oleander. Pretty flower and poisonous as hell. It was easy to find in Louisiana." I shrug. "And dear ol' mother just so happened to have some shoved down her throat while I had her tied up one night. I could have done it in a more discreet way, but I wanted her to know who was killing her. I wanted her to feel powerless and scared." I circle Ivy, her eyes tracking me. "Over the years, I grew bigger and stronger, but she always seemed to still view me as a weak and scared little boy. Well imagine her surprise when I finally used my strength and overpowered her."

Grinning wide at the memory, I continue, "I watched her die an agonizing, and quite disgusting death. Honestly, she might have choked on her own vomit before her heart stopped. Once she was dead, I untied her and carried her to her bed, tucked her in and placed more Oleander in a small vase on her bedside table as well as in her hand. And then I left and never looked back." I wipe off some lint on my shoulder and meet Ivy's wide eyes. "The coroner called it suicide. I called it justice."

"So, after that, you continued... killing... women?"

"I did. I made a list. Every woman who came through during those three years. They kept talking and I kept listening, taking notes. Names. Faces. Jobs. One by one, I hunted them down."

"Did you get all of them?"

"All but one." I stop, let the silence stretch, then lean in with a grin. "That's enough for tonight."

CHAPTER NINETEEN

Spending most of the week in the greenhouse with Venom feels like slipping into some alternate reality. The place is magical enough on its own, but with him and me actually getting along... it almost feels like a dream.

Venom hasn't touched me again since the night before Evelyn's birthday, at least not how I've been wanting, which has only made me even more painfully aware of how close he gets to me while showing how to tend to his plants or how my body reacts to him snatching my wrist in his firm grip to stop me from touching something poisonous.

The tension between us is much thicker than the air in the greenhouse and at times it feels like someone actually has their hands around my throat, stealing my air. But in reality, it's more complicated than that. It's

Venom who has rewired me, body and mind, making me crave everything about him.

I enjoy listening to him speak. With his accent and velvety tone, it's relaxing. He effortlessly calms me with his voice. Especially now as he reads passages to me from a book I've never read while we sit in the quaint seating area in the greenhouse at a round ornate vintage metal table. Thick tufted cushions keep my ass from feeling the discomfort of the hard metal chair.

"It was not the thorn bending to the honeysuckles, but the honeysuckles embracing the thorn." Venom reads aloud. He sets his book on the small table and takes a sip of his whiskey.

His throat bobs as he swallows, and my gaze follows the line down his smooth neck to his golden chest, exposed where he leaves the top of his shirt undone. Maybe it's from the heat in here. Maybe it's his way of tempting me, letting me imagine what's hidden beneath.

When I look back up, his piercing blue eyes are locked on me. He smirks and sets his glass down.

"What kind of tree is this?" I ask, distracting myself with the pretty little tree next to us with delicate pink flowers and berries.

"It's a southern crabapple tree."

"Everything is so beautiful, I don't think I could ever get sick of being in here."

"Mmm, I agree. But of all the creatures and plants I have encountered, you are the most beautiful."

I press my lips together to hold back a smile.

"Stop being nice. It's unsettling."

"I can be nice."

"I'm surprised you can go two minutes without insulting me somehow."

"Now, now, sweet beast, don't tempt me," he drawls. I roll my eyes and finish the sweet tea Evelyn made.

Venom moves, coming to stand in front of me. I look up through my lashes, feeling nervous at the way he's staring at me; like he wants to consume me.

His hand slowly moves toward me and my brows furrow before he delicately reaches into my hair. His fingers, now curled into his palm, stop in front of my face. He smiles, then uncurls his fist. A small pale blue butterfly flutters out of his hand, around us, then disappears somewhere into the trees.

I stare after it, smiling.

Venom holds out his hand. "Come."

I slip my hand into his and he walk us through the greenhouse.

"So, not all plants are poisonous here," I say.

"No."

"Then why do you have them?"

"For their beauty, of course. Some men want to be surrounded by beautiful women. I want to be surrounded by nature's beauty."

A surprising answer from him again.

Venom leads us over to his wall of pets. "I think Black Betty is sorry for biting you," he says as he strokes a finger over her large glass home.

"I'll take your word for it."

He walks over to another enclosure and sticks his hand in and pulls out a bright green snake.

Oh god.

"Would you like to hold her?"

"Absolutely not." I take a step back away from them.

"Come now, she's no worse a beast than you."

"No way."

"Afraid?" he asks with a menacing smile.

I huff out a laugh. "No."

"I don't know why you insist on lying to me when you're so terrible at it. It's alright to be afraid. It shows you respect their power."

"Well, I'll respect their power from the other side of the glass or from here, thank you very much." Before I can even react, he closes the distance between us. "Venom... don't you dare!"

"Don't move, darlin'. Stay very still," he says as he places the snake on my shoulder, way too fucking close to my face.

"Venom! Oooh my god, oh my god. It's moving. Why is it moving? Where is it going?" The snake's scales against my skin feel cool and smooth, like silk moving across my flesh in waves.

"She's just exploring, getting to know you. Or perhaps about to wrap around your neck and strangle you. There's really no telling."

"Venom," I warn with a harsh whisper. My arms instinctively rise, not knowing what to do with them in this moment. The snake slithers around my right bicep as I suppress the urge to scream.

"Relax, sweet thing. You're safe."

"I don't feel very safe right now," I say, trembling.

"I'm here. You're the safest you ever could be."

"I question your definition of *safe*. Please, Venom, take her back before she kills me."

He chuckles, then reaches out, lifting the snake into his hand and winding her around his arm.

"This is sweet Cora. She's a Green Tree Python and non-venomous. You were perfectly safe."

"Oh. I thought they're all poisonous. You could have told me that sooner instead of letting me think I could have been bitten and face death again."

"Yes, but where's the fun in that, darlin'?"

"Ugh. Your soul is most definitely damned."

He chuckles. "Oh, I went to hell long ago and never returned. Besides, I think I've done worse than this to damn my soul."

"Right. Is this because I said you were being nice? Fine, I take it back."

He laughs again. "You are quite enjoyable."

"I'm glad I amuse you." I say, placing my hands on my hips.

"Among other things," he says, still not looking at me, his hand stroking down Cora's body. He sets her back into her home, then finally faces me, sliding his hands into his pockets with a smile that sends my heart racing.

Why do I have to be so damn attracted to him? It makes it difficult to stay mad at him.

We continue staring at each other, the tension only growing like it usually does between us. Although he looks casually menacing and unbothered, I feel like I'm about to lose my damn mind if not my self-control first.

"See something you like?" he asks with a smirk.

"Can't say I do." More lies.

"Look a little more closely."

"No thanks."

"Afraid of what you might find?"

My cheeks flush. He knows how to push my buttons. The ones that annoy me *and* the ones that tempt me.

"Can't imagine there's much to find in your shallowness."

"Ouch. The beast shows her teeth."

I turn and stalk away.

Before I make it out of the greenhouse, my arm is pulled, and I'm pushed up against the wall with his arms caging me in.

"Where are you running off to, darlin'?"

I let out a frustrated sigh. "I just... I don't know. I need some air."

"I'm not sure if you've realized, but it's everywhere around us. There's plenty to share."

I bite my lip as I shake my head. "I just... I never know if you're trying to seduce me or make me fear you."

"Why can't it be both?" He grins.

"God, Venom, what are we doing? What do you even want?"

His eyes search mine before he tilts his head, a finger trailing the side of my neck. He tucks a strand of hair behind my ear and heat pools low in my stomach.

"Isn't it obvious?" he murmurs. He shifts his stance but keeps me pinned between him and the wall. For a heartbeat, he almost looks nervous.

"I want you in the worst way, darlin'." His thumb drags slowly across my cheek. "The kind of way that brings powerful men to their knees, that causes kingdoms to fall and the world to burn. The way I want you leaves me feeling desperate. And a desperate man is a dangerous man." He takes a steadying breath, his striking blue eyes locked on mine. "But I promise you this. The safest place your heart could ever be is in my possession."

I look at him, stunned, trying to keep my composure. "You want my heart?"

"I want *all* of you."

Okay maybe I'm not the one who already lost their mind.

"But I've been terrible to you." I shake my head in a mix of confusion and embarrassment. "I've been so unappreciative, I've attacked you countless times."

"Yes. And when you attack me, I crave your death at my hands." His fingers slide lower, wrapping softly around my neck. "I want to watch the light fade from your eyes, feel your last breath against my skin like a gentle caress. But do you know what I want more, sweet beast?"

His hand returns to my face, thumb gliding over my lips. He presses his forehead to mine, drawing in a breath before continuing.

"I want you. Christ, Ivy, I want you so badly. I want you by my side every day, every hour, infuriating me with your wicked tongue and beastly ways. Therefore, as much as I thought I could, I cannot kill you. And I will not be without you. I already told you"—his voice drops to a purr—"you are mine."

"Venom," I whisper, his name sounding more like a plea.

"When you're ready, I'll be here," he says, then releases me from his intoxicating hold and walks out, leaving me breathless and weak.

I can't deny my feelings toward him, feelings that just keep growing no matter how hard I try to bury them below the surface. They want to bloom and thrive, and I just keep smothering them, hoping they go away.

It's not working. I'm losing the battle between my own heart and mind.

But what do I want out of this situation? Do I even know anymore? Could I still leave and be satisfied with freedom if my... heart... stayed behind?

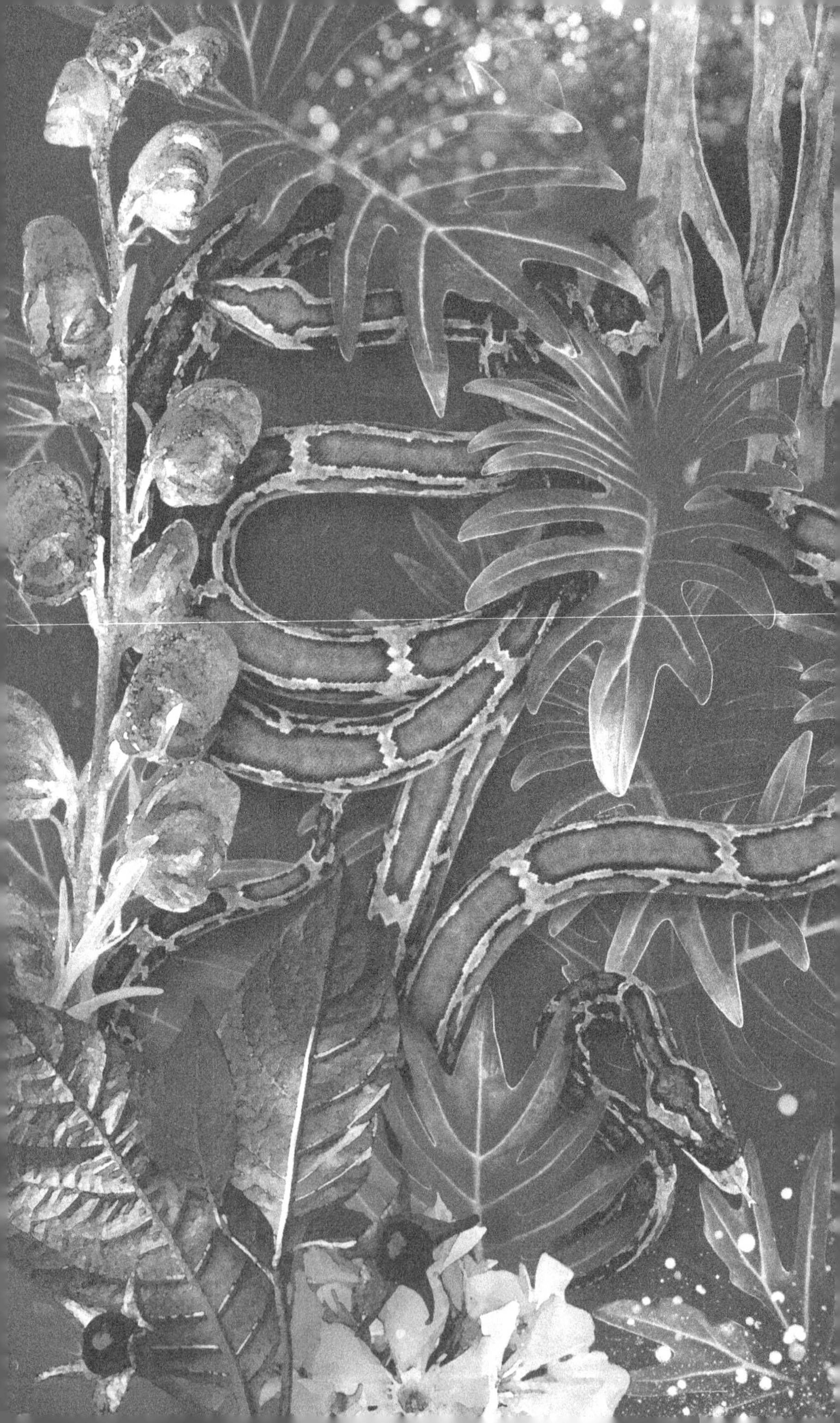

CHAPTER TWENTY

Leaving Ivy after just revealing my ultimate truth to her is agonizing. Not knowing if the feeling is mutual is even worse.

Pure torture.

But that's what this whole experience has been.

Torture.

I can be a patient man, but with her, my self-resistance has been tested beyond measure.

It's been hell. That's what my feelings for Ivy are. Absolute hell. With her blazing red hair, eyes that glow, a smile so seductive even the devil would be jealous, and a heart so fierce, she leaves me wanting nothing more than to burn in her eternal flames.

I crave her.

I need her.

I'm a man addicted to whatever poison she's injected

in me. I don't care if it's finally the lethal dose that kills me.

I've never truly experienced love. Love had always been something that felt not quite attainable, like a melody distantly heard, but too far out of reach to truly experience it in all its beauty. Love is a language I've never spoken. But this feeling seems like it could be that emotion.

If not love, then it sure is madness.

I grab another glass of whiskey before I make my way to my other *office*, this one being far less green and *alive*.

A notification pops up on my phone before I reach my desk, a particular name screaming at me through the screen. I have certain alerts set that will notify me any time *special* individuals are mentioned in articles or the news. Although this one seems to have notified me almost too late.

Staring at the name and the event being hosted, I smile wide. Placing a toothpick in my mouth, I kick up my feet on my desk and read further.

A masquerade charity ball is being held in Georgia on Halloween weekend by a wealthy tech entrepreneur and his philanthropist wife. They are raising funds for a new non-profit that will provide all the necessities for orphaned children.

How sweet.

This is certainly a welcome surprise, an opportunity I can't pass up.

I think this is the perfect time to offer my *charity*.

The greenhouse is calling to me again. It's time to work.

CHAPTER TWENTY-ONE

I spend the evening helping Evelyn cook dinner. Lately she's been teaching me recipes from her Italian heritage. Within the past few months, I have learned so much from Evelyn and of course, Venom. My mind swirls with all the new knowledge I now possess.

I feel different, as if instead of being plucked like a pretty flower, I've been watered and tended to so I can grow and thrive.

This place no longer feels like a prison, but an actual home with people in it I care about... as frustrating as one may still be at times.

My mind is still flustered with the way Venom left me earlier. I've been trying to keep myself busy to avoid facing what he told me and more importantly, how it made me feel to hear it.

"You seem distracted," Evelyn signs.

I look into her concerned eyes and sigh. "I'm sorry. I am a bit," I say out loud.

"Does it have something to do with a particular handsome blond in the greenhouse?" She raises a brow and smirks.

"He sure knows how to leave a lasting impression."

Of course it's about him. Everything I've been feeling since coming here has to do with him. The bad, the good, and the fucking scary. And damn if the idea of giving him my heart isn't the scariest thought I've ever had.

I shouldn't want him. Craving him feels like a sin. Loving him could surely be a death sentence. But there's a part of me that strangely trusts what he said—that my heart would be safe with him. I *want* to give it to him, which is even more frightening.

I've spent my whole life feeling like I'm holding my breath or just never having enough air to satisfy the parts inside of me that ache. But with Venom, it's like I can finally let everything go and... breathe.

Venom sees me in a way no one ever has. I want to give him the piece of me no one has ever owned. In fact, I want to give him all my broken pieces. Something tells me he'd be the one to glue me back together.

It already feels like he has partially mended my pieces. Although he has certainly bled in the process of dealing with my sharp jagged edges.

Evelyn leans forward, eyes soft. *"It's okay to feel what you're feeling. You have brought out a new side to him. He can be hard to read but I've been with him long enough to know better. And our charming boy has been lighter. Happier."*

"Really? I feel like I've been doing the opposite."

She smiles. *"Venom is not like other men. You challenge him. He needs that."* She gives me a light push on my shoulder.

"He does seem to enjoy that," I say with a smile.

Her expression suddenly turns serious. *"But I have one request. If you're still planning on leaving, don't tell him you're in love with him. Please. Do him that one kindness and just go."*

I laugh. "In love with him? I'm—it's not—I—"

I shake my head, not knowing how to even respond to that. I look back to the counter where the tomatoes are waiting for me to cut. Suddenly my hands feel too sweaty to hold the knife properly to cut them. I rub them against my pants and look back to Evelyn with, no doubt, flushed cheeks. She simply gives me a knowing smile.

I nod, then get back to cooking dinner.

"Your cooking skills have improved," Venom says from down the table.

"Is that a compliment?"

"It is. Hold it dear, who knows when there will be another. You've also gained weight."

"That's not typically something you should say to a woman, but considering—"

"Considering you were nearly starved for nine months..."

"Yes, that. I welcome the gained weight."

"So do I. It looks good on you. I'll never complain

about having more curves on your body to admire.”

“That sounds an awful lot like another compliment.”

He shrugs, and I take a bite of food to stifle my growing smile, and we stare at each other. There are so many times I wish I was a mind reader to truly know what Venom is thinking, like right now. He stares at me like it’s me he wishes he was eating and that thought alone has my cheeks flushing and breaking eye contact.

We continue on in silence until I decide to do something I haven’t done before.

I pick up my plate and cup and walk to the opposite end where Venom sits. I pull out a chair and take a seat right next to him.

He eyes me curiously. “You’re awfully close, darlin’. Aren’t you afraid the viper may strike? Or is it I who should fear the teeth of the little beast next to me?”

“Would you like me to bite? I can’t promise it won’t hurt.” *Is this flirting? Am I flirting with Venom?*

“You sank your teeth into me long ago, and it’s a pain I do so welcome.”

I bite my lip and look away. His hand shoots out, thumb pressing against my mouth, and my gaze snaps to those piercing blue eyes.

“Now, now,” he murmurs. “Save the biting for me. Release your pretty little lip.”

I obey. He drags his thumb over the spot where I’d held it captive, his gaze lingering on my mouth before lifting to my eyes.

“You are a wicked temptation,” he says, thumb still tracing my lips. “Fill my glass with your poison and I’ll drink it gladly… and beg for more."

"What if I ask for something else instead?" My words come out breathy.

He tips his head, studying me then raises his brow. "Go on then."

I swallow down my nerves and give in to the heat blossoming in my chest.

"Kiss me."

Venom's eyes darken with a predatory hunger. He stands, knocking back his chair in the process, pulls me from my seat and presses me against the wall by my throat. My mouth parts with words I want to say but I'm hushed by Venom's lips crashing against mine.

His hand travels into my hair, pulling tight, holding his prey in his hungry grip as he devours me. Our tongues dance together, tasting each other and speaking unspoken words.

I fist his hair and pull, causing him to groan in pleasure into my mouth. His arm slinks around my waist and he lifts me. My legs wrap around him.

He tastes of whiskey and forbidden fruit.

I want more.

"Venom," I moan as I break away enough to catch my breath, leaning my head against the wall. He rests his head against my chin as his chest rapidly rises and falls. Then he kisses my neck and sets me down, taking a step back.

I look at him, both of us breathless and still hungry. His eyes bore into me as he clenches his hands, seeming to fight against something within him. Perhaps the same feeling I was trying to fight.

"Come to a ball with me," he blurts out.

I shake my head in confusion. "What? A ball?"

"Yes, a charity ball in Georgia. Next weekend."

"That's a bit far, isn't it?"

"We'll be flying private. This is important and I want you with me."

"Ok," I softly say.

He runs a hand over his pale blond hair, smoothing it back in place, then leaves the room without another word or glance.

I succumb to my weak knees and slide down the wall until my ass hits the wood floor and sit there, still catching my breath from the kiss.

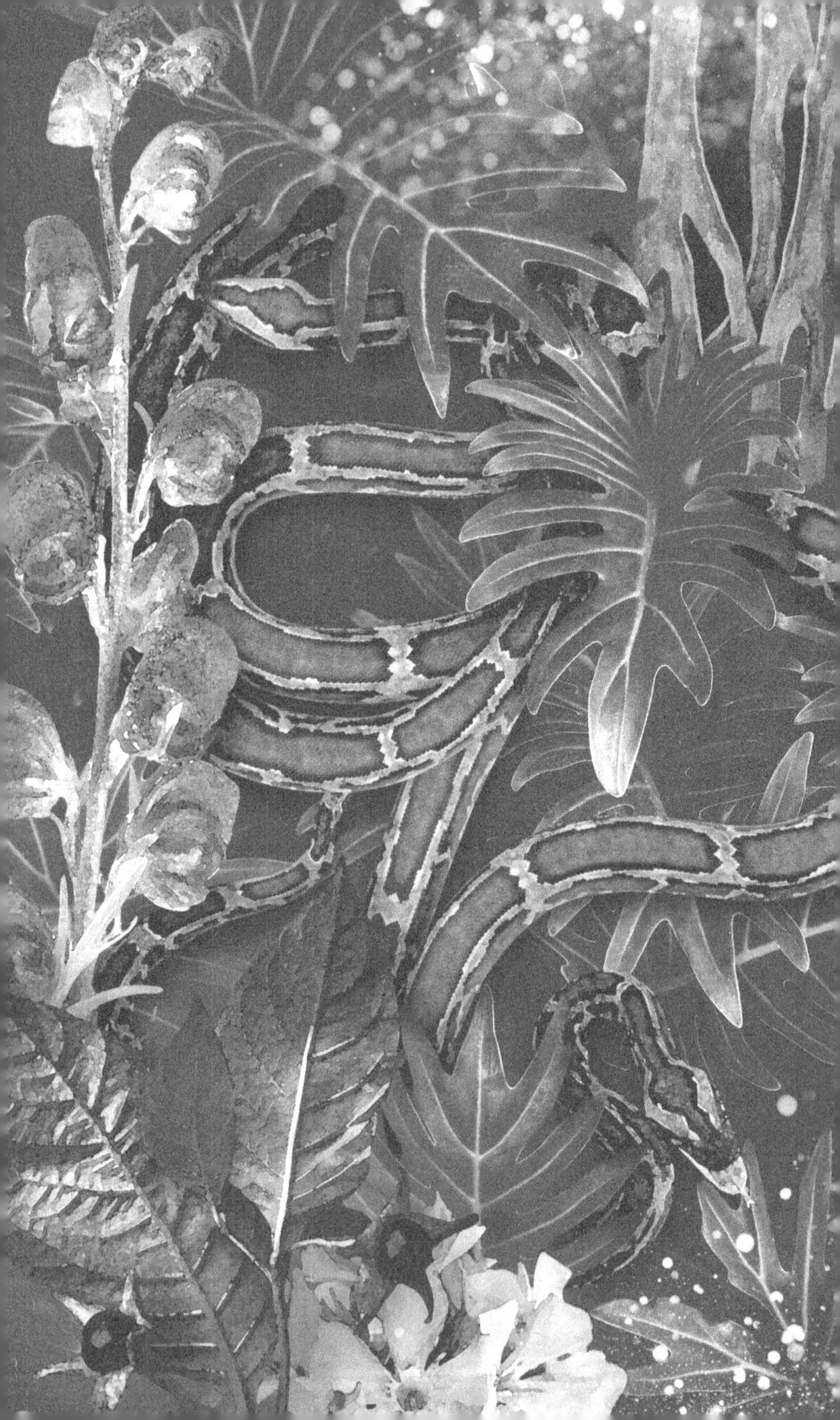

CHAPTER TWENTY-TWO

Considering the plane ride was Ivy's first time flying, she did rather well for our trip from Pennsylvania to Georgia. Although the constant pressure of her fingers digging into my arm might suggest something different. It was amusing and rather enjoyable.

"Here, Evelyn picked this out for you," I tell Ivy as I deposit the garment bag on the lounge chair in our hotel room.

"What do you think of it?"

"Don't know. Haven't seen it."

"She gave me this." She holds up a bag of what I assume is makeup and hair products. "Hopefully, I can make myself look less *beastly* and fit among the wealthy," she says with a smile but stares at the floor.

I grab her chin, making her meet my eyes. "Darlin',

no matter what room you enter, you will never fit in. Be proud of that. You will always stand out like the flame of a flickering candle in a dark room. You are luminous," I say as I stroke the freckles scattered on her cheek. "Your glow could lure even the most resolute men to burn in your eternal flames."

A tension-filled silence grows between us as our eyes lock. Her mouth slightly parts, but before she can speak, I walk away.

She gathers her things and walks to the bathroom, closing the door behind her. As she's getting ready, I dress into my black-on-black suit and wait.

After nearly an hour, the bathroom door opens. I stand from the sofa and turn her way.

My gaze catches first on her bare leg, then travels upward along the curve of her thick thigh to the high slit in her emerald gown. The fabric clings tight over her hips, lined with shimmering crystals that draw the eye to her slimmer waist. Sheer panels trace her sides before the dress widens again at her chest, cleavage spilling in a way that makes my mouth dry.

With her copper hair pinned up, her neck and shoulders are bare, exposed, vulnerable. I fight the urge to lean in and mark her beautiful flesh as mine.

I finally meet her tender eyes. Pieces of her hair frame her face in loose waves as the rest sits high in a bundle of flames. My breath hitches as I take her in, lost for a moment in her.

I step closer, drawn to her intoxicating allure. Her makeup is light enough that her freckles still show, a detail that makes my chest tighten. A flush of pink warms her cheeks, and the dark liner framing her eyes makes them blaze, tempting me to drop to my knees before her.

"My, my. So, the beast becomes a beauty. You are a sight to behold."

With flushed cheeks, she whispers, "I can't get the zipper completely up on the back though."

"Allow me." I move behind her, zipping the rest of her gown up. It's lower cut in the back and strapless so some of her scars are still visible. I gently trace one with my finger.

She moves to step away, clearly uncomfortable as she fidgets with her hair and stares at the floor. She meets my eyes but seems unable to form the words. I pull her to me. "You have nothing to be ashamed of." Moving to her back once more, I trace another thick scar with the back of my finger. "Suffering can teach one so much. These are your story." I press a kiss to one and a visible chill runs through her. "Your scars are signs of resilience, and you shouldn't ever feel ashamed of that, little beast. Just as the freckles on your face mark your beauty, so do these. You've been through the fires of hell and yet still bloomed." I trace a few more and press another kiss to a scar before coming to stand in front of her again. "Oh, and one more thing. You will wear these." I pull out a set of serpent earrings, showing them to her.

Her face lights up. "They're beautiful."

I move to place them on her myself, brushing a finger along each ear.

"So, I really look alright then?"

"More than alright. Dare I say you look like a little viper, ready to sink your teeth into your prey. You are deadly, darlin'." I press a gentle kiss to the inside of her wrist. She smiles wide as I release her. Taking a step back and raising my arms, I add, "Now, how do I look?"

"Absolutely *venomous*." She smirks.

"Perfect," I purr. "Let's go to a ball."

AFTER PASSING THROUGH the valet, Ivy and I ascend the front steps of the Georgia mansion belonging to Mr. and Mrs. Beck, passing by glowing pumpkins, candles of various heights and burgundy and orange mums.

How *kind* of them to open their home to the public for this charity ball. Although, they should have been more careful about who they let in.

"There are a lot of people here," Ivy says as we enter the grand ballroom that's overly decorated to fit the Halloween theme.

"Yes."

Ivy continues saying something, but my attention falls elsewhere as I scan the dimly lit room, looking for my target. "Venom?"

"What?" I ask, looking back at the beautiful woman by my side. Her green lace mask embellished with tiny ruby and clear crystals covers the top half of her face. The color of her mask matches her dress perfectly, making the golden rays in her green eyes stand out even more. She holds up two glasses of wine that someone already came by with. Perfect. I take the glass flute from her and swing back the liquid in one go.

"Are you alright? You're acting a bit weird."

"Me? Acting weird? When have I ever been normal?"

"True, but you just don't seem like yourself right now. Is it all the people?"

I look back around the room, everyone wearing some sort of mask, but I'd still recognize who I'm here for. "Not quite enough. I think we're missing some."

One in particular.

"Right."

Ivy signals a waiter passing by with a platter of something wrapped in bacon. She grabs two of them and the man hands her a napkin before continuing on. "Here," she says, holding up the food by the toothpick stuck through it.

I take it from her, then bring it to her mouth. "Open." She opens up for me while maintaining eye contact and once the snack is in her mouth, she brings her teeth together, and I slide away the toothpick and place it between my lips.

A woman walks past me, brushing my shoulder. She looks back, powder blue eyes shining through her rabbit mask, and smiles at me. Although I'm used to grasping the attention of women, this one seems different. She's not the blonde I'm looking for here, but something about the way she just looked at me, like she knew who I was, stirs a curiosity through me.

The mysterious woman keeps walking, the tops of her rabbit ears disappearing into the crowd.

I push away the urge to follow and find out who she

is. I can't let myself get distracted; she's not the one I'm here for.

Looking back at Ivy, who is still curiously taking in the large room of people, I smile. "Let's get you another drink, darlin'."

IVY

GLANCING AROUND THE grand room, I take in the dark elegance. I have to say, whoever did the decorating deserves an award. Tall windows are draped in black and gold velvet, and dim chandeliers cast a mysterious, intimate glow. Red and black candles flicker everywhere, their clove-and-apple scent mingling with other spices while shadows dance on the walls. Pumpkins glow on the floor and tables, with tiny ones floating overhead like eerie lanterns.

Guests drift past in flowing gowns and tailored suits, each wearing a mask—animals, demons, or simple gilded designs. The anonymity of it all makes every passing glance feel like a silent appraisal, unsettling and electric.

To my left, a low fog seeps from a hidden machine, adding to the gothic haze. When I look up, a man in a wolf mask is already watching me. He gives a wolfish grin before disappearing into the crowd. I brush off the chill and let my eyes wander over cobwebbed tables covered in lace, vases filled with dark crimson roses, and a masked live band playing a slow, haunting melody that completes the Halloween ball's spell.

Across the room, I spot Venom. I watch him as he mingles with the colorful people around him. Next to them, they blur as he stands out like a carved shadow.

The black-on-black suit sharpens his wide shoulders and narrows at the waist. Sharp and sleek. His pale hair, slicked back, gleams against the darkness, and his snake mask covers half his face without dulling his beauty. Even half-hidden, he radiates danger—the kind of temptation that ruins you while you crave it all the same. Heat blooms through me.

As I sip my red wine, his eyes lock on me. Even from a distance, they strip me bare, pinning me with my own truth. His gaze slides down my body and back up, a slow, deliberate stroke. When our eyes meet again, he smirks.

Fine. Since he likes games so much, let's play. I swallow back the rest of my wine, set the glass on a table then turn to the nearest man and strike up a conversation. He could be handsome to some under his black raven mask, but truthfully, no one in this room compares to Venom. Sweet and dangerous. There's no doubt in my mind he could have any woman in this mansion and my god, even with their faces partially concealed, it's clear there's so many really beautiful women in here. My stomach twists at the thought, then eases when I realize his eyes are still on me, and I like how that feels.

"Great event, huh?" I say to the man.

Gosh, I don't even know how to make small talk. I feel awkward as hell right now, but I sneak a glance at Venom, who's lost his smile and is looking very intently at me and my new *friend*.

"Great event for a great cause," he says before letting his gaze linger too long on my chest.

"My name is Ivy."

"John." He holds out his hand.

I slip mine into his. "It's nice to meet—" Before I can finish, someone grabs my wrist, pulling my hand away from John.

"Excuse us," Venom says with a hint of annoyance as he pulls me away. I can't help but start laughing all the way until he pulls me down a dark hall and pushes me against a door.

"Something funny, darlin'?"

"That really didn't take long," I say while giggling like a tipsy schoolgirl.

"You were purposely trying to make me jealous?"

I nod, staring at his black mask adorned with three snakes. "It worked. Rather quickly, I might add."

"Let me make things very clear, little beast. Be careful with your childish games, because any man you allow to touch you tonight will end up dead before the evening ends. Understand?"

"No punishment for me?" I ask with a raise of my brow.

His eyes darken to that hungry hue again. "I didn't say that now, did I?"

"Maybe I—" Another voice draws our attention. Venom goes rigid at the woman's voice reprimanding someone over broken glasses.

"You know what? Just get out of here. You're fired," the voice from around the corner says.

Venom, like a moth drawn to a flame, slowly walks toward the way we came, where the woman is. I round the corner and find him just standing there, staring at the woman's back. When she turns around, I spot Venom's hands clenching at his sides.

What is happening right now?

The older blonde, wearing a fox mask, saunters toward us before realizing we're standing here.

"Oh, excuse me. I apologize if you had to hear that. Incompetence is everywhere."

Venom doesn't respond, but he slips off his mask while staring at the mysterious woman. Suddenly her expression changes from confusion to surprise. She pushes her mask up, eyes wide.

"Marcus? Is that you?"

I think Venom's not going to respond again when he finally speaks.

"Mrs. Beck."

"Oh, please. We don't need formalities." She waves her perfectly manicured hand in the air.

"*Caroline*," he says flatly.

"That's better. It's truly you, isn't it?" She takes a step back, looking him up and down, nearly salivating, then steps closer once again. "Well, you have certainly grown, Marcus. More handsome in every way."

Why is that name familiar?

"Mmm. Wonderful charity event you're hosting."

"Helping young lost souls find their way is dear to my heart. I never forgot our time together, you know. I was glad I could help *you*. How long has it been since I last saw you? Must be well over ten years now. Perhaps we could reacquaint ourselves again, properly and privately. Find me later?"

Oh my god. This bitch. It's *her*. *The* Caroline. The first woman to sexually assault him.

"Perhaps," he says.

Perhaps?

What the fuck.

Caroline's red lips form into a smile, and when she walks past Venom, she strokes a hand down his arm, and I nearly lose my motherfucking shit. I step to go after her when Venom grabs my arm, pulling me back against him.

"Now, now, beastie. None of that."

"What? But why? Fuck that bitch!"

"Unfortunately, that's been done."

"Don't make those kinds of jokes, Venom. This is fucked up. *She's* fucked up. Did you know she was gonna be here? Is this why we came?"

"Yes. Now, keep your voice down and get back to the ballroom."

"Please tell me you're here to kill her?" I whisper.

"Now you approve?"

"She deserves it!"

"I do love your enthusiasm regarding murder, darlin'."

"*Her* murder."

"Go on now, entertain yourself. I need to take care of something long overdue." Venom walks away from me; toward the direction Caroline went.

My heart slams so hard it feels ready to burst out of my chest.

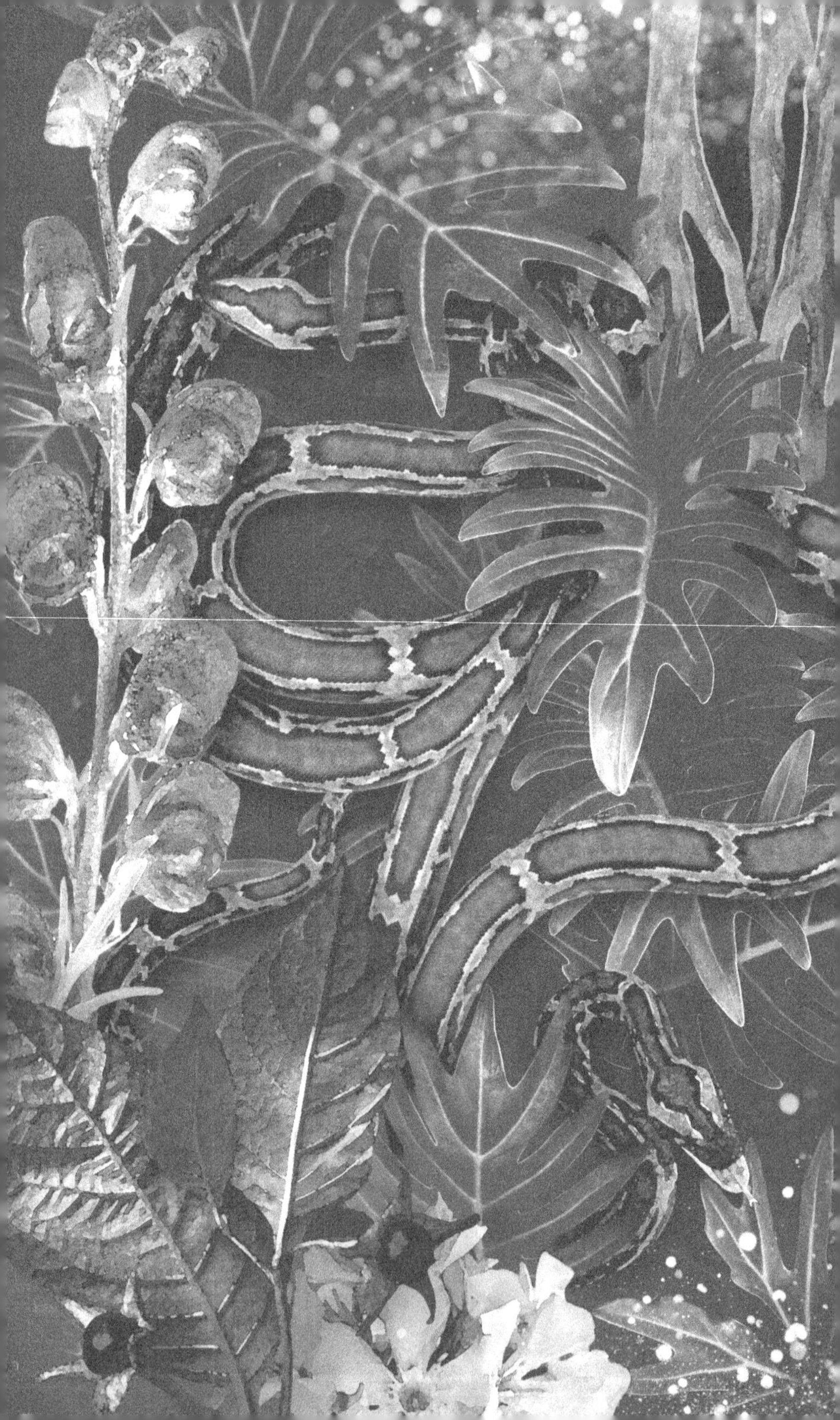

CHAPTER TWENTY-THREE

By the time I catch up with Caroline, she's making her way up a mahogany sprawling staircase in the back part of the mansion, a twin to the grand staircase located in the front of the home. Wide at the base and curving into two different directions with the banister wrapped in black garland, crimson ribbon and perfectly placed red roses. When she looks back and spots me following her up the wide steps, she smirks.

Over the years, I could have found her and killed her, but I saved her for last. Knowing she was still out there, living simply because I deemed it so, was satisfying enough. Until the time came that I was ready to end her existence.

And that time is now.

Caroline enters a room, leaving the door slightly ajar.

Before I follow in after her, I check a couple other rooms, finding a bathroom first and preparing what I need for this moment.

I push open the door she disappeared behind and close it behind me. The room is dimly lit by a lamp on a bedside table.

Of course she brought us to a bedroom. Even with a house full of people and her husband somewhere downstairs, her cravings have always overpowered anything else.

She takes a seat on the bed and lifts her leg through the slit of her crimson dress, pointing it at me.

"Help a dear friend out. These damn heels are killing me."

Those gold stilettos won't be her demise tonight.

I step closer, taking her ankle in my hand and begin to unlace her heels.

"You know, I never forgot our time together either, Caroline. I might have been a toy to you, but now it's my turn to *play*."

"I've always loved playing with you, Marcus. I never stopped thinking about you."

"Aren't I a little old for your liking nowadays?" I drop her bare foot, and she lifts her other one up.

"Don't be silly. We have history. I remember what a sweet one you were."

"I'm certainly still sweet." *Just laced with poison now.*

"I paid extra to be your first. Did you know that?" She gives me a full smile, filled with sickening pride.

"I did not," I say, trying to hold back my disgust.

When her other foot is free, she pushes herself onto the bed and motions to the spot next to her.

"Come lie with me. Like we used to." I remove my suit jacket, then place a knee onto the king-size bed and prowl over to her, lying on my back beside her. "Do you ever think about our first night together?" she asks as she begins to run her fingers over my chest. My body stiffens at her touch, my stomach turning.

"Often." Memories of that first night begin to flash through my mind. The images, the feelings. After all these years, I still seem to be able to feel affected by them.

Surprisingly after sharing my story with Ivy, the nightmares I would experience did occur less. I suppose she was right about letting it out and letting it go. Although, I couldn't let it completely go with Caroline still being out there.

But now, she's here. She might think she's still the predator amongst us, but she has no idea the kind of creature she helped create.

The prey has become the predator and I'm as *venomous* as they come.

"I'm so curious what your body looks like now underneath these clothes. My goodness, you feel so strong," she says as she squeezes my arm. She sits up a bit, leaning toward me, and begins to unbutton my shirt. "Let's have a proper look at you, shall we?" When my shirt falls open, her eyes light up at the sight. She doesn't know it yet but she's hungry for poison. "Oh my, you've truly grown so much. And you got a tattoo? Is this your only one?"

"It is."

"A snake. That's… nice. I do wish you left your skin flawless and pure."

Ain't nothing pure about me anymore.

"Sorry to disappoint."

"Oh no, no. You're perfect. Let me show you how perfect I think you are." She drags her nails down my torso until she reaches my belt, and I clench my jaw.

I'm not even hard yet. Her touch is having the opposite effect on me. Unlike how it was back then. But I need her to think I'm into this. I need her to believe I want her.

I picture Ivy.

My sweet beast.

My feisty little viper.

I replay the moment she asked me to kiss her. I replay feasting on her sweet pussy on my dining table.

My cock hardens just as Caroline pulls it free.

"Oh, Marcus. I have missed you."

I swallow the bile in my throat and focus on the woman with fire for hair, who slithered her way into my life and into my h—

"I wonder if you taste the same," Caroline says, interrupting my thoughts.

But before her mouth descends upon me, I move to stand at the edge of the bed, my pants falling to my ankles. I harshly grab her blonde hair to hide my trembling hand.

Am I really ready to feel another woman's mouth on me after all these years? I've avoided it ever since leaving my mother's prison, never wanting another touch to drag me back into those memories. Control was the only way to survive.

So I kept it simple. Quick fucks. Quick exits. Enough to take the edge off, to quiet the craving for release, but never more than that. Never anything that could strip me bare.

I stare into her eyes—empty and cruel—the ones that haunted me for so many years. I curl my lip in disgust but just as quickly switch back to a neutral expression.

She created this monster. Now I'm ready for her to finally suffer those consequences.

I pull her toward me. "I'm not a boy any longer, Caroline. Give me a taste and see for yourself."

"Oh my, I do like this feistier side of you," she says, looking at me with excitement.

I fist her hair tighter and she groans. Then I pull her toward my cock as she opens her mouth wide.

My length sinks into her and I push her further, making her take all of me until she's gagging at my intrusion at the back of her throat. I release her just enough so she begins moving her mouth over me, sliding her tongue all around, savoring my taste.

I do hope it's sweet enough.

I tip my head back and imagine Ivy instead of this wretched woman whose mouth I never wanted to feel again. But in a sense, this is poetic justice.

Breaking away from my cock she says, "Marcus, you taste absolutely delicious."

"Do I now?" My satisfying grin is more for me than her.

Her mouth dives back around me.

The air in the room suddenly shifts and my attention

snaps to the slightly open door, where Ivy stands in a state of shock staring at Caroline sucking my cock.

Fuck…

Caroline stiffens and begins to choke as I push her away from me and run after Ivy.

CHAPTER TWENTY-FOUR

Of course I was going to follow him. In what world did he really think I was just going to go back to the ballroom and wait for him. But now I'm regretting it, because what the actual fuck.

My stomach drops and I suddenly feel a flood of nausea run through me as I stare at him and Caroline. This is *not* what I expected to see. I'm not sure what I expected actually, but it sure as fuck wasn't Venom getting his dick sucked by his past assaulter.

I meet his eyes, and he has the nerve to look remorseful.

My eyes begin to water, but I hold back the tears. I just don't understand. This is so fucked up. I shake my head at him and turn from the room, stalking down the hall, intent on strolling out of here and going who knows where, just away from *this* and him.

"Ivy! Ivy, wait!" Venom's voice cuts from behind me. He catches my arm, and I spin on him, slamming my fist hard into his chest.

"Leave me alone!"

"It's not what you think."

"Oh really? Your dick wasn't just in her fucking mouth? Are you still playing games with me?! You tell me you want my heart and then you fuck another bitch's mouth, and *her* of all people? Do you have feelings for her?" I ask incredulously."Let's go." He grabs my arm again and pulls me back toward the room, but I yank free and push at his chest as hard as I can.

"No. No fucking way! I'm not having some kind of twisted sit down with you two. Fuck that."

He steps face-to-face with me, nostrils flaring. "Shut that pretty mouth, darlin', and listen or rather... *watch*." Then he effortlessly throws me over his shoulder and takes me back into the room. He sets me down and locks the door behind us. I look over to Caroline who now lies collapsed on the floor, grabbing at her mouth and throat.

Venom saunters over to her and squats beside her.

"How do I *really* taste nowadays, dear ol' Caroline?" She tries to speak but only red foam bubbles from her mouth as she spasms on the floor.

Oh my god.

She reaches for him, and he swats her hand away like a pesky fly. "You don't get to touch me anymore. You're despicable. I've waited for this moment since the first time you laid a finger on me. I wanted you to die the same way you killed the boy in me."

Caroline's tear-stricken eyes widen as she chokes, her body convulsing as she claws at her throat, searching for air. Venom stands and turns his back to her, walking toward me as she finally falls still. Dead.

"I'm sorry you had to see that. I needed to handle this my way," he says, avoiding eye contact.

"I… I thought—"

He meets my eyes. "It's alright." He pulls me into him, wrapping his arms around me and kisses my forehead. "There's only one woman I crave."

I shake my head and look back to the dead woman on the floor. "You laced your dick with poison?" I ask in surprise.

"A special little concoction I made just for her."

"That is twisted as fuck."

He grins. "Come now, darlin'. I'm starving."

Before making our way back to the main event, Venom stops at a bathroom to clean himself up. Once we enter back into the ballroom, I expect everyone to look at us, to *know* we—I use the word *we* loosely—just did something terrible, but everything is as it was, everyone unaware that one of the night's hosts is dead upstairs after choking on a poisonous cock.

After picking off more hors d'oeuvres together, Venom disappears for a bit, promising he would be right back. I sit and glance around the room. My eyes land on the same man I saw earlier in the far corner, the one with the wolf mask, and once again, his attention is already on me. Goosebumps pebble across my skin. I look away for a moment before checking once more to see if he's still staring.

He is.

Something about him seems strangely familiar.

I shift in my seat, the unease growing.

Someone approaches me from the side and says something over the music. "*Cherry*."

My head snaps to him but the rest of my body stiffens. "What did you just say?"

"I said, here's your cherry bomb, miss," the waiter says as he hands me the drink. "Extra cherries."

My brows pinch. "I didn't order anything," I say as I accept the drink.

"Curtesy of the gentleman over there." He points behind me and then walks away.

A cold prickle crawls down my spine, sharp as icicles, as I turn to find him—the man in the wolf mask. Or someone else. My gaze darts frantically over the crowd, over bodies swaying and drifting like ghosts on the dance floor.

Cherry.

I could die happy if I never heard that word again.

What a shitty coincidence to drag my thoughts back into the past, stirring memories I'd rather avoid.

I push the thoughts away and set the drink on a nearby table, not interested in it or who it came from.

Venom comes into view again, stealing my attention and putting my nerves at ease.

He holds out a hand to me. "Dance with the devil?"

Smiling, I slip my hand into his. The music currently playing is a sweet, soft melody played by the live instrumental band, perfect for a slow dance.

"You're no devil by the way. I would know. But if you were, what would that make me?" I raise a brow at him. He leans in and whispers in my ear as we settle onto the dance floor.

"The devil awoke and called out my name.

"What I heard was an angel whose voice was so tame.

"I loved her at once, what more could I do?

"Filled with sweet poison, you would fall too."

I lift my eyes, studying him with intrigue. "A poem? What's that supposed to mean?"

"Well, isn't it obvious? You're the devil, darlin', not I."

I bite the inside of my cheek to suppress a smile, but my eyes betray me, and he grins wickedly.

"And what's that talk of loving the devil?" He ignores my question and spins me. I giggle as I twirl. "You know, I've never danced with anyone before," I say as Venom wraps his arm around my waist and pulls me closer.

"Never? What about school dances?"

"I never went to my prom. I wasn't allowed to go."

"Well, beast, if you were wanting to feel beautiful in a stunning dress and dance with a handsome fella, consider your wish granted tonight."

I smile at him and then rest my head against his chest. He moves his hand lower, to the small of my back as we slowly move in a trance to the music. His body feels warm, the steady beat of his heart and his earthy cool scent, comforting. I could rest against him like this for more than one song, for a whole night, for… ever.

"Venom? I say, looking back up to him.

"Hmm?"

"Thank you."

"For what?"

"Just… everything." Then I put my head back against him and sway with him until the song ends with an abrupt crash of glass.

Everyone's attention moves across the room to where a man collapsed against the champagne fountain and violently jerks on the floor in a pool of sharp glass and liquid. The champagne begins to turn a shade of pink as the man bleeds from various locations, including his eyes and ears.

Stepping closer, I recognize the man whose raven mask hangs halfway off his face. It's John.

I turn back to Venom who is now casually leaning against the bar and downing back the rest of a drink. He looks at me and shrugs.

Unbelievable.

I stalk toward him. "Are you gonna kill anyone else tonight?" I harshly whisper at him.

"If we don't leave now, most definitely. I'm having a blast, but I think the party is over. Off we go, darlin'," he says while holding out his hand to me once more.

And once again, I take it without hesitation.

We're almost back to the hotel when Venom stops the car on a dark road.

"Get out of the car."

"What? Why? Hey—"

He turns the radio music up loud and steps out.

Oh my god.

I open the door, but before I get out, Venom's outstretched hand greets me. I laugh and take his hand.

"You're joking."

"As much as I love humor, I'm very serious right now. Our dance was rudely interrupted. We need a redo." He grins wide.

Smiling like a schoolgirl whose crush just asked her to prom, I let Venom lead me onto the road, lit only by the car's headlights, his arm snug around my waist. We begin to dance to "Dancing in the Moonlight."

I can't help but laugh at how ridiculously romantic this is. Does he even realize that?

Venom smiles bigger than I've ever seen as he repeatedly spins me around and dips me at the perfect moments. My hair eventually slips free from its up-do, as he runs his fingers through my wild strands.

He looks so carefree. No false amused facade, just pure joy. His bright eyes sparkle, and I find myself laughing and smiling so much my cheeks hurt. My eyes fill with happy tears.

Just me and Venom, on a lonely dark road under a Georgia moonlight, with a fall breeze swirling around us, dancing in front of the car's headlights.

No words needed. Just smiles and laughs and starry glances.

Seems so simple, but it's the best moment I've ever had in my life.

CHAPTER TWENTY-FIVE

Once we arrive back in our hotel room, Venom heads straight to the shower.

Walking over to the full-length mirror, I stare at myself a bit longer. I really did feel beautiful tonight. Still do.

I reach behind me to try to unzip myself, but it catches on the fabric. I awkwardly try to pull and pull, barely even able to reach it in the first place but then decide to just wait for Venom to help. Wearing this gorgeous dress a little longer won't be so bad.

I remove my heels and pace the room, replaying the entire evening in my mind, especially how it ended. This is certainly not a night I will ever forget.

Venom strides out of the bathroom in just a towel wrapped low around his hips. This is the first time I'm seeing him completely shirtless in full lighting; the first time I get to truly admire his snake tattoo. I've glimpsed the snake's head before, but now my gaze follows the ink as its body slithers down his chest and coils around his torso. The scales are etched with such precision they look almost alive. And then there are his abs—cut like stone, impossibly perfect. I've never seen him work out, so I have no idea how the hell he maintains them, but damn, I'm impressed.

Venom clears his throat. "Eyes up here, darlin'."

I blush and turn away. When I look back at him, he's still staring at me.

"Did you have a nice evening?" he asks with an amused grin.

"You didn't have to kill him, ya know."

"Not this again," he says as he strides over to sit on the couch. "I think I've made myself clear."

"But that's insane! You can't go around killing every guy who talks to me."

"He touched you, to be clear."

"It was an innocent handshake. And what about the guy in the grocery store? He didn't touch me."

"No. But I didn't like him."

I throw my hands up. "Ugh, you're impossible."

"And you're beautiful."

"Don't. Don't compliment me to distract me and change the subject!"

He walks toward me with his unsettling predatory grace. Considering he's nearly nude and stalking toward me with that look in his eyes, my nerves spark, sending a buzz through my veins.

"Ya know, you should come with a warning label, darlin'."

"Oh really? I'm not the one with a poisonous dick," I counter. He ignores my comment.

"May cause inappropriate thoughts."

He steps closer.

"Irrational behavior."

Another step as my heart begins rapidly beating.

"Severe addiction."

He reaches me, pressing me against the wall, and leans in to whisper in my ear.

"Possibly even death."

His words caress my ear and send a heated rush blazing through me.

I meet his electric eyes when he pulls away. "Is there a cure?"

"For this type of affliction, no. Even if there was, I wouldn't want it."

"So what do you do about it?" I ask breathlessly. My god, I want this man. I want him so damn bad I feel like I might spontaneously combust if I don't have him.

"I accept my fate."

"I'm sure you could get over this affliction."

Grinning, he says, "There's no getting over you, darlin'. I've never met a more beautiful creature or tasted such sweet poison. I'm hooked and at your mercy."

"Are you asking for my mercy?" The tension between us thickens to something almost palpable.

"Never."

The room suddenly feels hotter, and a wave of

confidence washes over me. I push past him and take a seat on the chaise lounge.

I bite my lip. "You want me? I should make you beg."

His brow shoots up in amusement. "I'd gladly fall to my knees before you and beg if that's what you want."

The thrill of this sends my adrenaline spiking. "Then do it," I challenge.

With a devilish smirk, his fingers toy with the knot of the towel, unhurried, his hungry gaze locked on mine. The air thickens, heavy with the challenge, before the fabric slips free and falls to the floor. Heat scorches my cheeks, my breath catching in my throat, betraying the nerves I was trying so hard to mask. My lips part at the sight of him—hard, dangerous, utterly venomous.

He lowers to one knee. Pauses. Smirks, savoring the moment and teasing me further. My eyes travel up and down his body, taking him all in. Then he sinks the other knee to the floor.

I swallow back my nerves once more, securing my confident mask back in place. "Now crawl to me."

"Oh, you wicked beast. Just know that when I reach you, it's *my* turn." The feral glint in his eye sends my nerves spiking again.

He drops his hands on the floor and begins to crawl toward me. Slowly and gracefully with a hungry and menacing expression.

This isn't the carefree soul who was dancing in the middle of the road with me not too long ago.

This is the predator.

And now I'm reminded how dangerous this man is.

In so many ways. Ways I'm not sure I'm prepared for, but I'm finally ready to find out.

He calls me a beast, but he looks as if he's going to be the one devouring me.

With every second he gets closer, my body reacts, my senses and every nerve buzzing with excitement. The tingling sensation between my thighs becoming painful, unbearable.

He just about reaches me when I lift my leg up and place my bare foot on his shoulder, halting him in place.

He shakes his head and snickers. "Were you trying to stop me before I got within striking distance? Because you made a grave mistake."

I furrow my brows in confusion and that's when he grabs hold of my ankle and yanks me onto the floor. I yelp as he grabs the bottom of my gown and pulls, ripping the fabric down the center until my bottom half is fully exposed, then he tears away my panties, and without hesitation, descends upon my eager pussy.

My back arches, a moan slipping out as his wicked mouth finds my throbbing, sensitive flesh.

"Christ, darlin', I've been having withdrawals from this sweet thing," he murmurs against the inside of my thigh. He presses a kiss there, then returns to my pussy, giving it his full, devastating attention.

My fingers slide through his pale hair as he devours me. Gentle teeth toy with my clit, and the sensation nearly tips me over the edge. I clamp my thighs around his head, but he pries them apart and, to my shock, slaps my aching pussy. I cry out, pleasure sparking bright. His tongue sweeps through me, then he's sucking my clit again, fingers gripping my thighs hard enough to bruise. I don't last long. I shatter, hard, with this venomous man between my legs.

"Oh god, Venom. Fuck," I gasp.

"Delicious." He kisses the inside of my trembling thigh. "I'd be a happy man dying between your legs."

"No more death tonight." I cup his face, nerves surging before I swallow them down. "I want more."

"I wasn't done with you anyway, darlin'. But you're gonna have to be clearer. I want you sure. Say the word, little beast, and I'm yours."

I bite my lip. His gaze drops to my mouth, then returns to my eyes.

"I'm sure. I want all of you, Venom. I want it to be you. Right now."

His smile widens. He reaches under the couch cushion and pulls out a knife.

When the fuck did he stash a knife there?

He slides the blade to my lower belly where my split gown ends and slices through the rest of the fabric.

"I liked this dress!"

"I'll buy you a new one." He lifts me, leaving the ruined dress on the floor.

"What are you doing?" I laugh.

"I'm not letting your first time be on a hard floor when there's a perfectly good bed a few feet away." He reaches the bed and tosses me onto it. I squeal, laughing as he climbs over me. His broad frame cages me in. My gaze skims his carved body, down to the thick length hanging between his powerful thighs, then back up to the gleam in his eyes.

"You're nervous."

It isn't a question.

"Yes, but not because I'm unsure. I just—well... you're not small."

He chuckles. "You're already loosened up and wet. I'll go slow, darlin'. Tell me to stop whenever you need."

I nod. He lowers, sucking and licking around one nipple before taking it into his mouth. A soft moan spills from me as he gives each nipple attention, then he positions himself at my entrance.

Dark heat flashes in his eyes as he slides his tip through my slick. I gasp when his swollen head pushes in, then he eases the rest of himself inside. I stretch around him, taking him. There's a brief ache, a pull, but it feels incredible.

"That's it, darlin'. You're doing great."

He settles fully, and I have never felt so full. In every way.

"Oh, god, Venom. You feel... fuck... you feel so good inside me." He starts to move, slow and deliberate, letting his thick cock glide out and back in. "More, Venom, I need more."

My senses spark, all of me aflame.

Desperation floods me. I wrap my legs around him, trying to draw him deeper. He chuckles.

"Greedy little beast." His hands lock on my hips as his pace builds, his thrusts driving deeper. My head tips back on a moan.

Venom drops his mouth to my breast. A sharp sting blooms—he's biting me. He doesn't let go, holding my breast between his teeth as he fucks me, pleasure and pain braiding until I'm lost to it.

Gruff sounds rumble from his chest as he keeps sinking into me, again and again. He's as deep as he can go, and somehow it still doesn't feel like enough.

He releases my aching breast, soothes it with a suck and a lick, then kisses the tender spot. One hand buries in my hair; the other wraps the back of my neck in a firm grip.

Pressure coils tight in my core as our eyes lock.

"Eyes on me when you come."

"Mmm," is all I manage.

His hand slips down between us, finds my clit, and starts to play. I nearly detonate on the spot.

"Oh my god. Fuck, fuck, fuck. Don't stop. I'm gonna come."

"Do it. Come for me, sweet beast."

I surrender. Pleasure crashes through me, my body clenching around him as I climax. Venom follows, groaning, shuddering, both of us clawing at each other as we fall apart together.

We ride the waves until they ease. He rests his forehead against mine while we catch our breath.

"You're fucking perfect," he says, kissing my forehead before sliding out and dropping beside me.

He doesn't leave. He pulls me in, holds me tight. I feel cherished. Chosen. Then he slips to the bathroom and returns with a warm cloth, cleaning me gently. He presses a quick kiss to my pussy when he's done and settles back beside me.

We drift off in each other's arms and wake in the early hours.

"Good morning," he rumbles, voice sleep-rough. "It is morning, right?"

"It is," I say as we lie facing each other.

He tucks a strand of hair behind my ear, kisses my forehead, then rolls to sit at the edge of the bed.

I gasp, my heart constricting.

Morning light slips through the curtains and lays his past bare across his back. It's the first time I've seen it.

What the fuck.

His head turns to the side. "What's wrong?"

"Your back," I whisper as I reach out to touch the jagged pale scars.

"Ah, yes. My back..." He looks away. But the words are said so flatly, void of emotion, but I know too well, that must not have always been the case.

"Your mother?"

"Yup, that would be her handy work over the years."

"Oh my god, Venom." I had no idea the extent of his mother's abuse but his story is heartbreakingly painted across his back. I reach out and trace a few of the lengthy scars, as well as the larger patches that look like burns. "Why didn't you tell me when we talked about mine?"

He turns fully. "It wasn't the time. We were talking about you, and I didn't want you feeling bad for me when you've already carried so much."

"But so have you," I say, chest heavy.

"Yes. Turns out we both have. And here we are. Whatever we've been through led to this. To last night. I wouldn't change it."

I cup his cheek and kiss him.

While I shower, Venom orders room service. It won't be Evelyn's eggs Benedict and French toast, but it will do. My belly aches for food. And for him.

"They said thirty minutes," he calls when I step out.

"Any ideas how to pass the time?" I ask, letting the towel slip to the floor.

The corner of his perfect mouth ticks up. "Not a single one. You?"

"Maybe." I cross the room, stopping in front of where he sits on the couch. Water still drips from my hair, down my body. He leans in, tongue catching a drop on my belly and licking up to my nipple. He toys with it, and I cradle his head, fingers in his hair like he's the most precious thing.

"Sit back."

He does, and I sink to my knees. His eyes intensely study me. When I wrap my hand around his hard cock, his fingers snap around my wrist, tightly. I meet his gaze. There's softness there, a vulnerable edge.

"Is this okay?"

He inhales, steadying. "Sorry. I—I haven't let anyone—since—"

I release him at once. "Oh my god. I'm sorry," I whisper, looking away.

"No. Hey—look at me." He lifts my chin. "I want you to. After I freed myself, I never let another woman touch me there, let alone put their mouth on me. Besides Caroline, last night, which was certainly not for pleasure beyond finally getting to kill her. With others, it's always been simple. Nothing more."

I nod in understanding. "I get it. You wanted to feel in control."

"Partly. But you, sweet beast… you're the only touch I crave. The only one I want to have all of me. The one I'll give up control for."

Emotion floods me. He guides my hand back to his thickness. I trusted him, and now he's trusting me.

I stroke him slowly as I stare up at him. His eyes flutter closed; a soft groan slips out.

"The sight of you on your knees with your hand around my cock might be my undoing, darlin'."

I smile, continuing to work him as he reaches out and places a hand to my cheek. Then I take him into my mouth. His body tenses for a beat, then eases. His hand buries in my wet hair, grip firm, as I savor him, mouth and hands moving in sync.

"Christ, Ivy," he breathes.

His hips rock, pushing deeper, the head nudging the back of my throat. I moan around him, eyes watering.

Gripping my hair tighter, he pulls me off his cock and slams his lips to mine. The kiss is raw, messy and filled with hunger.

I climb into his lap and begin peppering kisses along his jaw to his neck, nipping gently.

His groan of pleasure lets me know he likes it.

"Don't go easy on me, darlin'."

Smiling against his skin, I bite harder where his neck meets his shoulder. His answering hiss and moan has my pussy begging to be filled.

He fists my hair, tilting my head. "You're such a wild little beast."

"But you like it."

"I *love* it," he corrects.

Reaching down between us, I begin stroking him again. He pulls me toward him and kisses me with fervor before releasing my hair and grabbing a hold of my hips.

I then line him up and sink down onto him slowly. His slick cock pushes into me to the hilt. My god, it feels so much deeper this way.

Grabbing onto the back of the couch, bracing myself, I begin to move up and down his length, riding him. His hands help guide me, but he's letting me control this.

Control. Something I'm not used to having.

"Christ, darlin'. Look at you."

His hands skate up my sides and grab a handful of my breasts before leaning back. My fingers move to his neck as instincts take over—rolling, grinding.

His head falls back on a groan, arms stretched along the couch. The sight of him letting me take him, being pleasured by me, sends pressure building in my core once again.

Keeping a hand on him to steady myself, I let my

other fall to his chest, tracing his smooth golden skin and snake tattoo.

I've never been more attracted to a man before. I've never felt this way toward anyone.

Venom slithered his way into my life, saving me in way I never knew I need to be saved.

Leaning in, I sink my teeth into his neck once more. He moans, surging forward, burying his face between my breasts. His arms lock around my waist, holding me tight as I pick up the speed.

"Mmm, I can't take much more. You feel incredible. Deadly perfection. Let me feel you come around my cock again." My head tips back, breathy sounds spilling. "That's it, darlin'. Fuck me."

He grips my ass hard, tugs my hair with the other hand, sending flickers of pain to my scalp, which only sharpens the pleasure I feel in my pussy.

"Oh god."

"That's it. Keep going. Be my sweet little beast and come for me. Make a mess of me. I want your juices soaking my cock again."

"Ahh—fuck." Pleasure surges through me in electric waves. I grip his neck, eyes locked on his as I gasp.

His baby blues flutter shut for a moment before he meets my gaze again. His body jerks as he comes, jaw slack, brows drawn, bliss wrecking his face.

I collapse against him. We hold on to each other as we come down from the high.

A knock sounds. "Room service."

"Ah, shit."

Giggling, I slide off him and dart to the bed as Venom's essence runs down my thighs, then I dive under the covers.

He wraps my towel around his hips and opens the door. A short brunette wheels in a cart piled with platters and coffee. "Enjoy," she says on her way out. Venom hands her a fifty before she leaves.

Moving the cart closer to the bed, Venom starts uncovering all the platters.

"This is a lot of food."

"I got everything they had. Wasn't sure what the beast would want."

I smile. "Food coma, here we come!"

He chuckles as he tosses the towel away, and climbs in beside me. We eat until we're painfully full, then fall asleep together again.

For so long, sexual acts were a form of punishment. Control. A weapon. Although I never had a dick inside me before Venom, men would still use me in ways that left me feeling disgusted, ashamed, angry. They would take out their deviant sexual desires on me, leaving their filth on me to dry until I was permitted to shower.

What Venom has made me feel regarding sex and just as a woman in general is nothing short of magical.

I feel truly cherished and safe opening myself up to him in this way. My heart and body.

I chose him.

I *choose* him.

And it feels amazing that he chose me too.

CHAPTER TWENTY-SIX

We make it back home in one piece even though I insisted something was wrong with the plane and we were going to die.

I admit, I may have overreacted a bit, but it freaks me out how something so big can just be flying through the air.

Venom comforted me as best he could, which was sweet. The first few weeks of knowing Venom, I never thought I would use that word to describe him, but he has peeled back so many of his layers, slowly revealing to me the man he truly is.

The door slams shut behind us as we walk into Venom's house, causing him to look back at me. "Sorry, that door is heavy as shit."

"If you go around slamming doors, I'm gonna think

you're upset with me, darlin', and then I'll have to try to make up for whatever I did wrong," he says as he pulls me into him.

"Oh. Well then, never mind. Maybe I am upset," I tease.

"Mmm." He grabs my face and kisses me.

When we pull away, something from our peripheral vision catches our attention.

Evelyn is now standing in the foyer staring at us with a smile on her face.

"We're home," I sign and smile at her.

"*Yes, I felt the door close from the other side of the house. I thought I would be walking in on something much different.*"

"She kissed me, for the record," Venom quips, and I swat his arm.

Evelyn just continues smiling as she watches us, looking rather pleased with this new progress in our relationship.

"How's the ladies doing?" Venom signs and asks aloud.

"*Doing well. They all behaved. And how about you?*" She raises her brows.

"Did I behave?" He looks over to me, grinning, then back to Evelyn. "Hardly."

She shakes her head. "*I'm glad you're both okay. Are you hungry? I can put something together.*"

"That would be great. I could definitely eat," I say.

"Mmm, yes. I could eat as well," Venom says, then eyes me with a playful expression causing me to blush.

Evelyn nods and walks away toward the kitchen.

"Behave!" I scold.

"You should know that's not something I'm capable of. Especially when I still have the taste of you on my tongue, sweet beast."

My thoughts instantly go back to the plane ride when part of Venom's method of comforting me was eating my pussy until my body was trembling from what his mouth was doing instead of how turbulent the ride was.

Feeling flustered, I shake my head. "I'm gonna go help Evelyn."

AFTER EATING, VENOM, Evelyn and I spend some time in the greenhouse. We both seem to have missed it, and I love when Evelyn joins us. It feels amazing to be back in here, surrounded by such beauty and the familiar scent. Venom checks on his pets and plants, tending to some in need of extra love while Evelyn sticks by me.

"*These are my favorite*," Evelyn signs, smiling at a section of purple hood-shaped flowers with long bodies.

"What's it called?"

Evelyn begins to spell it out when Venom walks up behind me. "Monkshood. Although you might recognize it by its other names, Wolfsbane or even Queen of Poisons."

"I've definitely heard of Wolfsbane before. Wasn't aware what they looked like. Wolfsbane is poisonous, right?"

"Right. Aconitine, a neurotoxin, is found in the

Monkshood plant. I use it often. Ev has always said they looked like the most beautiful wildflowers."

"They are beautiful." I look to Ev and sign out loud.

"Beautiful and deadly," Venom says. "Just like someone else I know." He kisses my cheek and walks down an aisle.

I look back to Evelyn and see her smiling at me. My cheeks flush and I look away.

Evelyn touches my shoulder, getting my attention again. "*I'm going to bed. Goodnight.*"

"Okay, night."

I continue watering some plants when suddenly something catches my eye, something with blue iridescent scales. "Venom! Shit, shit, shit. Venom!" I yell.

He comes running over. "Christ woman, why are you hollering like a rooster at dawn?"

"There's a snake! In the plant." He pushes away some of the leaves and inspects the area. "There! Right there!" I point to the thing.

"Oh, it's just Mya. She's quite alright. She likes to take her naps in the foliage."

My eyes widen. "You mean, there are snakes just roaming around freely?"

"Of course, darlin'. I don't hold my pets prisoner. Some even find their way into the main house. The ones on their best behavior are free to go where they'd like." He winks.

"You mean the ones that aren't venomous?"

"Sure. If that's what makes you feel better."

"Venom!" I throw my hands up in frustration. "I just don't want to almost die again."

He chuckles. "Leave them be and you'll do just fine. I do think eventually y'all will become friendly." He pats my head.

"Doubtful." I roll my eyes.

Placing a finger under my chin, he tilts my head, so I can meet his eyes. "We did, didn't we?"

"Something like that." I can't help but smile at the thought of how far we've come.

He leans in closer. "I still bite though," he says in my ear, causing a shiver to dance up my spine.

I bite the inside of my lip to distract myself and move to put some distance between us when he grabs my arm and spins me back to him.

"Don't run off just yet." His finger gently grazes my cheek as he stares into my eyes. "My heart is reckless for you. I'm a mad man, darlin', ready to give my life for just one more taste of your poison."

I can't resist him. This beautiful complex man standing in front of me is my weakness. I want him as much as he wants me and now that we've gotten a taste of one another, we're addicts, constantly craving for more, even if it ends us. Because now, as an uneasy feeling rushes through me, I realize if I were to be without this man, I would simply die. "Take what you need," I whisper.

He grabs me, bends me over a table full of lush green plants, thankfully not the one Mya is napping in, and pulls down my pants. His hands stroke over my ass, kneading and smacking it. I whimper when I feel his teeth sink into the tender flesh of my ass before he kisses the same spot. I close my eyes and arch into him. He chuckles and descends to his knees. A finger grazes over my seam before I feel his warm tongue slip between my pussy from behind as he continues kneading my ass cheeks.

"Mmm, yes," I murmur.

My body begins to shake when his tongue spears into me. A moment later, he replaces it with his fingers, reaching deeper inside me and drawing out more pleasure as he focuses on my clit. I grip the edge of the table, vines from a plant tickling my face as he gets his fill of me. My ass is smacked again and bit hard while his fingers still pump into me. "Oh, fuck."

He pushes up my shirt, leans over me and begins peppering kisses along my back, still maintaining the rhythm between my thighs. My hair is roughly pulled back, forcing me to look at him with a groan.

"Christ, you're such a good little viper. Now come for me. Give me your sweetness." His voice is deep and smooth but teeters on the edge of becoming feral.

With my body bent over a table of plants and Venom's fingers fucking me, I come. He drops down and replaces his hand with his mouth as he sucks up my juices.

My knees nearly give out, but Venom doesn't let me fall. His mouth lingers between my thighs until he's had his fill, then he rises, gathers me against his chest, and carries me from the greenhouse straight to his bathroom upstairs.

We sit in a warm bath, Venom behind me as he washes my hair so tenderly, even stopping to kiss the scars on my back.

"I admire you," he says.

"What?" Where's that coming from?"

"I was just thinking about how you've been given endless opportunities in your life to break or be strong and you have showed up standing tall with teeth bared every time."

I smile.

After a moment, I break the silence. "You know… you were never the villain."

"You didn't know me before all this," he says solemnly.

I turn toward him and straddle his lap. "Well, I know who you are now, the person whose always been there underneath everything. The man you've become. And it's far from a villain."

"Does that mean I get a happy ending, after all?"

Smirking, I wrap my arms around his neck. "Time will tell, I suppose."

A silence fills the room as we stare into each other's eyes. He pushes a wet strand of hair away from my forehead before his eyes search mine, and then he kisses me. I grip him tighter, my hips pushing into him as the kiss grows passionate.

We break apart, and I look into his blue eyes again. An undeniable feeling washes over me.

I love him.

I'm so fucking in love with him.

AFTER BLOW-DRYING MY hair, I find Venom already in bed. He reaches into his nightstand and pulls out a battered, familiar book. Is that—

"Yes. I told you it was one of my comfort reads as a child."

"You kept it all these years?" My surprise bleeds into my voice.

"All three of my favorite. Every now and then I pick one up and read a few chapters. Just to feel that same magic I felt as a lost child."

"That's actually really beautiful."

"Not as beautiful as you, darlin'. Now come closer." Still naked, I crawl between his legs and rest my head on him. He opens the book and begins to read. While his voice threads through the story, I trace invisible shapes across his thigh, circles and spirals and nonsense patterns, and he combs his fingers through my freshly dried hair. I've never felt more at peace.

This is what it feels like to love someone.

The thought hits me so hard I sit up before I can stop myself. "Venom?"

"Hmm?" He lowers the book, giving me his full attention.

"I need to say something." His brows furrow, curious. I straddle him. His eyes dip to my breasts before climbing back to my face. "I love you." Something flickers across his eyes—too quick to name. I give a nervous laugh. "I'm in love with you, Venom. You have my heart."

His mouth opens as if he's going to speak but closes again. Instead, he smiles, grabs the back of my head, and kisses me. In the next heartbeat he rolls me beneath him, sliding into me with slow, deliberate care.

It's not rushed and not rough. Each movement feels

like a vow, like he's trying to tell me something without words. For a moment, I believe he is.

When we're both spent and breathing each other in, he stands, pulls on sweatpants, and leaves the room without a word.

He might have just made love to me, but he didn't say he loved me back.

He didn't say it back.

I stare at the door after it clicks shut. Did I misread everything? Am I a fool for giving him my heart? I was sure he felt the same.

The longer I lie there, the more unsettled and hollow I feel. I slip out of his bed and retreat to mine. Alone.

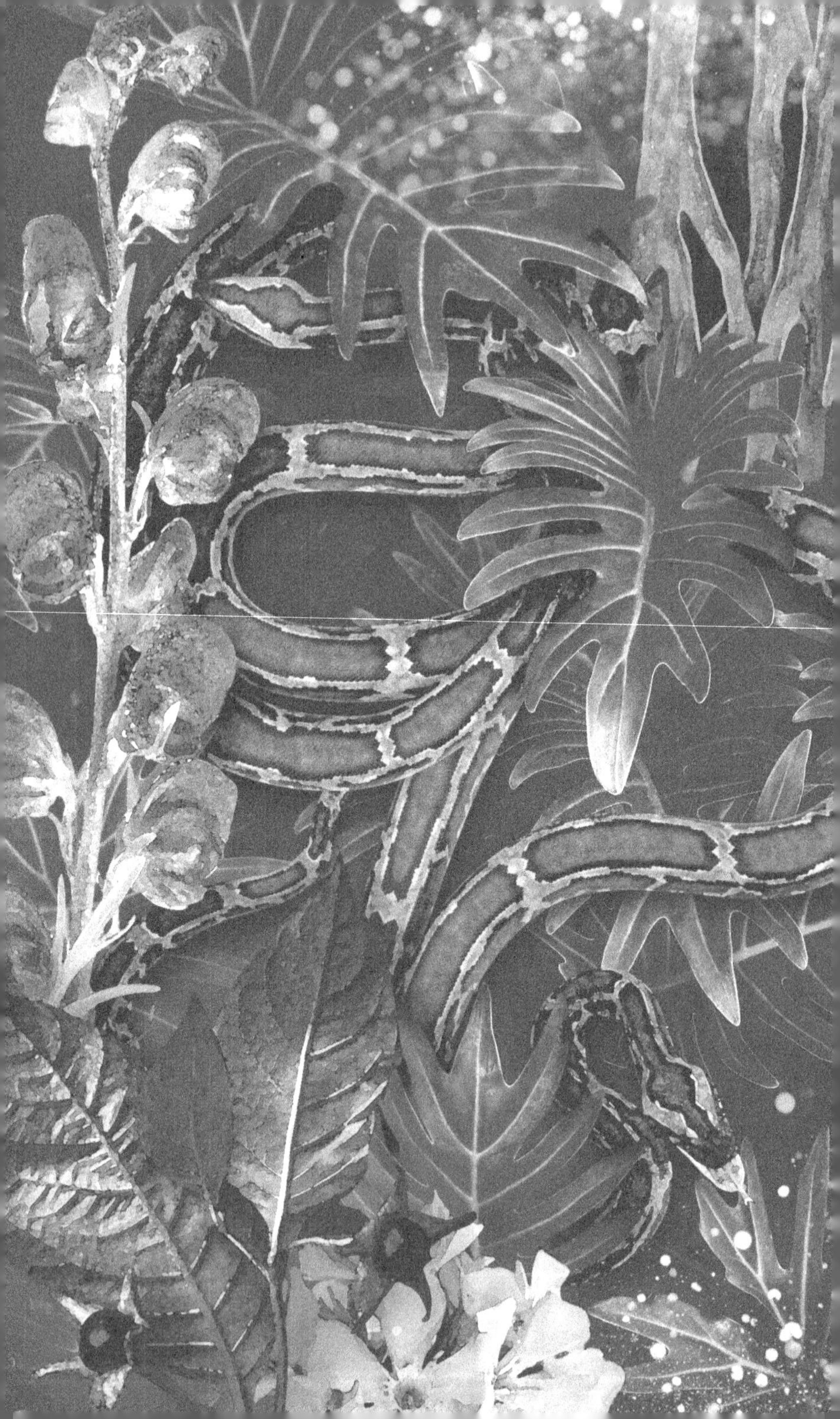

CHAPTER TWENTY-SEVEN

The regret is like a whisper in my ear until it's screaming so loudly, I flinch.

I should go back up there right now and tell her. Tell her how painfully in love I am with her. But I can't. I can't move from this spot I planted myself in within the comfort of my greenhouse.

Hearing her tell me she loves me set my feelings on fire. Absolute burning agony. Because what popped into my head at such an inopportune time was how I have yet to give Ivy her freedom. She told me she loves me while I still hold her captive in my home, and that nearly wrecked me.

Will she still love me when I tell her she's free?

Will the sound of freedom be louder than the love she feels for me?

For a moment, she was almost mine.

I fall asleep in my recliner, among my plants and pets, where I've always belonged.

MORNING ARRIVES QUICKER than I expected.

I follow the sound of laughter, Ivy's addictive laughter, until I reach the kitchen and find her and Ev sitting at the table. Evelyn is smiling at her as Ivy covers her mouth to stifle her giggles.

"What's so amusing this early?"

"I was just telling Ivy about that time Mya tripped you in the greenhouse and you fell ass-first into the rose bush. I had to pull thorns out of your ass for an hour."

"I don't think that's something she needed to hear about, Ev."

"It most certainly is!" Ivy says through laughs. "I can picture it so clearly."

"My ass? If you want to see it, I'll gladly show it to you."

Evelyn grins, a sweet dimple appearing in her cheek as Ivy catches her breath from her laughing fit.

"Can I talk to you?" I ask Ivy.

Her face turns serious, then she slowly rises from her seat and follows me into the other room.

"Evelyn is going into town later for some groceries. If you'd like, you can go with her."

She eyes me suspiciously. "Okay."

I hand her the keys to my Mercedes. "And when

you're done, you're free to leave. The car is yours. You can go wherever you want."

"What?" Her expression nearly transforms to that fiery anger of hers I know well.

"I'm saying you're free, Ivy. You're no longer my prisoner. Isn't that what you wanted?"

She flinches with what appears to be shock and then it turns to anger. "Are you stupid?" she asks, placing her hands on her curvy hips I love so much.

"Excuse me?"

"I mean, you must be. I just told you I'm in love with you last night and now you're telling me I am free to leave?"

"You've asked for your freedom many times before," I remind her.

"Yea, that was before! Before... everything. You must be joking. Tell me you're joking, that this is just another game."

"No more games, Ivy. I don't want to keep you prisoner any longer," I say; my patience for this difficult conversation nearing its end.

"You don't want to keep *me* anymore?"

"Ivy—"

"Stop calling me by my name! Call me beast or beastie. Call me yours. Just don't call me by my name right now." Her eyes begin to well up, her expression looking pained.

I step closer to her and press a hand to her cheek. "I never saw you coming, little beast. You surprised me and I'm not used to that."

"And now you're just pushing me away, after everything?" She blows out an exasperated breath. "You told me my heart was safe with you! If I loved you harder, could it be enough? Could I be enough to make you want to keep me?"

I step away from her as if I've been slapped and shake my head. "It has nothing to do with that."

"Fuck, Venom." She throws her hands up. "It has everything to do with that!"

"Stop."

"No, what the fuck are you thinking right now?"

I run a hand through my hair. "That's the thing, darlin', when it comes to you, I can't fucking think clearly. I can barely form a coherent thought. You cloud my judgment; you make me second-guess everything. You're poison pumping through my veins and I fear what will happen when it finally reaches my heart."

She steps forward, placing a hand over my chest. "Just let me in."

I turn away from her in frustration. "You think I haven't let you in already?" I pull at my hair before turning back to face her. "You've gotten closer to me than anyone ever has. I wish I could say it was by choice but you"—I place my hand over hers on my chest— "you've managed to sink your vicious teeth into me, releasing a type of poison I'm not immune to. It pumps through my veins, the chambers of my heart. Your delicious poison has filled my lungs; your wicked touch tames the flames inside me and silences my demons." I clutch her hand tighter. "Make no mistake, sweet beast, you are deep within me. So much so that if I were to try to cleanse you from my system, I would most definitely perish. This is who I really am. A man, utterly consumed by the woman he loves." She takes a step back, both our hands falling to our sides. "But at my own peril, I have to free you and let you go."

"So, you love me?"

I close the distance between us and grab her face. "Yes, you infuriating little beast, I fucking love you. That is why I cannot keep you prisoner any longer. I can't allow you to love me while I still hold you captive."

"So, I'm free? Right here and now, I'm a free woman?"

I let her go and stand tall, clenching my jaw, hands fisted. "Yes."

"Okay."

"Alright."

"I'm going to the store with Evelyn later and then… I'll be coming back… *home*. To *you*. Because that's what I choose as a free woman. I choose *you*. I choose *us*." She steps closer and places a hand to my chest. "I don't love you because I've been your prisoner, Venom. I fell in love with you under a glass dome ceiling surrounded by nature, between fighting and stolen glances, I fell in love with you in a room full of books sharing our pasts and truths. I fell in love with you slowly but deeply because you *see* me and I see *you*." She lets out a breath. "I love you and I don't want to be without you, ever."

My heart nearly explodes out of my chest at her words and the way she's looking at me. No woman in my life has ever looked at me the way Ivy has lately, especially right now.

Everything that matters to me lies within those vibrant green eyes.

"And so, the beauty fell in love with the beast. I, being the beauty of course," I say, smirking.

She rolls her eyes. "Shut up and kiss me already."

I grab her by her nape and slam my lips across hers.

Her soft moans fill my mouth as I pick her up and set her down on the living room couch.

Desperate to be inside her, I take her quick and hard.

CHAPTER TWENTY-EIGHT

"Okay we're heading out," Ivy calls out.

I round the corner and grab her wrist, pulling her into me. "As much as I enjoyed our last chase, just come back to me now, darlin'." I kiss her forehead, let her go and turn my attention to Evelyn. "Ev, watch out for this one. Oh, and make sure she picks out some stuff other than gummy bears. I'll see y'all later."

As I'm watching Ivy and Ev pass through the front gate, my phone buzzes in my pocket. I pull it out to see a text from my favorite operations officer from a high-ranking organization.

Alice

I just received word that Deborah is leaving the country early tomorrow morning. Probably personally moving… the product. We need her taken care of tonight. We'll give you an extra 50K to make it happen.

Me

Since you asked so sweetly, consider it done.

I've worked with Alice for many years. Although we have never met in person, I've become fond of her, or rather, what she stands for as well as the organization she works for.

Wonderland.

That's what they call themselves. And of course, the woman at the top is called the *Red Queen*. I've never even spoken to the Queen and she's rarely ever mentioned. I'm sure I could dig up more information on them if I wanted to, but I have no interest in that. We have a mutual respect. My reach is far, but they are on a much higher level. I often thought they might be a branch of the CIA or FBI, but I might never know and that's alright by me.

Although I was supposed to have another two weeks before I made a move on Deb, I'm always prepared.

Death is always in my pocket.

Deborah lives a couple hours away, but I should still be home by tonight to greet my sweet beast when she returns. I look out the window once more, the car gone from sight, then head to my greenhouse.

I select a couple of vials, along with some syringes and extra blades and fill the custom pockets of my black suit jacket with them.

Time to play.

FROM HER UPSTAIRS bedroom, I hear Deborah's garage open and close, signaling she's home. I look at my phone once more which has the current view of her security cameras, and watch my prey make her way closer and closer to *me*. I slip my phone back into my pocket and wait.

The bedroom door opens as she walks in and flicks on the light, closing the door behind her. She begins to unbutton her silky blouse, not noticing I'm sitting on a rather comfortable chair in the corner of her large bedroom as she strides into her walk-in closet. A few seconds later, she returns, slower this time, a worried look crossing her face as if she now senses something in her room that does not belong. Or rather, *someone.*

That's right Deborah, you should be concerned.

Her eyes land on me and they go wide as she grabs her chest in shock.

"Oh my god. Who the fuck are you? What are you doing in my house? Get out! Get out right now before I call the police!"

"Hush, darlin'." I shift in my chair, stretching my legs out on the stool, making myself more comfortable.

"I said get out!"

"I heard you, unfortunately." I pull at my ear. "Has anyone ever told you your voice is like nails on a chalkboard? Christ, woman, who would ever listen to you speak for more than a few seconds without stuffing something in that big mouth of yours to shut you up. If I knew how wretched your voice was, I might have reconsidered taking this order."

"Excuse me? Who the fuck are you?"

"Oh, I see we are past niceties." I place a toothpick in my mouth then stand. "I'm the person sent to kill you, darlin'."

Tipping my head slightly, I smile wide at her.

She stares at me for a moment, probably considering if I'm joking. When she realizes I am not, fear replaces her anger and she bolts for the door.

I whip a throwing knife and it lands in the door right before she reaches it. She jerks back in surprise, stumbling in her heels and rolling an ankle before she drops to the floor. In desperation she crawls for the exit once again and I throw another blade, sending into the door again. She turns and pushes her back up against the wall, heavily breathing.

"What the fuck do you want?! I have money, I can pay. I'll give you more than whoever hired you. I can give you whatever you want!"

I casually walk closer to her and squat down to her level. "What if what I want is to watch you slowly die? Does the offer still stand?"

"Please! Please don't do this. I—I have a family!"

I chuckle. "You have two adult children who don't

even speak to you anymore, darlin'. Dare I say it's because of your voice alone, but I think it might have to do with your extracurricular activities or simply just being such a cunt of a mother. There's a lot of you around ya know. Quite unfortunate. For you, that is."

She spits at me.

Why do they always have to spit? Is that really so satisfying?

"Foul. Now you've upset me, Debbie. Can I call you Debbie?"

"No," she growls.

I stand, wiping away what spittle of hers landed on me. "Here's what we're going to do, Debbie. You're going to continue your little nighttime routine and I'm going to watch. If you reach for your phone, you die. If you try to run out of here again, you die. Are we clear?"

"You just want to watch me, like some freak, and then you'll leave?"

I smirk. "Most definitely."

Stepping to the side, I motion for her to get up and continue what she was doing before she was interrupted by my presence. She eyes me suspiciously but rises onto shaky legs and limps her way back to her closet. I follow with a smile.

I watch her remove her long form fitting skirt, leaving her in just her beige bra and matching panties. I eye her up and down as I lean against the closet doorway. I get a scowl from her in return and then she reaches behind her back and unclasps her bra. She turns before letting me get a full view of them but reveals her ass to me in the process instead.

Certainly not as plump and delicious as Ivy's. The thing is barely non-existent. She then slips on a light blue nightgown, with a plunging neckline.

"Did you choose that one just for me, darlin'? I'm truly honored."

"Fuck you."

"I'll have to pass, all offense to you."

She lets out an annoyed grunt and I move away from the door as she walks out and goes into her bathroom next. I stand in the doorway again and watch.

My phone buzzes in my pocket and I quickly take a peek at it, seeing it's my sweet beast.

Ivy

I love you. We hit some traffic due to an accident, but we'll be back soon. I hope you aren't missing me too much.

Me

Missing you terribly. I had to step out for work but I'll see you when I'm home. I love you.

My attention snaps back to Debbie, who is now pumping foam into her hand and begins to wash her face.

Mmm, almost time.

I've learned Deb here does love her skincare routine.

I play with the toothpick in my mouth, anticipation building.

She dries her face and looks over at me with another scowl before continuing. Reaching for her La Mer cream, she uses a small little tool, scooping some out and begins to rub it into her face, neck and chest.

"You missed a spot."

She gives me no response, just stares at herself in the mirror as she applies the cream.

She suddenly stops, hands hovering just an inch away from her skin. And then she screams.

My head tips and I close my eyes, savoring the sound of this vile woman's agony. Then I let out a satisfied sigh and look back at her. "Ah, there we go. That is certainly better."

Frantically, she grabs a towel and tries wiping off the cream, but it's too late. She watches herself in the mirror, horrified, as her skin reddens, blisters and then begins to melt.

Her initial scream was pleasing to finally hear, but now her continued high pitched noises are very unpleasant to my ears, maybe I should have chosen a quicker death. Although, this child trafficking bitch definitely deserved something slow and painful.

I move toward her to get a better view of my work when she tries to grab at me. I shove her away and she stumbles back, tripping over the bathroom rug and falling ass first into the tub with a thud. She makes the mistake of attempting to use her hands to try to stop what is happening to her face, but that only causes the flesh bubbling on her hands to stick to the melting skin on her face.

Debbie's pain-filled screams grow softer, her body moving in jerky motions as she tries to claw herself out of the tub.

This is certainly a messy one. Blood and other liquid oozes from her face down to her neck, mixing with liquified skin. Her mouth moves, where I imagine her lips were once, trying to say something, but it just comes out as gurgled sticky noises.

She finally stops moving. The bathroom becomes quiet except for the continued sizzling of her flesh.

I pull out a syringe, cover my nose and lean into the tub to quickly inject the high dose of venom into her arm, taking an extra step to make sure she's quite dead.

And then I turn away and make my way downstairs.

As I pass the kitchen, I swipe up a delicious looking apple. Before I reach the front door, I hear a faint sound coming from down the hall to my right. A hollow banging.

Last time I followed a sound after killing someone, I found my little wild beast.

Do I want to see where this leads me?

I place my hand on the front door handle and stop.

Well, fuck it, let's have a looksie.

As I walk toward the end of the hall, the banging gets louder. I reach the door and the noise stops.

I try the knob. Locked.

I let out an annoyed sigh then take a step back and kick open the door.

The room is dark and quiet now, but I find the light switch on the wall and flick it on.

A child, in nothing but dirty underwear, huddles in the corner of the room. Bruises scatter his frail body and his messy brown hair shields his eyes.

I take a step toward him and the poor boy pulls his legs even tighter to himself in fear, shaking.

"Now, now. It's alright. I'm not here to hurt you."

I crouch down to his level and wait for him to lift his head.

One big cerulean eye meets me, while the other remains closed in an angry bruise. I clench my jaw, griding my molars before I speak.

"What's your name, boy?"

He studies me for a moment before whispering, "Damon."

"And how old are you, Damon?"

"Nine. Are you a policeman? Are you here to save me?"

"I'm no policeman, but I can help you."

"The lady—she'll be back soon," he says with deep rooted fear.

"She's already returned." His one eye goes even wider and he looks to the door. "It's alright. She's dead now."

"Are you like... one of those superheroes?"

"I would prefer you not call me *that*. You can call me, Venom."

"So, you are a superhero!" he says excitedly.

"No, no. Not that *Venom*. I don't have a parasite in me. We just share the same name. Although I will say, I'm much better than him." I give him a wink then stand and hold out my hand. "Can you walk?"

He smiles and stands, slipping his small hand into mine.

"Was it really bad for her? Can I see her?"

Surprised, I look down at him with furrowed brows. "I'm not sure you want to see what she looks like *now*."

He stands taller and with determination says, "I do. I want to see her."

"Well alright then, but I don't want to be blamed for any nightmares you have." I'm sure I'll hear shit about letting a child see a dead body from Alice, but I can see in this boy's eyes why he wants to see her, that he *needs* to see her. As I did with my abusers. If this is the closure he needs, so be it.

"I already have nightmares," he says softly.

Me too, kid.

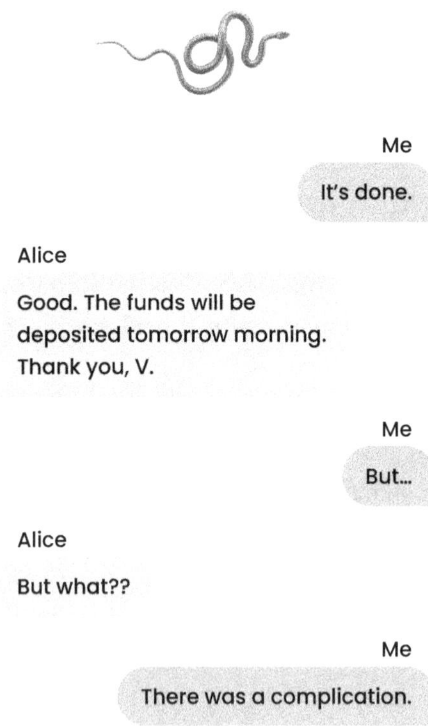

Me

It's done.

Alice

Good. The funds will be deposited tomorrow morning.
Thank you, V.

Me

But...

Alice

But what??

Me

There was a complication.

Alice

Since when do you have
complications?

Me

The… product… is currently
asleep in my back seat.

Alice

Fuck. Our intel did not disclose
he was being held there. This
must have just happened.

Me

He's pretty banged up and
needs to be checked out. And I
am not the one to hold his hand
through all this. I might have
scarred him already.

Alice

I got this. Can you meet me in
two hours? I'll take a chopper.

Me

Send me the address.

DAMON ENDS UP waking up a little while before Alice is
set to arrive and uninvitedly crawls his way into the front
passenger seat.

"I'm cold," he says, rubbing at his thin arms. "And hungry."

I toss him the apple I stole from dead Debbie and then step out of my car and begin to unload the pockets of my jacket, tossing the items onto the driver seat. Damon's eyebrows raise as he takes in everything.

"Don't touch any of that."

"I knew you were a superhero," he says with a proud smirk.

"You really gotta stop calling me that, kid." I lean in and hand him my jacket. "Here, put this on."

He's drowning in it, but at least he'll be warm. I also turn up the heat and press on the seat warmers.

After collecting my *tools*, I put them in my bag in the trunk and then join the boy.

"Do you have family? Someone who might be looking for you?"

He shakes his head. "Mom and Dad were killed. And then the men took me." A tear rolls down his dirty bruised face and I find myself wishing I could bring Debbie back alive just to kill her again.

"Well, there's a very nice lady coming to get you. She'll take care of you."

"I can't go home with you?" He looks at me with such hope and I'm suddenly thrust back into memories I don't want be in. I shake my head, pushing away where my mind is going.

This boy in front of me reminds me too much of myself. I need Alice to get here now.

Headlights appear as a car pulls up directly in front of

mine. Someone gets out and moves to stand in between our cars; a shadow carved out between the two sets of headlights.

"Is that her?"

"I'll be back right back. You stay here."

I climb out and walk over to the person, their face becoming clearer with every step.

Long blonde hair, tightly tied back in a ponytail, slim porcelain face with light rosy cheeks, powder blue eyes, and a smirk, greets me.

"Alice," I say with a nod.

"Venom."

"Never thought we'd meet."

"Oh, we've sort of met." She smiles; bright pearly teeth drawing my attention to her mouth.

"Is that so?"

"Georgia, the ball."

The instant she says it, I remember. "The rabbit mask. Of course. You should have said hello."

"I was working, and I assume, so were you. Although I didn't expect you to bring a date."

"My date nights always involve a little mayhem." I grin.

"Wouldn't expect anything less." She looks past me to my car. "Is the boy okay?"

"Hungry, bruised. Could have broken bones, other internal injuries, but he's walking and talking."

"Thank you, Venom. I'll take it from here."

She begins to walk to the car.

"What will you do with him? Just… curious."

"We'll help him heal and find him a loving home and hopefully his trauma won't affect too much of his future."

"One's trauma is complex."

"Speaking from experience?"

"Of sorts."

She gives me a soft smile.

"Will you ever tell me your real name?"

"I have."

"Well alright, *Alice from Wonderland*," I say sarcastically.

She smiles again and then moves to open the door to greet Damon. She crouches and introduces herself and exchanges more words before helping him out of the car.

"I'll be in touch, Venom," Alice says as she walks back by me, hand in hand with the boy. He stares at me as he passes and before he makes it to Alice's car, he lets her hand go and runs to me, colliding into my side and hugging me.

"Thank you for saving me, superhero."

I so desperately want to correct him again, but I don't.

Instead, I place my hand on his back and give him a couple taps. "It was nice to meet you Damon, go on now and make Alice get you whatever meal you want, don't skip dessert."

He looks at me with a big smile and runs back over to Alice who is smiling at me too. She gives me a nod and turns away.

CHAPTER TWENTY-NINE

I put my phone away after texting Venom, telling him we're stuck in traffic, and look over to Evelyn in the driver's seat. She frowns when she looks at me.

"I hope you and Venom didn't have dinner plans."

"It's alright. We'll get there when we get there," I say with a sigh. She looks back to the road and I place a hand on her arm to get her attention again. She looks back at me, and I ask, "Were you ever married?"

"No. But I was very much in love once upon a time." Her expression changes and I know that means it ended badly.

"We were high school sweethearts. He was my soulmate. But fate had other plans for us. He died from cancer. Too young. It wasn't enough time with him. No amount of time would have been enough with Frank."

I rub her arm, offering comfort. "I'm sorry."

She places her hand over mine then signs, *"I still cherish the time we had together and the memories we made. Those will live on forever. And I know I will see him again one day."*

"I believe that as well. How did you meet Venom anyway?"

"Frank and I owned an Italian restaurant together. Venom used to frequent it often. But after Frank died, I was at a complete loss. My whole world exploded and I couldn't go on for a while." She shakes her head, looking down, lost in the memory. *"I sold the restaurant, but I still needed to work and make a living somehow. That's where Venom came in. Being a regular, he knew the situation and he knew how much Frank's loss affected me. He offered me a position as his live-in housekeeper. He said he needed someone discreet, someone he could trust. Also made me promise to make him his favorite Italian dishes from the restaurant."* Her smile reaches her eyes, and I laugh because of course Venom would add that in there.

There's a pause and Evelyn's expression softens as she takes a steadying breath before her hands rise again. *"He saved me in a way, from myself, from my spiral. And bit by bit I crawled out of my dark hole. I had a purpose again, someone who needed me."*

I don't know why I'm suddenly tearing up, but I hold them back. "He needed you too, Evelyn." Tears brim her eyes, and I reach over and give her a hug. I meet her eyes. "Thank you for sharing."

"Of course, my sweet girl. And I'm glad you see Venom as I do."

We smile at each other and then the cars in front of us begin moving.

Finally.

I can't wait to get home to Venom.

THE GATE LEADING to the rest of Venom's driveway is wide open. It is supposed to close automatically but must have gotten stuck after Venom left.

"*Venom will have someone take a look at that. It acts up sometimes. Nothing is without fault.*" Evelyn signs.

As we drive closer to the house, I can't help but feel that something is off, more than just the gate being open.

Evelyn parks the car in front of the stairs leading up to the front door and pops the trunk. I step out of the car and a gentle breeze blows, stirring the tiny hairs on my arms and causing goosebumps to rise across my skin. I slip my sweater on, pulling it tighter over my shoulders.

As I take a few steps toward the back of the car, another breeze lifts strands of my hair from my face, and I catch a scent of smoke. Cigarette smoke to be exact.

Strange.

Neither Evelyn nor Venom smoke.

Something deep in my gut grows heavier, unsettling my nerves further as I glance around the property, taking in everything within view.

Nothing but tall trees swaying in the wind.

Evelyn pauses before walking up the front steps, holding two grocery bags in her hands. She looks at me with concern.

"Sorry, I'm alright. I'll grab the rest of the bags." She continues staring for a moment longer as I walk to the trunk and lean in to grab more.

The crunch of footsteps and the sound of glass hitting cement instantly lift my head. Evelyn stands in shock, the bags now on the steps with their contents spilling out.

She is not looking at me. She is staring past the front of the car, toward the garage.

Slowly, I stand and step around the car to see what has her so frightened.

Four men stand only a few feet from the garage, guns aimed. One flicks his cigarette to the ground when his eyes meet mine.

Oh my god.

They begin walking closer, turning their aim to me as well. I look back at Evelyn and meet her eyes. The fear in the sweet old woman's gaze is enough to bring me to near tears.

"You," the man with a full dark beard, says, pointing at me. "Step away from the car and keep your hands up. And you," he looks at Evelyn, "get down from the stairs." He gestures with his gun for her to move.

We do as he says, Evelyn and I coming shoulder to shoulder to stand before them. She grips my hand and squeezes tight.

I swallow my nerves and force my voice to remain steady. "What is this about?"

"We've been looking for you."

"Me? Why?" This can't be right.

"You'll find out soon enough. You're coming with us.

And if you make a fuss, we have approval to use physical force."

"In other words, I'll happily knock you the fuck out," another man chimes in with a sinister smile.

I glare at him as Evelyn lets go of my hand and moves to stand in front of me.

I grab her shoulders and try to move her back. "Evelyn, no!" But it is no use. She can't see my lips from here, and she doesn't budge from her protective spot.

The men laugh and my buried anger resurfaces. I try to move around Evelyn but she spreads her arms to block me. I know I could overpower her, but I don't want to risk hurting her.

"There has to be some mistake. Please, I'm not who you're looking for!" I plead.

The bearded man smirks as he eyes me up and down. "Nah, you're definitely her." He glances at his watch. "Time to go. We're behind schedule."

They all move forward and my adrenaline spikes as I pull at Evelyn's arm, trying to drag her away. She still doesn't move.

The bearded man reaches us first and presses his gun to Evelyn's forehead. "Move out of the way, you old hag."

"Please! Don't shoot her! I'll come! Okay." I throw up my hands in surrender. "I'll come willingly, just don't hurt her."

Evelyn turns toward me and quickly, with both hands, signing for me to run, to call Venom.

I shake my head in disbelief.

I am not leaving her.

"Stop moving your fucking hands!"

She doesn't hear him, but Evelyn turns back to the men with her chin held high. A fist flies out and crashes against her cheek, sending her to the ground.

"Evelyn!" I scream.

My fury explodes. I charge the bearded man and drive my knee into his groin. His gun goes off as he stumbles back, swearing and clutching himself.

Hands grab me from behind. I twist, clawing and kicking, grunting and yelling as I fight, seeing nothing but red. Hoping I can cause pain to at least one of these motherfuckers.

A body slams into me and I am knocked to the ground. I get on all fours to push myself up, but a boot drives into my stomach and I collapse, clutching myself as nausea rips through me.

Two men close in, wrangling my legs as I thrash. I glance over and see the others stomping on Evelyn and dragging her up the steps.

"No! Evelyn!" I scream, reaching for her.

Arms lock around my waist and haul me back. My screams grow raw until I can't even tell if I am still screaming, only watching in horror as one of the men pulls out a large knife and drives it into Evelyn's stomach.

A dark bag drops over my head. Something cracks against my skull, and everything goes quiet.

CHAPTER THIRTY

I pull up to my gate and let out a sigh. This damn gate. I take a mental note to get it upgraded asap.

It's dark, but I'm picturing my beast waiting for me in my greenhouse and I smile at the thought.

I never had someone who truly loved me to come home to when I was growing up. Eventually things changed and Ev would be the one waiting up for me some nights, making sure I was alright. It was different having someone care like that about me. And now, knowing Ivy is the one waiting for me to come home, it's a feeling I never want to get used to. To see her eyes light up when she sees me, take in her familiar summer scent, to feel peace amidst the chaos of my mind and work life in the arms of my favorite little viper.

My home within a home.

My headlights catch on my other car that Evelyn used today, still parked in front of the stairs like she usually does after coming home from grocery shopping, and the trunk is still open.

I reach into my pocket and pull out a knife.

Something isn't right here.

I stop the car and step out, slowly walking the rest of the way, focusing on any little movement or noise.

Before I even make it to the trunk, my attention is pulled to a sound coming from the front steps.

My eyes widen as I see Evelyn lying in an awkward angle on the stairs.

"Ev!" I run to her, kneeling in a pool of blood beside her and pulling her into my lap. "Oh, Ev."

I take in her injuries. Bruised, bloody face, bleeding wounds to the stomach and... her hands. Her fucking hands have been cut off.

No.

I can't fix this.

I can't fix this.

The realization steals my breath and forms a tight grip around my heart like a boa constrictor coiling its body around me and squeezing, tighter and tighter.

Evelyn looks at me with a pained and broken expression. Her face is splattered with blood, red tears streaming down her cheeks.

She lifts her arm, slowly moving it as if trying to sign but all that remains is a bloody stump.

My heart breaks even more.

"Fuck, Ev. Shh. You're going to be alright," I try

reassuring her, or maybe it's more for myself.

She shakes her head at me. She's always been able to tell when I lie.

A gurgled cough escapes her, more blood seeping from her mouth.

"Where's Ivy? Is she okay?" I ask through a trembling voice.

Evelyn points her arm straight toward the driveway.

And I nod in understanding.

Taken.

Someone came here and took something precious from me and hurt the only real mother figure I ever had.

I squeeze my eyes shut and swallow back the lump in my throat. I caress her hair as I stare back down at her. "I'm going to help you now, darlin'. You won't be in pain any longer," I say, barely able to keep a steady tone.

She nods, and a tear escapes my eye.

"Christ, Ev. Who's gonna keep me in line now?"

The corner of her mouth ticks and she lifts another bloody arm pointing toward the driveway again.

Ivy.

"I'm going to get her back. I promise; I'll get her back."

I tip my face to the sky, blinking hard, refusing to let the tears win. Not yet.

Not until I tell her. I look back to her, my sweet Ev, and my chest cracks open. "You're the only real family I've ever had. The only one who stayed and showed me kindness, love. Thank you… f-for everything, you crazy old bat. I-I love you. Christ, I should've said it sooner."

Her brows pinch, tears streaking down her face, mixing with the blood smeared across her cheeks, but her eyes—those eyes—hold me like always. Like I'm hers. Even when I've been a thorn in her side. She remained an anchor for me.

My stomach twist and my hands tremble as I pull out a syringe of aconitine, from her favorite plant. It takes three tries to steady my hand enough to press the thin needle against her neck. My throat burns like shards of glass have been placed inside me as I whisper, "It will be quick, darlin'. The purple wildflowers will take you to Frank." A strained small smile grows across her blood coated mouth. "I'll see you soon, Ev."

The plunger goes down. And my world goes with it. She trembles once. Twice. Her smile falters, before she exhales a last, rattled breath.

"No," I choke, pulling her against me, my forehead pressed against hers. "Please, don't—" My body heaves, but she's already gone.

A soft breeze blows and everything becomes eerily still, no noise, just a suffocating silence as if Death himself has arrived to take my Evelyn away forever.

I kiss her cold forehead; my lips wet with my own tears. "Goodbye, old friend."

I hold her a few moments longer before I compose myself, steeling my emotions and carry her inside to place her on the couch. I cover her with a blanket, then make a call to someone who will assist with her body with care and respect.

There's another important matter that needs my attention now.

Getting my little beast back and making whoever took her suffer.

IV

CHAPTER THIRTY-ONE

"Wake up, Cherry."

The voice pulls me to consciousness, and I slowly open my eyes, blinking away the fuzziness.

"There we go," comes the voice again.

I look to my right, eyes landing on black suede shoes and dark slacks on long legs. I follow them up until I reach a disturbingly familiar face.

No.

I'm dreaming.

I'm dead and this is my hell.

I shake my head and frantically blink, trying to rid myself of the image before me.

He crouches to where I lie on the floor and that's when I realize my hands are also tied behind my back.

"It's true, Red. Your eyes are not deceiving you. We are reunited at last." He opens his arms wide as if this is some welcomed reunion.

I awkwardly sit up and move myself further away from *him*.

"It can't be. I shot you. In the head!" I say, shaking my head in denial.

"You sure did. And we'll discuss your punishment for that later. And for all the effort I've gone through trying to find you. But I can't deny how much I've missed you, my sweet cherry." He brushes a finger along my cheek, and I flinch away.

"How… how did you survive? It's not possible."

"Aw, Red, I'm starting to think you're disappointed."

"I am," I growl.

"I see you haven't lost your fire. Good." His satisfied smile widens. "You should work on your aim; you just grazed my skull. Maybe go for the heart next time. Although, you running away from me sure felt like you ripped open my heart." He brushes his hand down my hair and looks lovingly at me as I curl my lip in disgust. "But you also made me look like a fool!" He slaps me hard across the face enough to send my body back to the floor.

"Fuck you! I should have unloaded the whole clip into your fucking face!"

For a moment, he looks disappointed, sad even.

"Maybe you should have, but perhaps there's a part in you that didn't want to really kill me. Perhaps my sweet cherry developed feelings for me, after all."

"Not a fucking chance."

"You've been gone far too long. I think you need to be retrained. That's fine. I'll happily break you again until you're behaving properly. But for now, I'll give you some time to think about your mistakes." He walks to the door. "We'll catch up soon, Red. And I want to hear about everything you've been up to and how you ended up in the Southern Poisoner's home. Oh, by the way, you looked ravishing at the ball. It was hard to resist taking you right then." He smiles and leaves.

Oh my god. He was there.

The image of the man in the wolf mask who was watching me flashes before me, and I sharply inhale. It was him. And the cherry bomb… fuck. I should have known! I'm so stupid! I lay my head back and stare at the ceiling.

This is my fault. Again.

Something in me cracks and I start laughing. Laughing until I'm almost crying.

My luck can't possibly get any worse.

Once again, I'm in the hands of this psychopath. A dead psychopath. At least he was supposed to be dead.

Nikolai is alive.

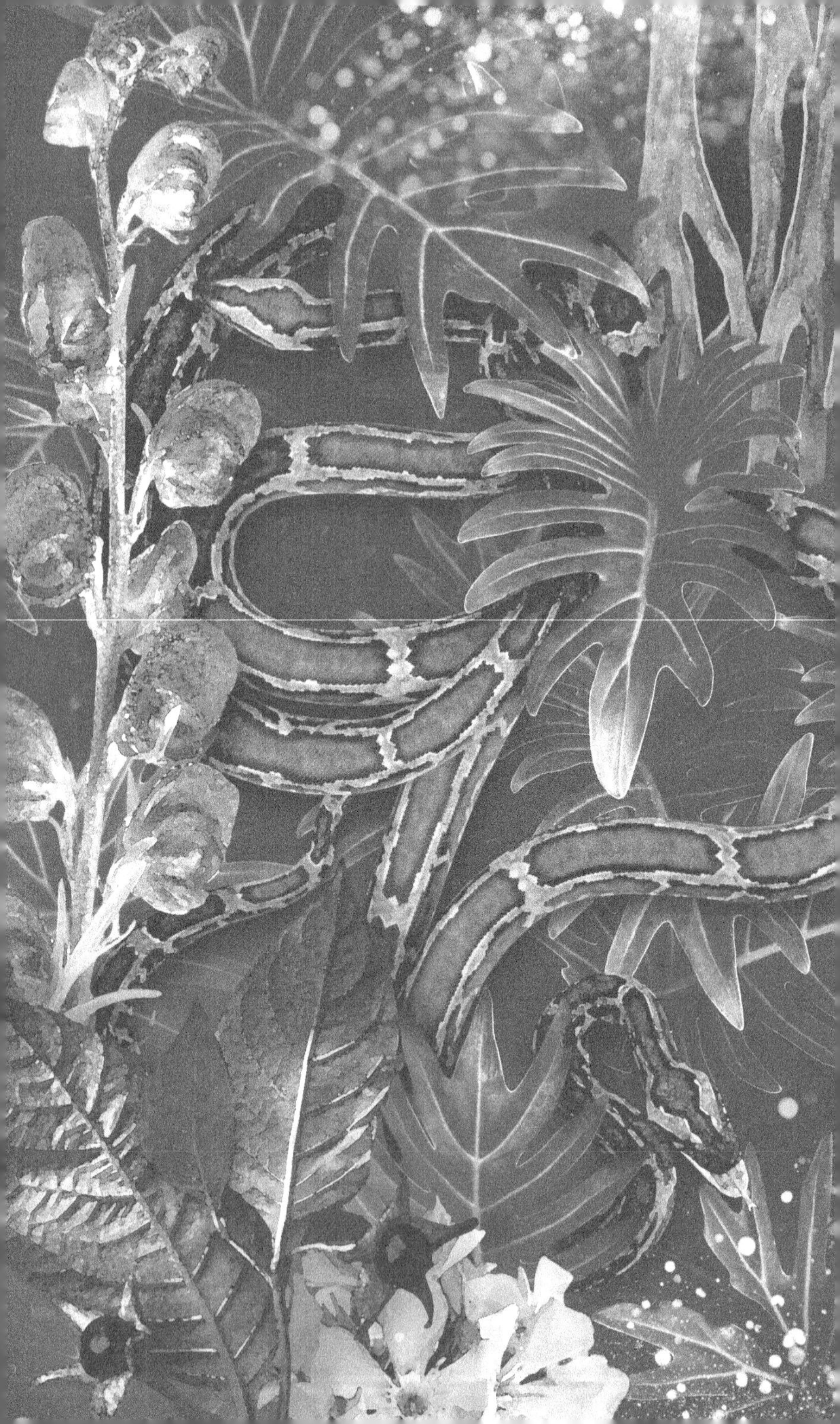

CHAPTER THIRTY-TWO

The bottle of whiskey smashes into the wall and shatters into pieces. Dark liquid drips down the wall as I run my fingers through my hair and pull at the roots.

"Fuck!" I shout.

It's been three days. Three fucking days and I haven't been able to locate Ivy.

I've watched the surveillance system outside my house dozens of times, looking for any more clues. I've repeatedly watched those four men hurt the two important women in my life. I've listened to Ivy's gut-wrenching screams for Evelyn so many times that when I close my eyes at night, that's all I hear.

I've tried to ignore this pain I feel and push it deep down inside me where all the other dark parts of me lay shattered like that whiskey bottle. But these jagged pieces are ripping me to shreds as they try to be suppressed.

Why can't I find her?!

My phone rings and I answer it right away. "Tell me you have something."

"Sorry, Venom. I've been working overtime on this for you, but I've looked into all your possible enemies, and I do mean *all*. There's nothing. They're clean."

"She couldn't have just disappeared, Luther. You're the best at finding people. Are your talents dwindling due to old age?"

"Look, Venom, I consider you a friend and I want to help you. I'm trying, but you gotta give me a little more information here."

Luther Bommer is well known amongst people in my line of work. There also happens to be an Interpol red notice out on him. Impressive, really. Luther isn't just skilled at finding people who don't want to be found, but he also happens to have an incredible talent for crafting bombs and that is where his passion truly lies.

"I've told you everything I know."

"And her enemies? You might not be the only one with people out there wanting to hurt you."

"They're dead. The couple who took her, the man who had her before, they're dead. I took care of at least two of those deaths myself."

"And what about the buyer she was sold to who never ended up getting her?"

I let out a frustrated sigh. "I didn't look any further into it. Those types of men would just move on to the next."

"Maybe. But we should check every possibility. Give me a couple hours and I'll get back to you."

With all the enemies I have who might have wanted to do this, I never considered her enemies being a possibility.

I pace the first floor again, passing by Mya who has curled herself around the base and stem of a lamp. The light's reflection glimmers across her scales, making them shimmer beautifully. I'm happy she's at least here with me, even though I haven't wanted to step into my greenhouse, because it has become nothing more than a reminder of Ivy.

I keep expecting to creep up on my little beast, to make her jump and watch her cheeks flush so beautifully. Or to find her admiring the plants, whispering sweet words to them as she caresses their foliage.

Every room holds memories of her.

The silence in my home was once comforting. Now the silence is so loud it physically hurts, threatening to destroy what little I have left of me.

I open a new bottle of liquor and take a long drink, slamming it back on the counter before collapsing into my recliner. Resting my head against the back, I stare at the ceiling and replay my happiest moments with Ivy, starting with the night we danced together in the middle of the road in Georgia.

I run a hand over my face and, before I realize it, sleep takes me.

A FLASH OF red hair disappears around the corner. "Ivy?!" I quickly scramble to my feet, stumbling after her. "Ivy!"

I round the corner, entering the kitchen, but it's empty. The sound of the greenhouse door closing sends me racing down the hall, nearly tripping over myself. I rub my weary eyes. I probably shouldn't have drunk so much.

I throw open the door and there she is, standing with her back to me.

"Ivy? Are you okay?" She doesn't respond or move. I step closer to her. "I thought you were gone." Placing a hand on her cold shoulder, I turn her.

"Christ!" I stumble back, catching myself on a table of potted plants. I look at my sweet beast in horror.

Her eyes are replaced by wildflowers and blood drips from her nose. Her mouth opens wide in a silent scream and that's when snakes, dozens of small snakes, begin to slither out from her mouth. But just as quickly as the snakes appear, maggots take their place, consuming her whole body as her skin turns to a shade of death, likes she's been rotting in the earth.

"Ivy! No!" I reach for her again, but just when my hands grab her, she bursts into a dark cloud of dust—

I jolt awake in a panicked frenzy, gasping and toppling off the couch. I frantically look around the room for Ivy.

Fucking nightmares.

Bringing a hand to my throbbing head, I groan and stand. The room sways and I stumble a step then spot the shattered bottle of whiskey on the floor.

"Ev!" I stumble to the foyer. "Ev!" I know she can't hear me but where the fuck is that woman. I turn back to the living room, spotting the blood-soaked couch.

Memories flood me, sending me to my knees.

When Evelyn's body was taken, sent to be cremated, I was asked if I wanted the couch to be disposed of, but I declined. I'm not sure why. But looking at it now—a piece of her, a reminder—is like a knife to the gut.

"Ev," I solemnly whisper, shaking my head in disbelief. "Fuck!" My voice echoes through the empty house, bouncing into the empty hole that's been left inside me.

My phone dings from a text and I quickly scramble to my feet and pull it out of my pocket.

Luther

Gabriel or Nikolai sound familiar?

I rack my brain.

Nikolai.

Yes. The first man who held her captive.

The one who whipped her.

The one she killed.

Me

Nikolai. That's the man Ivy killed.

Luther

Are you sure?

Me

**What the hell are you saying?
And who the fuck is Gabriel?**

Luther

Nikolai is alive. And Gabriel Moore
was the head of a large sex
trafficking ring over in Boston with
connections in multiple other cities.
He was the one helping to locate
Ivy for Nikolai, his business partner,
but he ended up being murdered
in March last year. I guess that put
a damper on things. But Nikolai
found Ivy anyway and purchased
her from that couple in Virginia. He
was supposed to collect her the
next day after you found her.

My heart constricts. The man who tortured Ivy has her once again.

Me

Send over his information.

Luther

He lives in New York. But he's not just
a nobody. He's Nikolai Petrova. Has
connections to the Solntsevskaya
Brotherhood.

Me

And? You say that as if I haven't
taken out members of the
Bratva before.

Luther

I'm saying, it's not gonna be
easy. He won't be alone.

Me

Sounds like a good time to me. Now tell me, how long would it take you to deliver me some custom items that go boom?

AFTER TALKING TO Luther, I pull up an old friend's number.

There's one more person I need to talk to.

The line rings a couple times before it's picked up.

"Hello?"

I smile, hearing her voice again. "Hello, little minx," I purr.

"Venom? How'd you get this number?"

"Still asking silly questions?"

"You can't see me, but I'm rolling my eyes right now, just so you know. What's up?"

"I need your help, darlin'."

"My help?" she asks with surprise.

"If you gotta include the skeleton man, fine. Probably best anyway. My—a friend of mine has been taken. I need some assistance with getting her back before it's too late."

"A *female* friend?"

"Are you jealous, little minx?"

"Just surprised." I can practically hear her smiling on the other line. "What happened and what exactly do you need?"

Once the plans are set with the others, I get to work

in my lab, creating a fresh batch of my specialty—Venom's Kiss. It's a potent and lethal concoction of neurotoxin, hemotoxin and myotoxin, thanks to Black Betty and Sally. It took years to perfect Venom's Kiss due to the complexity of the toxins and the mix of proteins and enzymes, but it is my most venomous and favored cocktail. The quick dose first affects the nervous system, shutting it down and halting breathing, then internal bleeding commences, and muscle tissue begins to break down, securing death.

It's absolutely glorious.

CHAPTER THIRTY-THREE

TWENTY YEARS OLD

Mother strikes me again with the galley whip she purchased a few years ago specifically for my punishments. She even proudly displays the short whip with its black braided handle and multi-tailed end, hanging it on the wall in the living room to serve as a constant reminder to fear her.

Except, I don't fear her anymore.

There's not much she could do to me—take from me—that hasn't already been taken.

I became a hollow shell.

Now at twenty years old, the hollowness that was once inside me has been replaced with anger. Filled with hatred. And I've bloomed into a monster.

Before my mother has a chance to bring the whip down on my bare back again, I turn, grabbing her wrist tightly and twisting it to the side.

She cries out in pain, a shocked expression taking over her dull features.

Still holding on to her wrist, I slowly stand, eyes fixed on this woman who gave me life, only to make me wish for death.

Her expressions become more horrified when I crack a sinister grin.

"What are you doing? How dare you! You disobedient child!"

I drop her wrist and send the bottom of my foot into her sternum, kicking her back. Her whole body lifts off the ground for a brief moment as she flies backward, crashing into the glass coffee table, shattering it.

She howls in anger and pain as shards of glass stick out from her flesh.

Blood.

Beautiful crimson blood weeps from her pale skin and my smile only grows at the sight.

"I'm no child anymore, Mother." I saunter over to her and crouch down to where she sits in a pile of glass. "I would like to introduce you to the monster you created."

She reacts, lifting a bloody arm to try to hit me across my face like she has done countless times. I catch her wrist again and tsk. "There will be no more of that, Mother." I haul her to her feet by her arm and drag her into the kitchen as she hollers her empty threats.

Pulling out zip ties from a drawer, I strap her down

to a chair, stuff a cloth in her mouth, then give her a little pat on her head. "I'll be back soon. I need to go pick some flowers."

275

CHAPTER THIRTY-FOUR

My knees ache as they rub into the hard floor. I look up to check how my wrists are doing, still tied above me on a hook dangling from the ceiling.

The door opens and Nikolai walks in, coming to stand in front of me.

"How's my sweet cherry doing today? Ready to submit?"

"Never happening."

He harshly grabs my jaw, forcing me to look at him. "Always so stubborn. I think I've been too lenient with you. I've been so thrilled to have you back that I've forgotten what has worked to correct your behavior in the past. My apologies." He releases me, only to strike me with another slap before making me meet his dark eyes again. "I should shred that beautiful back of yours up. Punish you until you are screaming my name." My eyes widen and adrenaline spikes.

Not that again, anything but that. "Please, Nik."

His crooked smile grows. "I have missed your sweet pleas." He stands and shouts, "Adrian! Bring my whip."

No. No. No.

Fuck. I have to play this game for the long run. Who knows how long I'll be here this time. I doubt I'll ever have a chance to escape again. Nikolai won't let that happen a second time.

"Nik, wait. Please. I'm sorry." I try moving closer to him, my bruised knees pressing into the ground, making me wince.

He squats again and tips his head at me, eyes raking up and down my body. His beard is trimmed shorter now, and the sides of his hair have taken on more salt than pepper.

"Tell me, Red. Are you still a virgin?"

I swallow the lump in my throat and keep my gaze fixed on his dead eyes.

"Do you know how disappointed I'll be if my precious property has been destroyed? If my sweet, innocent cherry spread her legs to be a whore for the Southern Poisoner? You don't have to answer me now. I have a doctor coming who will give me my answer."

The door opens again and in walks Adrian with Nikolai's favorite whip, the Russian knout. He hands Nikolai the several foot long whip; a long thick wooden handle leading to twisted cords of leather with metal rings added to inflict extra pain. Panic begins to bloom inside my chest.

"Leave us." Nikolai uncurls the whip, letting it hit the floor in front of me with a *smack*, the sound sending painful chills through my body. "I've missed you. So much."

He then moves to my back, pushes up my shirt and unclasps my bra, leaving my back bare and ready for his torment.

"Nik. Don't do this. Please. Anything else."

His response is the all too familiar sharp sting across my skin that I thought I would never feel again.

But I don't cry. As much as I want to, I can't give him my tears.

I scream.

And scream more, until I pass out.

When I gain consciousness again, I'm met with Nikolai's vile face.

God, this nightmare is never ending.

My arms are no longer stretched above me but secured tightly behind my back now.

Groaning, I sit up and lift my chin to Nikolai. The whip lies a few feet away on the floor, easing my nerves just a little that it's not still in his hand.

"It hurts me to hurt you. You must know this." He grabs my chin. "I wish we could get along. Things are much better when we get along, no?"

I say nothing and hold his stare with hatred pumping through me.

Grinning, he releases my chin harshly, then begins unbuckling his belt.

My eyes drop to his crotch before I meet his twisted hungry gaze again.

"I truly have missed you. Your beauty. Your fire. That mouth of yours." He licks his lips as he removes his gun from the back of his waist, then lets his pants drop to his ankles.

I'll bite him. I swear I'll fucking bite him and rip his vile dick off. Even if it means I die here and now. He will never get away with violating me again.

"I can read your thoughts, sweet cherry. It's written all over your face. Don't do it." He waves his gun in front of my face before pressing the barrel into my forehead. "Shall I return the favor? Let your skull feel the burning kiss of a bullet?"

I press my lips together and swallow the bile and dread rising in my throat.

"Open that pretty mouth and behave yourself. Convince me to forgive your betrayals." With his other hand, he grabs a fistful of my hair, jerking me toward him. "Open!" he shouts, his voice echoing throughout the empty room.

I close my eyes and—

Gunshots ring out, causing me to flinch and Nikolai to drop his hand from my hair. I can hear shouting outside this room and footsteps running.

"Seems we'll have to continue this later."

Dressing up, he stalks out of the room, yelling to some guards in Russian.

CHAPTER THIRTY-FIVE

I t's time.

I take a deep breath, place a fresh toothpick in my mouth, and roll up the sleeves of my shirt to hide the blood splatter from taking out the security on the outskirts of the property. Then I make my way to the front of Nikolai's home.

As I casually stride closer to the front of the house, two men standing outside his door draw their weapon and step toward me.

"Who the fuck are you?" the one to the right says.

"Why, I'm the guest of the hour."

"We don't get guests here," the left guy says.

"I'm sure I'm expected," I respond with a grin and take a couple strategic steps forward.

"Stay right where you are!" The men look at each other for a beat before returning to me. "And your name?"

"The Southern Poisoner." I dramatically bow and they eye each other again. I don't miss how they push their shoulders back and tense. It only makes me smile even wider like the Cheshire cat.

I reach into my back pocket and both men take another step toward me and shout. "Don't fucking move! Take your hand out of your pocket!"

I lift my left hand up in surrender and then slowly pull out my right, holding a cigarette box. "Just getting a smoke, fellas." They ease up just enough as I throw my toothpick away, flip open the lid and bring it to my mouth to pull out a thin long cylinder. I toss the box to the ground and they eye what's in my mouth curiously. And then I blow hard, once, twice, the tiny darts sinking into dumbass number one and dumbass number two's necks. They both reach for their neck like they just got bit by a bug, pulling out the dart and throwing it to the side. But before they have any time to do much else, they both drop to the ground.

Oh, how I do love those darts. The Golden Poison Frog is certainly one of my favorite species, and thankfully, I received my order of the bright yellow wild frogs last week, just in time to extract their batrachotoxin for these darts.

"Gentlemen," I say as I step over their bodies and walk the rest of the way to the front door. A micro dose would have just paralyzed them, but the one I used, death already claimed them.

Reaching the door, I clear my throat, knock twice then place my hands in my pockets, fingers curling around the knives hidden in their custom venom-filled sheaths sewn into my pants.

A few seconds later, the door opens to reveal more armed men.

"Good evening, fellas. I'm here to see Nikolai." Once again, the men glance at each other for answers, but none speak. What kind of armed guards are these fuckers? "Honestly, is he truly not expecting me? I'm a bit offended." When they continue staring at me with furrowed brows, I add with a long sigh, "I'm The Southern Poisoner. Nikolai took something from me. More specifically, a pretty little thing with fire-red hair."

Their eyes light up with recognition. Some draw knives. Others point guns at me.

"Now, now, none of that. I came to talk."

With this many men armed, there's no room for mistakes or hesitation. Thankfully, speed and precision are my specialties.

One of the men leans to the side and looks behind me, spotting the first two guards on the ground. "He killed Boris and Ivan!"

I spare a glance behind me. "Oh, them? Were they your friends? The others around the perimeter are gone as well. My apologies."

A man with long hair tied back in a top knot grabs my shoulder. "You want to see Nikolai? Fine, it's your death sentence. Let's go."

"Check him for weapons," another with a full beard says.

Too late.

My knives come out fast, stabbing Top Knot in his armpit as he grips my shoulder, then I spin, slamming my elbow into another guard's face before slicing him across the stomach in a spray of blood. A gun goes off, but I keep moving.

My knives move in a blur of steel, fresh blades sliding into my hand as needed. They land in necks, thighs, and, for this next poor fella, I spin on my knee, slash his Achilles tendon, and when his knees hit the floor, I slice his neck open then bury my blade in his eye. I pull the knife free, eyeball still attached, and hold it up, admiring it in surprise. "Huh, well look at that."

The man falls back with a thud, and I nearly miss a bullet from another goon.

More shots are fired as they frantically try to shoot without true aim. One bullet lands into another guard's chest as I use him to shield me. I kick him toward the last armed man and, when they collide, I fling my knife. It spins through the air with a soft hiss, landing right in that vulnerable spot at the base of his neck. His body twitches, then falls.

I stand tall, catching my breath as I look at the pile of bodies now laying on the white marble floor, slowly turning a shimmering red. Some still convulse as my special concoction of venom courses through them. Others stare blankly at the ceiling, already dead. If the knife wound itself didn't kill them, Venom's Kiss surely will.

Running footsteps echo through the home. When I turn, over a dozen men stand armed, ready to shoot me into oblivion.

I raise my hands and smile. "Sorry about them. They were a bit rude."

One of the men steps forward, holding up his hand in signal to the guards to hold their fire.

"So, you must be the man who stole my cherry."

And there he is. Nikolai.

"Stole? Now I wouldn't use that word to describe it."

"I could easily kill you right now."

"You could." I shrug.

"Am I to respect that you have no fear?"

"Respect from you means nothing to me. I've come for my beast."

He laughs. "You kill my men, make a mess of my home, and expect me to give you what you want?"

"Oh, certainly not. I'm here to make an offer. Myself in exchange for her. Let her go and you can have me. I am far better looking and am worth much more money to my enemies."

"You think this is about money? You are mistaken, my friend. This is about betrayal and what happens to those who betray me. In fact, I am happy you are here, Poisoner. I have a new idea. Come, you will help me with something."

I quickly look at my watch, taking note of the time, then step forward with my hands still raised.

"Check him for more weapons. And if he moves even an inch, shoot him."

"Perhaps we got off on the wrong foot." I grin.

He gives me a disgusted look then turns away as I'm pushed from behind to follow Nikolai.

I'm brought into another large, nearly empty room. I'm not sure what Nikolai typically uses this room for, but the man needs an interior decorator.

The armed men take up spots around the room with one remaining behind me, a gun pressed between my shoulder blades.

Nikolai takes a seat in a chair that looks more like a throne. I smirk. So, he thinks he's a king.

If you come for the king, you best not miss.

And *miss*, I do not.

"Remove his shirt," Nikolai orders.

"We just met, and you already want to see me naked?" My, this is moving fast."

"Get your laughs in now. In a moment, they will be gone."

The guard behind me kicks the back of my legs, sending me to my knees, and begins ripping off my shirt.

"Now fetch the girl," Nikolai signals to the guard standing beside him.

My eyes follow him through a different door than where we came in and stay locked on it until it opens again, revealing my little beast, Ivy.

Her face is flushed, and some wild hair sticks to her face and neck with sweat. She looks around the room, eyes landing on me, and shock replaces any sadness she held.

"Venom!" She steps toward me but is jerked back by the guard gripping her. "You shouldn't be here! What are you doing?!"

"What's it look like? I'm being the hero, darlin'," I say to her with a grin.

Her eyes widen and she lightly shakes her head before Nikolai's laugh steals her attention, his voice echoing through the room. "Some hero you are."

"I admit, I'm out of practice. Not my usual go-to." I quip.

"Now, Red, the doctor hasn't arrived yet, but tell me, is this the man you gave my cherry to?"

Ivy presses her lips together in a tight line and doesn't respond.

Nikolai gives a nod to the guard holding her and he turns to slap her across her face.

My body seizes. It takes every ounce of control I have not to attack, to simply kneel here and wait.

"It was the sweetest cherry I ever had," I say, drawing Nikolai's attention back to me. "How unfortunate, you'll never get to know."

His face turns red, and a scowl forms as he looks to Ivy then back at me. He quickly stands and strides over with determined purpose and lands a punch to my cheekbone.

My head snaps to the side, then I smile back up at him. "Now you just broke rule one." I look to Ivy and give her a wink.

"Rules? You think you have rules here, Poisoner?" He chuckles as he glances around the room to his guards. Some laugh along with him. Nikolai throws another punch. Weak.

"Is that all you've got? Well, that's rather embarrassing."

Nikolai looks past me, "Get my whip." He then moves back to his *throne*, taking a seat.

A beat later, another guard takes the place of the

original one behind me, letting the end of a long leather braided whip fall to the floor with a light tap.

This should be a good time.

"Begin," comes Nikolai's stern voice as he sits back to watch the show.

"No!" Ivy shouts.

I look at her and watch as tears begin to flow from her beautiful emerald eyes and then I look away, bracing myself.

Oh, beast, don't cry for me.

Then the first lash comes, landing across my back and bringing old memories to the surface of my mind.

Pain is no issue for me, but as the lashes keep coming, it's the memories of a small boy being whipped, never escaping the abuse of a mother, that have me nearly breaking.

But... although the boy died in that house, the *man* escaped... or rather... the *monster.*

Now I smile wide as the familiar kiss of the whip greets my flesh once more.

CHAPTER THIRTY-SIX

The guard strikes Venom again. "Stop! Please! You're hurting him!" I yell, my voice cracking.

"That's the fucking point you ungrateful, disloyal bitch!" Nikolai spits.

Venom lifts his head, meeting my tear-stricken eyes.

Another whip lashes his back as he grits his teeth and flinches. "It's alright, beastie," he grits out. "Just saying hello to an old friend."

I shake my head through the tears and try to breathe through my constricting lungs.

I can't bear to see any more. Are they going to whip him to death?

More lashes land across Venom's back as he falls forward onto his hands. Sprays of blood scatter through the air along with the whip when it's pulled back.

Each lash strikes my own heart, the harsh cracking sound echoing inside my skull. My hands curl into fists as my eyes blur with tears. But I can't look away. I won't.

I feel utterly helpless as my screams lodge in my throat and my pleas fall to whispers.

His tormented eyes look at me once more before he hangs his head. Blood seeps from his body onto the marble floor and my stomach twists. Something inside me shatters.

Desperate, I yell, "Stop this, Nik! I'm begging you! I'll do whatever you want! I'll never leave you again! Just please stop!"

My pleas are ignored as Nikolai continues watching with a smug smile.

I can't let this happen. He's only here because of me.

It was supposed to be me!

Tears stream down my face as I watch Venom, beaten down, whip by whip, edging closer to something I'm not sure he could come back from.

Again, Venom looks at me. Sadness carved into his beautiful face as he takes in all my tears for him. "Don't go soft on me now, sweet beast. Show me your teeth," he says with a bloody grin.

He's right.

I'm not soft.

I'm not weak.

I'm his beast.

I sink my teeth into the guard's arm, tasting the metallic tang of blood, and break free when he pulls his arm away. I run towards Venom, throwing myself over him as the whip comes down, slashing across my back.

"Ivy! No!" Venom growls.

"I won't let them hurt you anymore!" I cry out as my already damaged back feels the sharp bite of the whip. But I'll take it. I'll gladly take them all for him.

Before another strike can come down, Venom uses what strength he has left and twists his body enough to grab me and pull me under him, shielding me.

"I'm supposed to be the hero here, darlin'," he whispers into my ear before his body jerks from the force of the whip. "Let me be the hero, Ivy."

"Sacrificing yourself isn't being the hero!" I say through a sob.

"It's not a sacrifice. It's a distraction."

"What?"

"Grab her!" Nikolai shouts.

Strong hands latch on to me and pull me away from Venom. He tries to hold on but the blood now coating us both makes his grip slip. "No! Venom!"

I kick and scream, trying to get back to him, but several loud noises disrupt the whole house.

Another boom blasts open the entrance to the room and what I see step through a cloud of smoke has my eyes going wide.

CHAPTER THIRTY-SEVEN

I keep my eyes fixed on my little beast. She's the only thing giving me what little strength I have right now. I'll let them take whatever they need from me.

I'll break for her over and over.

Explosions shake the building and Ivy's eyes widen at something behind me. I know what she must be seeing and relief washes through me.

Men scramble about. When I look over to locate Ivy through the smoke taking over the room, a long whip comes shooting out in front of me in a blur, but I still catch the distinct difference in *this* whip.

Metal and *bones*.

The room erupts further into chaos as men drop, some convulsing on the floor and others missing limbs, choking on their blood-curdling screams.

I twist the gem off my custom ring made specifically for this evening and turn it inward. Then I grab the ankle of the guard holding the whip and inject a heavy dose of venom into his leg. He falls back.

I quickly slip free the secret stash of small blades hidden in my belt buckle and throw them, pain burning across my back with the movement. I take out two more men before someone shoves me to the ground in the commotion.

Men scream in agony and fear. Guns fire. People flee, or at least try to.

When I spot Ivy through the haze, she pounces on a guard's back, digging her nails into his eyes as he screams. She's all claws and sharp teeth, and I fucking love it.

The man spins blindly, trying to throw her off of him. I whip my last blade into his neck just as Ivy falls off him and collapses to her knees, catching her breath.

Another goon with a bloody gash across his face suddenly takes notice of Ivy and lines up his knife to throw.

I instinctively reach for another blade, but I'm all out.

The little energy I have left is replaced with the visceral need to protect her, to keep her alive.

She won't die here.

No one else I love is dying.

She's closer to me than the guard, so with a surge of adrenaline, I run toward her, dropping to my knees in a slide as the knife flies through the air.

I reach her just in time, clutching her to my chest as the blade sinks right below my left shoulder blade. The force jerks me forward.

"Venom!" Ivy shouts in horror.

"Pull it out!" I groan.

"What? I can't do that!" she says in a panic.

"Pull it out, darlin'. Now!"

She reaches for the knife and yanks it out of my back. I feel the trickle of warm blood travel down, mixing with my other wounds as I quickly take the knife from her and whip it back at the guard who was storming closer, business end plunging into his left eye.

He stumbles back.

Then we watch as a whip of bone and metal wraps around his neck. It's given a harsh jerk, the sharp metal of the whip severing sinew and muscles, causing the guard's head to flop back, barely hanging on. He drops. Dead.

I grab Ivy again, clinging her to me. "Stay down and hold your breath!" I growl, then cover her head with my body as gunshots continue to ring out and more explosions wreak havoc through the mansion. Her nails claw into me as I feel her tremble beneath me.

Perhaps I had Luther make too many bombs, but I had to be thorough in this situation.

Ivy twists her head to look at me. Fear consuming her expression.

"I've got you. We're gonna be alright, darlin'. Give me your trust." She nods and presses her head back into me as I continue to shield her from the mayhem.

Silence soon falls.

I slowly uncurl myself from Ivy, looking her up and down, making sure she is unharmed.

Then I turn to stand and come face-to-face with a

hand held out. Following the outstretched hand, I look up and meet the eyes of…

The Bone Reaper.

"Did you purposely take your time?" I groan.

He helps me stand before saying, "I needed you to bleed a little first."

I force a smirk through the pain I feel.

Ivy sways, coughs, and collapses in my arms. "Do you have the extra dose?" I ask Reaper. Her coughing rattles against my chest. "Breathe shallow, darlin'. Just—hold on."

"Here." Reaper pulls the syringe from his pocket and hands it to me quickly.

Without giving her a warning, I inject her with the contents to counteract the poison she was exposed to when the bombs exploded.

"Sorry, darlin'. There's poison in the air. You'll be alright in a minute."

She nods, her eyes searching mine as she holds onto me.

A few moments later, Ivy is able to stand with little help from me and clearer eyes, although her skin is still a bit pale.

"Thank you," I say to Reaper.

"Hey! He doesn't get all the credit," a sweet voice calls out from behind Reaper. "The rest of the house is clear."

Sauntering over, covered in blood, is the fiery little minx, Charlotte.

"Next time you miss us, Venom, can we just do lunch instead? No need for all the theatrics."

"Oh, darlin', you know theatrics are my specialty." I chuckle.

She smiles and leans in to hug me, avoiding touching my torn back. "Good to see you again. Although I gotta say, you've looked better."

"Don't lie, little minx. You know you like your men bloody." Reaper grunts in amusement. "Nice whips by the way. I wonder whose unlucky spines those belong to."

"Thanks, it's an upgrade since my last set got ruined in a rather large house fire last year."

"Ah, yes, good times, great memories."

Reaper scowls, and I shoot him a wink.

"So, this is her?" Charlotte chimes in.

"Yes, this is Ivy."

Ivy clears her throat, her voice coming out a bit hoarse. "Hi."

"I'm Charlotte, and this big fella is Reaper."

"It's nice to meet you both. And... thank you," Ivy says.

"Yes, thank you for your help," I repeat again, trying to push through the pain.

"I owed you one," Reaper says through his bone mask.

My knees buckle, vision becoming hazy and weakness taking hold. It's now my turn to feel the effects this evening has had on me.

Ivy and Charlotte catch me before I hit the ground.

"Whoa there. He's losing a lot of blood. We gotta get him somewhere," Charlotte tells Reaper.

"Give me a second." He pulls out his phone and walks

away to make a call. A couple minutes later he returns. "Think you can handle a four-hour drive?"

"With you two? Doubtful."

"Four hours is too long, Venom," Ivy interjects, voice laced with concern. "You need a hospital, like now."

"Who has my phone?"

Reaper pulls out my cell from his pocket and hands it to me. I quickly select the contact, and it's answered on the third ring.

"Venom? Since when do you call me?"

"Since I need your help this time, Alice," I groan.

"Are you alright?"

"Just peachy." I stumble again, vision tunneling. I rapidly blink and shake my head as Reaper steadies me. "And by peachy, I mean I'm bleeding all over my new slacks and boots and I could use some medical attention asap." The words rush out of me.

"I see. You've been good to Wonderland, so send me a location and I'll send a chopper."

"You're the best, Alice." I end the call and slip my phone into my pocket.

"Come on." With Reaper and Charlotte now holding me up on each side, we make our way outside, Ivy following behind us.

CHAPTER THIRTY-EIGHT

I follow the couple, taking a few steps outside before something catches my eye as it comes toward me from around the corner of the house. But it's too late. I'm grabbed and the barrel of a gun is placed to my head.

"Leaving so soon?" Nikolai sneers.

My eyes meet Venom's. He stands taller now, clearly fighting through immense pain. His body is stiff and his expression is a raw mix of anger and fear.

This is the first time I have actually seen him afraid.

He clenches his jaw. I look to Charlotte, who stands just as still beside him, then glance at Reaper, who looks the calmest of the three.

"How do you see this playing out? Because from where I'm standing, you're already dead," Reaper says.

"That's the problem with bastards like you. You're all arrogant, thinking you've won before the game is over. I'm willing to bet my life that our Southern Poisoner isn't willing to risk the life of his lover. Are you now, boy?"

"What do you want?" Venom grits out through clenched teeth.

"To leave. With her."

"Not a chance."

"Then she dies."

"And so will you," Charlotte adds.

"As long as I can drag this disloyal bitch with me to hell, I can accept that."

I can't see a way out of this and I'm wondering if Venom feels the same according to how he's looking at me.

This is about to be over, one way or another. I feel the end coming.

VENOM

I DECIDE IN this moment that if Ivy dies, I will use up all the poison in the world to end everyone and then I will end myself. If fate sees to it that she dies here and now, then I will see to it the world ends, because there is nothing, absolutely nothing, without her.

Reaper steps slightly in front of me, giving me a view of his vest-lined back. A vest with pockets filled with small knives and one larger handheld scythe.

It looks like fate has other plans tonight.

I give Ivy a small smirk, trying to let her know it's

going to be alright. I can't very well pull the scythe out without drawing attention, but a small knife will do.

"Maybe I should introduce myself. I'm the Bone Reaper, and I was the one to kill your partner, Gabriel Moore, in Boston."

"Actually, that was me," Charlotte interjects with a little wave. "You should kill me."

"Charlotte," Reaper growls in warning.

I see what they're doing, trying to draw Nikolai's attention away from me and Ivy.

I use the opportunity and slip a small knife free from Reaper's vest. I grip it tight in my left hand and get a feel for its weight. This will definitely do. I will myself to push past the pain and steady my hand.

"You? You killed Gabriel?" Nikolai asks sharply.

"Honestly, it was one of my most enjoyable kills," she quips.

The instant Nikolai moves the gun away from Ivy's head to point it at Charlotte, I launch the knife at him.

I don't miss.

It lands in the back of his hand, making him yelp. He drops the gun, and that's when Reaper strikes, taking him down to the ground. All I hear is Nikolai scream as the unmistakable sound of snapping bones fills the air. I run to Ivy and shout to Reaper and Charlotte, "Put him in the trunk!"

I CONTINUE BLEEDING all over Reaper's car as he drives us

to a location I sent to Alice, two miles up the road.

"You should have put me in the trunk so I don't get blood on your seats."

"There's still time," Reaper quips. "You would even have some company back there."

I give him a bloody grin through the rearview mirror.

"It's okay, Venom. It's just a rental," Charlotte adds.

When I glance over to Ivy, I see her frowning, her eyes filled with concern as she holds on to me. "Don't worry, darlin', it will take a lot more to kill me."

She wipes a tear away. "This happened because of me."

"No more tears for me, little beast. This didn't happen *because* of you. It happened *for* you. And I would do a hell of a lot more for you than this. This is just a regular Tuesday for me."

She frowns. "Is there really such a difference?"

"Of course there is. Saying this happened because of you is putting the blame and responsibility on you." I groan as we hit a pothole and my torn back hits the seat. Ivy steadies me and I grit my teeth to continue. "You hold no blame for this, no responsibility. It was my decision to come for you. There was no way in hell I was just going to let you slip away. You've been mine since you walked into my home and sunk your poison into my veins. I told you there was no cure."

The corner of her mouth curves up in an almost smile, and then her voice grows softer. "Evelyn..."

My body tenses at hearing her name, the memories slamming back into me like waves on a shore, nearly sweeping me under until I'm lost in a sea of grief. But I grip Ivy's hand tighter, holding on to her, my new anchor.

I let out a pained breath. "I know. Now don't you dare go blaming yourself for that. There's only one person to blame and he's half-dead in the trunk." I turn toward her more, bringing my hand to her cheek. "Listen, I got to say my goodbye, and as it should have been, I was with her in the end. And believe me when I say she would be heartbroken if you blame yourself for her death. So don't. Don't do it, darlin'."

Her resolve breaks and she falls against me, sobbing. My back presses against the seat again and I wince, but no pain can compare to the feelings Ivy brings me. From very early on, they have overshadowed everything else, silencing the worst of my demons.

"I'm just so relieved you're okay. I don't know what I would have done if I lost you too," she whispers.

"I'm not going anywhere. And neither are you, ever again."

My breathing suddenly falters and my vision blurs with Ivy's sweet face disappearing from my view. I groan, and before everything goes black, I hear Ivy's voice screaming my name.

CHAPTER THIRTY-NINE

*T*he chopper took Venom and me to a rather sketchy looking building on the outside but inside was a state-of-the-art medical facility that I was so thankful for. Venom was treated right away and they tended to my back as well. Six hours later, we were cleared to go home.

Home.

I have a home. And it's with Venom.

Although coming face-to-face with the stairs I last saw Evelyn on was not something I was prepared to see.

I stand there staring at them, replaying the memories and feeling my world spin.

"Darlin', don't torture yourself. You've been through enough," Venom says, then holds out his hand. "We'll do it together."

I nod, take his hand, and together we walk up the stairs and into our home.

Our home.

Our home without Evelyn.

It's a bittersweet reunion, and all I want to do is get to the greenhouse and take a deep breath, so that's exactly what I do, Venom following close behind. For the rest of the evening, I tend to the plants while Venom rests in his recliner, watching me when I'm within view.

"You've become rather good at this."

"I had a good teacher."

"Come, sweet beast, take a break and sit with me."

"Will you read to me?"

"Always," he says, then pats his thigh, signaling for me to sit on his lap.

"I HAVE A surprise for you," Venom says when he finds me napping in the greenhouse.

I stretch and rub my eyes.

"Oh yea? Where is it?"

"Basement. Follow me."

Venom unlocks the door and pushes it open to reveal a completely dark room. He steps further in and a lightbulb flickers on.

My gaze travels to a chair. To the naked, hooded man tied to it.

He's bloodied and bruised and clearly has several broken bones. But it's the tattoos on his hands, fingers and chest that tell me who he is.

Nikolai.

It's been three days since I last saw him, but when Venom pulls off the black hood covering Nikolai's face, it's like I never left his mansion.

I had asked Venom what was going to happen to Nikolai and he only told me that he was going to be taken care of. I trusted he would finally meet his end. But here he is, lifting his swollen eyes to me.

"A gift," Venom says. "No one deserves to kill him except you. Reaper kept him until he could deliver him back here. I told him to keep him alive long enough so you could be the one to finally take what you deserve. He's all yours."

Nikolai groans and spits blood on the ground, nearly landing on my bare feet.

I meet his eyes again and a shiver runs through me as I recall every cruelty and how he stole my life from me, and right when I thought I finally gained it back, he showed up to steal it again.

He's taken so much from me.

He's taken Evelyn.

I clench my fist and feel a surge of adrenaline. Then I step to him and punch him in the face. It hurts, more than I expected but that doesn't matter right now. What matters is making him pay. Making him suffer. Making him wish for death only to have it dragged out by *me*.

I finally hold the power.

This is *my* life and no one controls it but me.

I hit him again.

And again.

And again.

I scream and unleash my rage on his face, until the images in my mind of his smug smile are replaced with how he looks right now. Bloody, bruised, and defeated.

I step back, chest heaving, trying to catch my breath and look over to Venom, finding him casually leaning against the wall fiddling with the toothpick in his mouth as he watches.

I look down at my split and bloody knuckles and then back to Venom.

"I need something else. Something sharp."

His grin widens. "That's my beast. Round two, coming right up."

He kicks a black bag over to me and I bend down to unzip it. It's filled with knives of all shapes and sizes and my eyes light up at the sight. "Hey, Venom?"

"Yes, darlin'?"

"Can you teach me how to throw a knife?"

"*Of course, darlin'.*" He saunters over to me and pulls a bundle of throwing knives from his bag. "If only we had a good target." He tips his head at Nikolai, "Oh look, how perfect. Will he do?"

"Definitely."

Nikolai lifts his messy face to look at us. It's hard to read his expression with how bloody and swollen he is but I imagine he's not too happy.

"Ffff... uuuhh... ck yyyou."

Venom positions himself behind me and walks me further away from Nikolai then places the blade in my hand. "This is the balance point. It's important to know that so you know how it will rotate. We'll start with a half-spin throw." He places his hands on my hips, "Put your right foot back, shoulder width apart and grip near the blade." His hand slides back up my body to my arm. "You're gonna bring your arm back, over your shoulder and step forward as you release it."

I do as Venom instructs. The blade of my first attempt bounces off Nikolai, but I keep trying.

"Adjust your grip, you're over rotating. Like this." He helps me adjust then steps back.

The blade flies through the air and finally sinks into Nikolai's belly. He yelps and I smile.

"Good!" Venom calls out. "Were you aiming for his stomach?"

"His neck, actually."

"That's alright. Keep practicing. You're doing great."

An hour passes and my back hits the wall as I slide down it and sit, taking a break. I look at Nikolai, several blades sticking out of various parts of his body, oozing more blood.

"St—op. No… more. P—please," Nikolai murmurs.

"Oh, but now I've finally got *you* to beg." I stand and walk over to him, gripping his hair and pulling, making him look at me. "You always loved when I begged, didn't you, Nik? How's it feel?"

"I—loved… y-you."

"Stop. You're incapable of love, you asshole. You're a monster. A disease that needs to be wiped out. The world will be a better place without you and I'm glad I'm the one who gets to end your existence."

Nikolai begins to lose consciousness when Venom steps forward and injects him with something. His eyes shoot open and he inhales an audible deep breath before rocking in his chair and shouting things in Russian.

"Adrenaline. To keep him a bit livelier for ya," Venom says.

I smile. "So thoughtful."

"If I may, I have an idea for round three."

"Okay."

"I'll be back."

When Venom finally returns, my eyes go wide at what he's carrying. Two snakes are wrapped around him, Black Betty and Sally, and more are in carriers.

I grin wide. "No way."

"Oh yes. Seems only fitting."

Nikolai sees what round three is and reacts. He begins bucking harshly in his chair and if it wasn't bolted to the floor, he surely would have been sent flying to the ground.

"No!" With a strained voice, Nikolai begins shouting in Russian again. "*Nyet! Nyet! Ne smey! Ty za eto sdokhnesh', ublyudok!*"

Venom steps closer. "No, Nikolai, you're the one dying when the rest of my girls here get a hold of you. You probably should refrain from moving. You don't want to upset them."

"You know Russian?" I ask Venom, surprised, but also not. He's a man of many skills and talents.

"I know many languages, darlin'. I've traveled the world."

"What did he say?"

"Just empty threats."

Nikolai goes completely still as Venom transfers his snakes onto him. They begin slithering their way around him as Venom begins to pull out the other girls from their carriers.

"Are these all of them?"

"All except Cora. And Mya must be taking a nap somewhere. Besides, these are the most venomous. We got neurotoxic, hemotoxic and cytotoxic venom here. His body is going to shut down, along with tissue destruction and he's going to bleed, a lot, from various parts. This isn't going to be pretty and if they all get him, it's going to be unlike any pain he has ever experienced or could imagine."

"Good. "

"One other thing, they don't all get along and can be a bit territorial."

"They're gonna hurt each other?"

"Possibly. Especially if they feel like they're competing. But hopefully Nikolai is enough of a distraction." Venom releases the last of the snakes then pushes me back toward the door.

Nikolai continues to remain as still as possible, with nothing but his panicked eyes moving.

The tension builds as we wait but then Venom walks over to him and gives him another dose of adrenaline and his body begins to involuntary move, tremors pulsing through him.

"No!" he growls.

And then the first of the snakes, Black Betty, strikes.

With every scream Nikolai releases, another snake sinks its teeth into him. He tries thrashing and shouting, but soon, the effects begin to take hold and like Venom said, it's not pretty but it's everything I wished to see become of Nikolai.

He loses control of his bladder, and by the smell, his bowels too. His body convulses, and as another snake wraps its body around Nikolai's neck, constricting tighter and tighter, his last breaths are stolen. His face turns a deep shade of red, then purple as veins strain beneath his skin from the pressure and ew—his eyes begin to swell, the whites of them turning red as blood vessels pop. They grotesquely bulge. The left in particular protruding unnaturally far, as if it might actually burst—

Nikolai's left eye flops out of its socket with a sickening pop, still hanging by a tiny cord of nerves and muscles, lightly swaying as the snake continues squeezing.

Another gasp leaves me when Sally snaps out, grabbing hold of his eye and begins to swallow it whole.

"Holy shit," I say while Venom chuckles.

"I do hope he was still conscious for that."

We watch just a moment longer as the blood seeps in crimson rivers from his gums, nose, and eyes… or at least where one use to be… as well as the other wounds I had already made.

Nikolai becomes unrecognizable as he dies a gruesome death.

I cover my nose. "Oh god, the smell."

"It's only going to get worse. I'll contact the cleaners. They'll take care of the rest after I collect my pets. But let's give them a bit more time with him even though I think he's pretty dead now."

"You think?"

"Come, darlin', how about a nice relaxing bath? I'll wash your hair and even braid it.

I lift on to the tips of my toes and press a kiss to his cheek. "Thank you for this."

I spare one more glance back to Nikolai, then close the steel door behind me, shutting my past away.

CHAPTER FORTY

Three months pass before Venom feels ready to go into Evelyn's room and sort through her stuff.

It still smells like her, and not that mothball old lady scent. The room smells sweet like honey and sugar and spices. Probably due to all the baking and cooking she loved to do. And for the first time, I smile at the good memories instead of the tragic end she had.

I look over to Venom who still stands in the doorway, taking everything in. Stepping closer to him I hold out my hand. "Together."

He takes it and I lead him further into the room and we slowly begin to pack up her belongings, smiling and laughing at certain things that bring us a flashback.

"Look, her sweater is still stained from that night you threw a meatball at her."

"I think she was actually upset with me for wasting one of her famous meatballs."

I laugh. "I can't imagine her ever really being mad at you."

"One sure way of that was to fuck with her food. I learned that early on. One time she was so upset with me, she refused to cook her Italian dishes for a week. Let me tell you about suffering..."

I look back down at her sweater. "She really did love cooking for us."

"And teaching you."

Smiling, I remember all the moments she took the time to teach me how to cook, even writing down the recipe so I would remember all the details. I'll cherish those recipes forever.

I open her bedside table and laying on top of a notepad, is an envelope with the name MARCUS written across it in Evelyn's handwriting.

"Uh, Venom, I think this is for you." I turn to him and hand him the envelope.

VENOM

THEY SAY THE hardest thing in life is having to say goodbye to someone you love. They're wrong. It's having to carry on without them for the rest of your life. Feeling their loss every single day, every minute, wondering when the pain won't feel so all-consuming.

I stare at the envelope for a moment then look back at Ivy. "She always called me Marcus..." I take a seat on the bed and then open it to see a handwritten letter.

I take a deep breath, then begin to read.

Dear Marcus,

If you're reading this, that must mean I'm dead. I do hope I went peacefully in my sleep due to old age but regardless, I will be happy to be reunited with my dear Frank. I hope you know you were like a son to me. Frank and I tried having a baby but after a few years, we found out I was infertile. It was a devastating truth we did not expect but we channeled our love into the restaurant. That became our baby, our pride and joy, and I know others could taste that in our food.

When Frank passed, as you know, I lost all hope and will to live. I had no one to care for, no one to care for me. But then you took me in and brought something into my life I thought I'd never have. A son. And for you, my boy, I wish you happiness and love. I hope one day you find someone who fills that hole inside you, makes you want to retire and choose love over all else.

Marcus, please know, you deserve happiness and love, and when you find it, hold it close and never let it go.

I love you always,

Your Ev

I clench my jaw to suppress my emotions. Too many damn emotions. Ivy seems to take notice and grabs my hand, giving it a gentle squeeze.

"You alright?"

"I will be. Here, take a look." I hand Ivy the letter and she quickly reads it and then throws her arms around me.

"I was right, by the way."

"About?"

"She really did care about you. I told you I could tell from that very first day by the way she looked at you with a mother's love."

"Seems you have a way of seeing people also. Although, I knew. Deep down I always knew, just didn't want to admit it to myself." I run a hand through my hair. "I've never known love in my life, only pain. That is until Evelyn and you entered my world." I put a palm to Ivy's face and push away her hair with my other. "I'm nobody without you, Ivy."

"You're the notorious Southern Poisoner. You're someone known and feared," she says proudly.

"It's nobody I want to be if I don't have you."

She reaches out, placing a hand to my face. "You have me, Venom. I'm not going anywhere. It's you and me, forever."

"Good, because if I need to put a damn leash on you, little beast, I will."

She laughs and kisses me. "I believe you. But maybe I can put a leash on you and take you for a walk around the greenhouse."

I smirk. "If you feel so tempted, do so at your own risk. I'm not one who can be tamed by simply being leashed."

"Neither am I." She grins wickedly and my chest flutters.

"I might have said once that I wanted to tame you, but truth is, darlin', I love you just as wild and beastly as you are."

Her lips crash to mine again and I scoop her up, carrying her out of Evelyn's room. What I want to do to her should not be done in there.

IV

CHAPTER FORTY-ONE

Venom told me I wasn't allowed in the greenhouse for two days. It was hard to resist due to my curiosity and simply just missing my oasis, but I obeyed.

"You're finally ready to let me back in?" I ask.

"I promise you; you'll think it was worth it."

"We'll see about that."

He stands behind me and wraps silk material around my head, concealing my eyes. "No peeking." With firm hands on my hips, he guides me into the greenhouse. Although my eyes are concealed, I'd always recognize the scent and feel of being in this place instantly. "Watch your step." I grab onto Venom's wrist as I almost trip on what I imagine might be a tree root. "I got you, darlin'. I won't let you fall."

"Just lead me into a viper's pit?" I say with a laugh.

"You entered the viper's pit long ago and did more than just survive." He presses closer to me, the heat of him warming my back, and whispers against my ear. "You thrived."

I smile and run my hand over his. "So, are we there yet?"

"Impatient?"

"Just really curious."

"Well, we're here." I feel him pull away from me and I instantly miss the feeling of him against my body. "You can remove the blindfold."

The blindfold slips from my fingers and falls to the dirt as I look at what's before me and take a sharp inhale.

Dahlias.

Dahlias everywhere, filling my whole view along with a blanket lying in the center of the arrangement. He spent the past couple of days planting all these himself.

A soft breeze blows through the greenhouse, stirring the lush petals of my favorite flower. Dark purples, delicate pinks, striking reds, oranges, soft yellows, and some so dark they look black, and there's even some with blue hues. It's a breathtaking scene and I mean it; my breath is lost for a moment like I've forgotten how to inhale air.

When I remember how to breathe and speak, my words come out in a whisper. "You remembered."

I feel Venom at my back once again. "I remember everything that has ever come out of that wicked mouth of yours." He leans into me and presses a kiss to the side of my neck then retreats.

I spin toward him to find him down on one knee and I freeze again.

"Oh my god. Are you about to propose?"

"Christ, no. A piece of paper to represent my love and commitment to you will simply never do."

I eye him suspiciously.

He begins to unbutton the rest of his shirt while staring up at me.

"Oh. Right here? Right now?"

He smirks and shakes his head. "Greedy for my cock, are ya?"

His shirt falls to the ground and I look him over, wondering what he is getting at. Then he takes my hand, turns it over and kisses my wrist. His eyes return to me and he smiles that devilish grin that was once so infuriating, but now it does something much different to me.

His brows scrunch together as his expression turns serious. "I love you. But it's also so much more than that. Those words will never be thorough enough to express what you mean to me." His eyes light up. "I craved you and when I finally got a taste, I realized I had been starving my whole life and now, sweet beast, I claim you as you have claimed me." Still holding onto my hand, he stands, and that's when I finally notice it.

A new tattoo.

Vines of ivy wrap and cling around the snake on Venom's body. They are intertwined, claiming each other in the most beautiful way.

My tear-filled eyes shoot up to his as my heart threatens to beat right out of my chest.

"Venom," I choke out.

"I do hope it's better than a typical proposal. I didn't end it with a question, because frankly, at this point, you don't have a choice in—"

I throw myself at him, arms wrapping around his neck. He lifts me and my legs wrap around him before I kiss him.

I kiss him deeply, like it might be the last time I ever feel his lips against mine.

He pulls away just to say, "That's certainly the response I was hoping for."

I grab the back of his head and push him back into me, sealing our lips again. A groan leaves him and I feel him smile against my mouth.

I hardly notice when Venom carries me over to another spot in the greenhouse and sets me down on my bare feet against the biggest tree in the greenhouse with ivy growing all over the trunk. "Don't move."

He begins pulling the ivy away from the tree and wrapping it around my arms.

"What are you doing?"

Before I know it, my arms are stretched in opposite directions and securely tied to branches above me by the ivy.

I'm sure I could break free if I wanted, but I'm too intrigued.

Then Venom pulls out a knife, flips it a couple times while staring at me, before coming over and cutting away my clothes until I'm left completely bare.

The air in the greenhouse is warm, but my nipples

still form into hard peaks, stimulated and eager for what Venom has planned.

Gripping my throat, he leans in. "Say you're mine."

"Make me," I challenge, with a bite to my lip.

His smirk widens and his eyes light up. "I was hoping you'd say that." Still holding my neck tightly, he presses a kiss to my forehead. "My pleasure, darlin'."

Venom pinches my nipple hard and I let out a whimper. He reaches to my other one and does the same, drawing the same response from me. And then he tweaks both of them between his fingertips at the same time while staring at me. I clench my thighs together and bite my lower lip to stifle my whimpers.

"What did I tell you?" He uses his thumb to pull my lip free from my teeth. "Leave the biting to me." Then his teeth press into my tender breast as he kneads my other in his firm grip.

I groan into his hair as my arm tries to move so I can grab him, touch him, but I can't.

"Are you to torture me?"

He stands tall once more and gently grabs my throat. "I mean to replace your past in every aspect, little beast. When you think of torture, it won't be of whips and pain; it will be of my fingers, my tongue, my teeth and my cock. You will feel pain but laced with pleasure." He strokes a finger down my cheek and across my lips "I will be your every memory. Because I don't just love, I consume."

"Is that a threat?" I tease.

"A promise."

"Then get on with it."

"That's my wicked beast." He grins then flips his knife out once more and brings it between my breasts.

I deeply inhale, staring into his pale sapphire eyes.

"Do you trust me?"

"Yes."

Then the blade gently presses into me with a soft sting as he drags it down a couple inches, pinching my nipple again at the same time. My mouth falls open with a light gasp and I watch his smile grow.

"You like seeing me bleed and in pain?"

"Only when it's followed by your pleasure." And with that his head drops to lick my small wound from bottom to top before planting his silken lips to mine as he steals my breath.

He steps back, breaking free from the kiss and slaps a hand across my breasts. I can't help but give him a light moan and begin rubbing my thighs together.

The pain he delivers pulls me closer, searching for the pleasure that follows. The tightness builds in my core, hungry for him.

"More," I plead.

"Such a greedy beast." He steps closer again, his breath sending chills over my skin. "Tell me, what do you want? My fingers between your juicy thighs or my tongue? Which will make you scream louder?"

"Both." I whisper. "Please, touch me."

"How can I refuse when you beg so sweetly?"

He suddenly lifts my leg, placing it onto his shoulder as I balance on one foot. Then he cups my pussy in his hand. "Is this where you want me to touch you, darlin'?"

"Mmhmm. Yes, please."

Then his fingers push into me and I let out a moan as my head falls back. I stare up through the tree's branches to the glass domed ceiling, feeling Venom's fingers fucking me and my eyes begin to roll back.

Venom clicks his tongue against his teeth, tsking. "Not yet, beastie." He removes his fingers and slaps my aching pussy twice. My body flinches and I groan, silently begging him to give me more.

He drops to his knees; my leg bent over his shoulder.

"My, my, I wish you could see how bad you're dripping for me." He runs a finger through my wetness as I look down at him. He then sucks it clean before giving me another slap.

"Fuck, Venom," I cry out. "Please, I can't take much more. Just let me come."

"But I've only just begun," he says with a playful grin.

I softly laugh. "You're gonna pay for this."

"I do love your threats, darlin'. They've always been adorable. Now let me get back to work here."

His mouth finally reaches my pussy, his tongue sweeping through me and I buck into him, desperate for more. I feel him chuckle against me before his tongue begins to move around my clit over and over in agonizing circles. Again, I try lifting my hips, pushing into him. His hand comes up, smacking my ass hard and then his teeth sink into the sensitive spot between my pussy and thigh. I nearly scream.

"That's it, beast, let it out. Scream for me."

His mouth returns to my pussy in eagerness, lapping

up my wetness before suckling on my sensitive bud. He's being gentle and slow now, savoring my clit, cherishing it with his lips and tongue. I moan and grip tighter to the vines of ivy helping to hold me up. "Yes. Please don't stop. Oh god." But right before I climax, Venom pulls away and stands. "No. No, no, no. Fuck, please Venom!"

He leans in, gripping my chin. "Tell me, do you prefer this kind of torture?"

A part of me wants to say no because this is fucking hell, but my god, it feels so fucking good. The mixture of pleasure and pain is intoxicating and I'm becoming delirious.

"Yes," I whisper, my voice feeling weak just like the rest of me.

"Good."

He begins unbuckling his pants and I smile wide when they drop and his beautiful erect cock frees. He grips himself tightly. "You want this?"

I nod.

His head tips low. "Use your manners, beast."

My pussy throbs and aches more than I thought possible. I need him inside me.

"Please. Please fuck me."

"*Of course, darlin'.* Anything for you." His wicked smirk grows.

He pulls me toward him and lifts, lining himself up at my entrance as my bent legs hang wide open for him. Then he impales me on to his glorious cock and I cry out, probably waking every creature in this greenhouse.

My legs wrap around him as he begins to pound into

me with reckless abandon. Fingers dig into my ass with a bruising grip and he moans against me as he loses himself inside me. I welcome the chaos of his love. I'll forever savor every twisted moment with him.

His love is a poison I've come to crave. He's made me an addict.

I'm addicted to Venom.

I hold onto him tighter as I near my climax and feel him reaching his. "I love you."

Suddenly I feel something moving on my arm. I look up and catch the sight of iridescent blue scales and the oval-shaped head that belongs to Mya.

I want to scream. I want to run. But I'm tied to this fucking tree and being impaled by a large cock. She slithers her way down my bicep and then onto my chest.

Oh my god.

Venom pulls back to avoid squishing her but he holds onto my hips still driving himself into me. I look at him with panicked, wide eyes.

"She won't hurt you, darlin'. *Trust* me, Ivy. Just let go," he says breathlessly. "Focus on me. Focus on *this*."

I close my eyes for a moment, letting my senses focus back to how Venom feels inside me. My head tips back as my bound arms hang from ivy with my bottom half being held up by Venom's strong hands as he fucks me, and I let out a moan.

As Mya's body slithers over my nipple, it strikes a nerve I didn't expect. The sensation tips me over the edge and I completely lose myself. Venom, taking notice of what's happening, pinches my other nipple once more then rubs at my clit as I break apart, bucking and writhing with my moans coming out as more of a scream as my orgasm shatters me with Venom following right after.

My heart pounds against my chest as Venom holds me close, both of us catching our breaths.

Mya begins to happily move herself onto Venom, coiling around his bicep.

A moment later, Venom speaks first. "Think you can stand for a second?"

I nod and he places me gently on my feet before transferring Mya back into the tree, then grabs his knife, cuts me free from the ivy, and scoops me into his arms. He carries me back over to the dahlias and lays me down on the blanket. And there, we lay together naked until the daylight shining through the glass domed ceiling turns into shimmering moonlight, wrapping us up in its silver glow as we fade into each other.

VENOM

CHAPTER FORTY-TWO

I enter the greenhouse, looking for Ivy, already knowing I'll find her there. When I do, I pause and continue quietly, watching her while trying not to draw her attention.

"Come on, it's alright. We're friends now, right?" she sweetly says into an area of orchids, holding out her hand. Mya slithers up into her palm and then around her wrist. Ivy giggles at the sensation. "Now listen, don't go biting me or I'm gonna be pissed and never talk to you again. Okay?"

"Well, I've bitten you and I remember you asking for more, darlin'."

She jumps, clutching her chest with her snake-free hand.

"Jesus, Venom. Can't you ever enter a room like a normal person?"

"What's a normal person to do? Stomp around and shout every time they enter?"

"I think you like sneaking up and scaring me."

I lift a brow. "I thought you'd never been frightened of me."

She rolls her pretty eyes and walks over to me. "What's up?"

"I just came to tell you they're almost here."

"I think it's really sweet of you for doing this," she says, placing a hand to my chest.

"I told you, the boy reminded me of myself, and if I can do anything to bring him a little joy, then I'll happily do that." She kisses my cheek. "At least something good came from that night. I can't wait to meet him."

I glance to my blue beauty, Mya, wrapped around my beguiling beast. "She looks good on you." I smirk, meet Ivy's eyes, then wink at her, causing her to blush.

Ivy's cell phone dings and she takes it out, smiling at the screen.

"Who has you smiling like that? That's only my job."

"Oh, it's just Charlotte." She shrugs and types something back to her.

"Just Charlotte? I'm not sure if I should be concerned or intrigued to see what the two of you could get up to," I say as I twirl a strand of her hair around my finger.

"We've just been talking girl stuff."

"Mmm."

She puts her phone back into her pocket and looks up at me. "Are you jealous?" she asks with a playful grin.

"If I have to keep seeing someone else make you smile

like that, then yes. Unbearably jealous, darlin'. I'll have to have a talk with her."

"Oh stop. Maybe you and Reaper can get more friendly too and we can go on a double date!"

"From what I heard, their last double date ended with a murder."

She beams. "Sounds like your kind of event!"

"This is true."

She laughs, giving me a light push. "Go. I'll meet you out there. Let me just put Mya back."

Pulling her closer by her hair wrapped around my finger, I kiss her deeply, then leave.

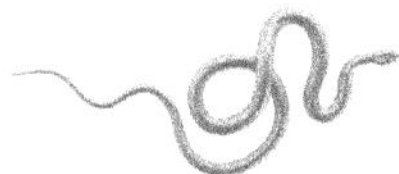

THE SOUND OF the car coming down my driveway has me quickly stepping outside to wait for our guests. I never thought I'd agree to something like this, but here we are.

Before the car even comes to a complete stop, the back door flies open.

"Damon! I told you; you need to wait until the car completely stops!" Alice shouts as she exits the vehicle.

The young boy bolts up the stairs and launches at me, attaching himself to me like a feral monkey.

I give him a couple of pats on the head and he finally lets go to look up at me with admiration.

"I kept telling them I wanted to see you again. Every day. Even more than once a day!"

"Persistence can get you far in life. So will a charming smile. Now, let's have a look at yours."

He tries mimicking my perfected smirk and I have to hold back a chuckle. "Well, we'll certainly have to work on that."

He looks so much better than he did that night I found him. I can now see both his eyes clearly—no more bruises and not so thin.

"I knew you lived in a castle!"

"It only looks like a castle on the outside. Unfortunately, inside is rather boringly modern."

"Do you have an underground cave or something?"

"I have something much better. Tell me, Damon, do you like flowers?"

He grimaces. "Flowers? Isn't that for girls?"

"Not my kind of flowers. Come, let me show you my lair and my pets." I open my front door and motion for him to walk in.

"Thanks for doing this. I know it's a bit unorthodox," Alice says as she approaches. "He was driving everyone nuts."

"It's no problem, Alice. You coming in too?"

"Ah, I think I should probably just wait out here and not cross any more lines. I have some calls to make anyway."

"I think we're well past lines, but alright then."

As Damon and I walk past the kitchen, Ivy pops out to greet us in a pretty floral mini dress and her typical bare feet.

"This is Ivy."

"Hi, Damon. It's so nice to meet you."

"Are you his girlfriend?"

Ivy laughs, her cheeks turning a light pink. "I am."

"You're a bit more than that," I say to her with a smirk before looking back at the boy.

"She's pretty. Prettier than Alice."

"She sure is. You're a smart kid. But watch out for this one. She's a pretty thing but as beastly as they come."

Damon scrunches his little brows together and Ivy swats my arm.

"Don't listen to him, Damon. He's gotten hit on his head a bit too much."

"From being a superhero?"

"Um, yeeeah, we can say that."

"One day I'm gonna be like Venom and save people too!"

Ivy smiles at the boy. "You know what, I think you'll be even better than him."

"Yeah? You really think so?"

"I know so."

Damon smiles so big at Ivy it melts something inside me. This boy, who has already been through so much at a young age, still has his smile. It's not lost. And I have this sudden urge to make sure he never loses it.

"Damon, do you like snakes?"

"Snakes are so cool!"

"Would you like to meet some of mine?"

"Yeah!"

I walk us to the end of the hall and open the greenhouse door, letting him enter first.

He takes a few steps in and then stops, taking in the surroundings.

"Wow!"

"Follow me and don't touch anything on the left tables." Damon eagerly follows me to the back of the greenhouse, with Ivy right behind him.

I take time introducing him to all the ladies and even find Mya for him to hold for a bit as well as Rose, my desert rosy boa. The kid shows no fear and again, it triggers my memories of me as a boy—unafraid of all the creatures I found in the yard, but the one fear I did have was from a mother who never loved me.

Although Damon did experience a true mother's love, it was not nearly long enough, and I just hope he finds people who will truly love him and protect him.

"Hey, Damon, I heard you like red velvet cupcakes," Ivy says with a playful grin.

"They're my favorite!"

"Well, red velvet cupcakes just so happen to be one of my specialties. Cream cheese frosting and all. Wanna help me make some?"

"Really? Okay, yeah!"

This kid's face lights up in the best way. Pure, unfiltered joy and excitement make his smile widen and his big blue eyes sparkle. It's beautifully contagious.

I quickly send a text to Alice, letting her know we're going to be a bit longer. She assures me she has plenty of work to keep her occupied while she waits.

As Ivy and Damon get to work on making the cupcakes, I sit at the kitchen table and watch them in wonder and maybe with just a bit of jealousy because Damon seems to be awfully good at making Ivy laugh. I used to sit here watching Ivy and Evelyn and now—my thoughts are disrupted when Ivy swipes some of the cupcake batter on Damon's nose and his contagious giggle echoes through the room. I smile and let out a small chuckle as I watch them, but then my thoughts pull me in a different direction.

If I hadn't taken care of dear Debbie when I did, I might not have found him in time. He could have been sold off to the next person and be lost for longer or perhaps even forever. He might not have gotten to be this version of himself right now, happy.

Damon helps Ivy clean up while the cupcakes bake, like a true little gentleman, and once they're done, we all eat one together and then Ivy packs some up for him.

"Alright, I think it's time we get you back to Alice."

He frowns, dropping his head and turns to leave with his fresh cupcakes in hand.

Opening the front door, I let Damon and Ivy walk out first. Alice quickly ends the call she's on and takes a few steps up the stairs. "Ready, Damon?"

"No," he simply says.

"Now that was the deal, kid. A quick visit and then you'll go stay with the Jamesons. They're really looking forward to meeting you."

"But I don't want to go. Can't I stay a little longer?"

"Damon, we have to stick to our deal, okay?" Alice says.

He looks down at his sneakers and toes a small pebble.

"But... I like it here. Why can't you and Ivy just be my new daddy and mommy?"

I swallow the lump in my throat and look over to Ivy for help, but all I see are tears threatening to spill from her eyes as she stares at the sad boy.

I look back at Damon and he looks up, finally meeting my eyes, and I lose all train of logical thought.

All I know, since the moment I saw this boy, is how much I want to protect him. I still see the innocence in him that I lost long ago as a child. I want to make sure he never loses that or his smile and forever feels loved and wanted. I want to give him what I never had.

I look back at Ivy and smile, thinking about how I know she would make a fierce and incredible mama. Protective and nurturing. But we can't rush something like this.

"Hey, Damon. Look at me." His stormy blue eyes meet mine as I kneel down to his level. "I heard the Jamesons are really nice people and they're gonna be real good to you. How about we set up another visit sometime? You can come hang out with Mya and Rose. Ivy can make more cupcakes. How's that sound?"

"I can see you and Ivy again?" he asks excitedly.

"Just say the word and Alice here will set it up."

"You promise?"

I smile. "You have my word."

He wraps his arms around my neck and I return the hug while looking over to Ivy, seeing her covering her mouth to hold back the emotions she's feeling.

I stand and face Alice.

"Alice, whatever the boy needs…"

She nods, not needing to finish my sentence to know my request. "Of course."

EPILOGUE

8 MONTHS LATER

Damon visiting us became a new routine, all three of us growing closer with each visit. He filled the empty hole in our home and heart that Ev left, with his wondrous spirit, infectious laugh, and incessant questions, always eager to learn. He quickly developed a passion for snakes and plants, making me so proud. It was like staring at a version of myself I could have been if not for the childhood I had.

Although the Jamesons were nice folks, it became clear where Damon truly belonged. And that was with us.

I left the decision ultimately up to Ivy, not wanting to push a child on her, but she insisted she wanted this too. She wanted Damon, wanted a real family with *us*.

We all needed each other in a sense, to help heal and grow, and we desperately wanted to give him the life we both never had.

Ivy and Damon healed old wounds I didn't know still lingered below the surface. My nightmares finally completely stopped as life had become so different, filled with more love than I ever had and never could have imagined.

After months of back-and-forth bullshit paperwork and court appearances, Damon was officially ours.

I'll forever remember the way his face lit up.

"It's done. You're ours and officially home. Welcome to the viper's pit, Damon," I said.

A high-pitched screech left his throat as he launched himself at Ivy and me, squeezing us tight before breaking down in a sob with tears of relief and happiness.

Ivy

"Another surprise?" I ask when we pull into town, and I begin to put the blindfold on.

"We have forever together, get used to surprises, darlin'."

The car finally stops, and I hear Damon get out of the back seat and then my door opens and he's grabbing my hand.

"Come on!"

I laugh and let him help me out of the car. "You guys are in on this together, huh? I'm not sure if I should be more concerned now."

"Dad said you're gonna love it."

"We'll see about that."

Venom comes over, wrapping his arms around me and I lean against him.

"I hope it's everything you dreamed of."

Then he pulls the blindfold free.

In front of me is the most charming building I've ever seen. It gives off that hidden gem vibe, like something you might find tucked away in an alley in Italy.

The doorway is framed with peonies, roses and climbing ivy as well as hanging ferns. There's a wooden ladder to the left with small potted lavender and succulent plants. Fresh cut roses ranging from soft pinks and deep reds to vibrant yellows and oranges sit in baskets on the ground.

I look back up to the vintage looking sign above the doorway which is surrounded by a garland of dried flowers and more ivy that intertwine with a stream of delicate lights. I cover my mouth to stifle a sob when I read the sign, the words sit curved above dahlias with a snake coiled around them.

The Blooming Viper.

I turn to look at Venom. "Is this—"

"Yours. All yours, sweet beast."

"You're serious? My own flower shop?" Tears cascade down my face, and I laugh with happiness.

He grabs me into his arms, kisses a runaway tear and licks his lips.

I fell in love with Venom's greenhouse right away— the beauty of it all. I used to think baking brought me peace, but the greenhouse, being surrounded by nature and helping things thrive, gives me a kind of peace I've never known, a kind of happiness I've never experienced.

Although the greenhouse has started to feel like *ours*, Venom gifting me my very own space—a place where I can feel not only peace and happiness but also purpose—is the most thoughtful and incredible gift I'll ever receive.

I kiss him, melting into him and feeling all the love he has for me.

"Ew, stop. Come on, let's go inside! I want to show you what I planted!" Damon says with excitement.

"Alright, alright, show me." I reach out my hand, and he takes it, running ahead and pulling me after him, leaving Venom to catch up behind us with a big smile.

And as I look back at him, still holding on to Damon's small hand, I realize I have everything I ever wanted in life, but thought I never would ever have. A family and a visceral love—and it's all thanks to the most *venomous* man I've ever met.

THE BLOOMING VIPER

ACKNOWLEDGEMENTS

Thank you to my readers! I originally had no plans to write Venom's story, but thanks to your support and excitement about this character, his story was brought to life! I hope you enjoyed it!

Thank you to my beta readers, Mel, Nikki and Kim! I loved hearing your feedback and suggestion on this story. Sorry about the tears though… haha.

Thank you to my street team, my little vipers! Y'all have been so amazing with your support and always hyping me up!

Thank you to my editor, Zee, who helped really polished this baby up, making it shine!

And finally thank you to my bestie, Mel, who has had to listen to all my ramblings, ideas and meltdowns. Love you!

ABOUT THE AUTHOR

Kayla Marie, a budding author from Massachusetts, has recently embarked on the journey of putting the swirling stories in her mind to paper. Specializing in the genres of fantasy and dark romance, she finds solace in the worlds she creates. When not lost in her writing, she can be found enjoying the company of her husband, children, and dogs. Whether engrossed in a good book, watching fantasy movies, or lost in her own daydreams, Kayla is always seeking refuge in another world.

Instagram: @enchanted.shelf